MARK OF
FIRE

MARK OF
FIRE

THE ENDARIAN PROPHECY
RICHARD PHILLIPS

Text copyright © 2017 by Richard Phillips
All rights reserved.

No part of this book may be reproduced, or stored in a retrieval system, or transmitted in any form or by any means, electronic, mechanical, photocopying, recording, or otherwise, without express written permission of the publisher.

Published by 47North, Seattle

www.apub.com

Amazon, the Amazon logo, and 47North are trademarks of Amazon.com, Inc., or its affiliates.

ISBN-13: 9781542046862
ISBN-10: 1542046866

Cover design by Shasti O'Leary Soudant

Printed in the United States of America

I dedicate this novel to my wife and lifelong best friend, Carol.

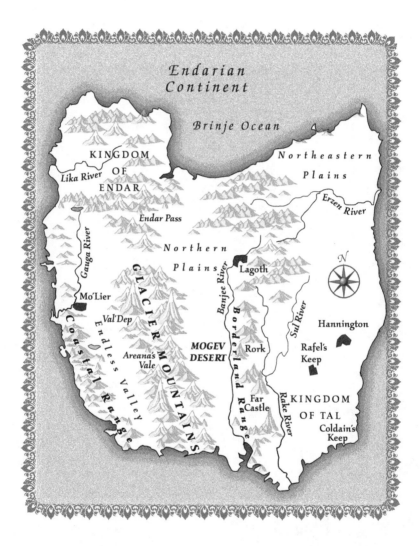

PROLOGUE

Kingdom of Tal—Outside of Hannington—Eastern Tal
Year of Record (YOR) 390

The sound of pigs squealing outside the woodcutter's house on the out-skirts of Hannington brought five-year-old Arn Tomas Ericson's head up as his father leapt from the dinner table. The inhuman laughter that accompanied the noise stood Arn's hair on end.

"Carl," Arn's mother said, her eyes wide with fear, "what's wrong?"

Arn's father grabbed his woodcutter's ax from its place beside the door. "Marie, bar the door behind me and close the shutters. Do not open them until I tell you."

Without another word, the man stepped out into the night, slam-ming the door shut. Marie immediately rose, dropping the door's bar into place and rushing to the lone window to close and bar the shutters.

Arn remained frozen, his fork full of mashed potatoes and gravy still halfway between his plate and mouth. His mind struggled to grasp his mother's terror. He wanted to ask her what had made the sounds, but when his father began screaming, Arn knew that he did not want to know.

Then his mother grabbed him by the arms and pulled him to his feet, sending the fork flying from his hand, splattering her blue dress with gravy. Too startled to speak, Arn felt himself being dragged across the room and lifted into the partially filled wood box beside the hearth. As sharp sticks poked his side and back, he opened his mouth to cry out but felt his mother's palm cover his lips.

"Stay silent," she whispered harshly. "Do not make a noise."

She shoved him down and closed the lid. A small shaft of light penetrated through a narrow crack but did little to push back the darkness that enfolded him. A tremor spread from Arn's hands and up his arms until his entire body shook. Outside, he no longer heard his father. There was a sudden blow against the cottage door. He heard the bar crack as the door crashed inward, followed by heavy footsteps.

Arn did not want to look but could not stop himself from pressing his eye to the crack. He blinked to clear the tears that blurred his vision. His mother stood against the far wall, holding a butcher knife, facing two men whose backs were toward Arn. The one on the left wore a black cape that swept to the floor, its hood pulled over his head. The other man was much bigger, with black hair hanging to his shoulders.

Arn's mother suddenly lunged forward, but she froze midstride at a gesture from the hooded man. Red bands of light wrapped her arms and legs, a glowing tendril reaching up to pluck the knife from her right hand. The hooded one gestured again, and Arn's mother floated up off the floor and back to the wall, as the tendrils spread her arms as if her palms had been impaled.

When the bigger man stepped up beside her, he turned to look back at his companion, and Arn suffered another shock, this one robbing him of his breath. The man was a woman but not like any woman he had ever seen. Her brown eyes looked human, as did her muscled body. But her jaws jutted an inch from her face, and when she opened her mouth, Arn saw teeth more like those of a wolf. His father had told him tales of these beings, the ones he had called vorgs.

She ran a very human-looking tongue over her lips and grinned.

"Well, my lord," she said in the rasping voice that matched the laughter Arn had heard from outside, "do you wish to go first?"

The hooded figure merely shook his head. "Be my guest."

When the vorg turned back toward Arn's mother and opened those jaws wide, Arn could watch no more. Instead he pressed himself away from the crack, again feeling a sharp branch poke him in the back. When his mother began screaming, the echoes formed an invitation to the pits of the deep.

PART I

Most believe that Endarians possess two forms of magic, time-shaping and life-shifting. In truth, these are both aspects of a singular ability: Exchange Magic.

—From the *Scroll of Landrel*

1

Hannington Castle, Kingdom of Tal—Eastern Region
YOR 412, Late Winter

The torches lighting the king's private audience chamber cast shadows across the table, the darkest of which came not from the king but from his magic wielder, Blalock. Earl Coldain despised Blalock even more than he detested his young king. Unlike his mighty father, King Gilbert was little more than Blalock's tool. Nevertheless, despite his monarch's many failings, Coldain would support him. The earl was, above all else, a man of duty.

"What of High Lord Rafel?" King Gilbert directed his question at Coldain.

"Sire?"

"What do you think of High Lord Rafel? Specifically, his loyalty to his king."

"Unquestionable."

The king leaned back in his chair, his pale hands clenching his royal scepter as his gaze traveled to the wielder standing by his side. "There are those who question it."

"High Lord Rafel?" said Coldain. "The hero of the Vorg War, commander of the king's armies? For over thirty years, he has served only the throne. He's the finest man with whom I have ever served. He saved this kingdom, and the people of Tal still adore him."

Blalock leaned toward the king, the scowl on his face drawing his lips into a tight line. "Perhaps even more than they love their king."

A sudden constriction seized Coldain's throat. So that was what this was about. Judgment was about to be passed on his oldest friend and mentor.

Gilbert's eyes locked with his. "It is what I have feared. I can feel it in your voice. Your own words condemn Rafel."

"Sire, reconsider! High Lord Rafel will meet any action against him or his people with extreme violence. His keep is second only to your castle here in Hannington in its impregnability, and his personal command numbers more than two thousand battle-hardened soldiers. A siege would last months and spread dissension throughout the kingdom."

"Consider your words carefully, Earl Coldain, before I begin to question the depth of your loyalty to the crown."

Coldain straightened in his chair. "Majesty, I know my duty, part of which is to give you my best counsel, then to execute your ultimate decision with complete commitment. My duty is my life."

"Well said." The king turned once more to his wielder. "Blalock, you have heard Earl Coldain's counsel. What say you?"

"The earl's concerns are valid. A direct assault on Rafel would indeed be disastrous." The wielder's eyes flashed beneath his brows. "But there is a better way to rid yourself of this problem and cow any other nobles whose loyalties to the crown may have died with your father. Send Blade."

Again, Coldain felt ice slide through his veins. Only a handful of people knew the face of the king's assassin, but everyone knew the legendary killer's name. "Blade was saved from the gallows and raised by Rafel."

Blalock's laughter echoed through the chamber's semidarkness. "Yes. And Blade turned his back on Rafel and everyone in his keep six years ago. Hasn't bothered to go back since. Blade is a dark soul. He will do what his king commands and, as always, he will be well rewarded."

"A most excellent solution," said Gilbert. "Earl Coldain, I want you to deliver the order to Blade in person. Tonight."

Coldain rose to his feet, forcing his body into a stiff bow. "As you command, sire."

"One more matter," said Gilbert. "Since Blade and Rafel were close, I want you to task Dagon to follow up, in case Blade is not as heartless as we think. If Blade fails me, Dagon is to kill Rafel and his spawn before assassinating Blade."

With a foul taste filling his mouth, the earl turned on his heel and strode from the room.

—✺—

Kragan, known as Blalock to the people of Tal, left the king's chamber without bothering to ask Gilbert for permission. They both knew where true power lay. After Gilbert's father, King Rodan, had died in a riding accident seven months ago, his title had transferred to his nineteen-year-old son. Although Rodan had been strong-willed, wise, and widely respected, the populace held his paranoid weakling of a son in barely veiled contempt. Little wonder, considering the delight the young king took in having anyone who he believed disloyal publicly executed.

Kragan did not begrudge Gilbert this last vice. But the king's incessant tantrums robbed Kragan of any shred of respect he might have developed for the lad.

With Rodan gone, Kragan was easily able to convince Gilbert to remove from power Gregor, the former king's gray-bearded magic wielder and chief advisor. Despite the furor Gregor had raised upon his dismissal, Kragan had moved easily into the graybeard's position as the power behind the young king. As long as the puppet monarch remained useful, Kragan would allow him to live. The day when Kragan would summon his vorg army to take this kingdom for his own lay on the not-too-distant horizon.

Turning to his right, Kragan placed both hands upon the wall, the large blocks of granite cold to the touch. His mind reached outward, grabbing the earth elemental, Dalg, and snapped it to his will. He stepped through the wall, releasing control of the elemental as he reached the other side.

An ancient stone stairway spiraled downward before him. The darkness was complete, yet he could see clearly. He descended the stairs slowly, caressing the wall with his hand as he went. Old Stone. Ancient stone. Very much like Kragan himself—frigid, hard.

The stairwell ended at a rectangular opening carved into the rock. He walked through and turned right, his long strides carrying him down the hall. He eventually turned left and climbed a short set of steps to an ornately carved ivory door, opened it, and entered a large chamber.

The floor, walls, and ceiling were of white marble. The torches that burned on the walls cast shadows that seemed to crawl within the stone. A four-post bed covered in red satin occupied the left wall. A chest-high pedestal with a small crystal vase stood beside the hearth.

In the center of the room stood a life-size statue of a young woman. The left sleeve of her blouse had been ripped away to reveal a shoulder that bore the red image of a fire elemental rendered in such detail that the flames seemed to flicker beneath his gaze.

He found himself staring at the intricately carved woman, the image of the one who had haunted his dreams since that day, centuries past, when he had killed the Endarian wielder, Landrel. He had taken the scroll that contained the prophecy and the drawing of this woman from Landrel's lifeless body. And the ability to create statues in her image had come to him unabated, sometimes feverishly.

For all these centuries, he had searched the world for her despite not knowing her name. Landrel had intended for his prophecy to torture Kragan by denying him such a vital piece of information.

Kragan glanced at the statue's perfectly carved face. Her name did not matter. He would know her by sight when he found her.

2

Rafel's Keep—A Week's Ride Southwest of Hannington
YOR 412, Late Winter

Carol stood in her nightgown, looking down from her balcony at the flickering torches spaced along the castle's dimly lit western wall. Their light barely penetrated the thin veil of snow that floated down from the darkness above. The guards moved slowly back and forth between the watchtowers, in a pattern designed to maintain alertness during the night's wee hours.

She left the overlook, returning to her bedroom where a fire blazed on the hearth, shivering as she turned to present her back to the warm glow. The room was high-ceilinged and open, lit by a candle chandelier and hearth flames. Bookshelves stretched across the far wall, the upper half accessible via the sliding ladder mounted on its grooved track.

Carol loved books by the scholars and great political thinkers of the age, many of which were outlawed in the kingdom of Tal. Some of the men who had written items in her collection argued that all people were born with basic rights, while other authors maintained that privilege was rightly granted by a king to those he deemed worthy. The former proclaimed that a king was no different from any other, that a ruler governed at the behest of the people, and that government's sole function was to serve the public. Carol thought that their ideas represented the coming world order.

These scholars held a far different vision of government than what existed within Tal, where land ownership was the result of direct grants from the king to men who had been given the titles of earl or lord. Chief among these noblemen, the title of high lord was given only to those who commanded the army of the kingdom of Tal. Even though a member of the royal family would technically outrank him, the high lord's authority was second only to that of the king.

Women of noble birth were referred to by the honorific title lorness, yet were denied direct participation in the government, forced to rely on wit and wile to influence the men who wielded raw power.

Carol's father had obtained these books for her. She was still amazed that she had been able to talk him into the seditious act. For her father to violate the law for his only daughter bespoke of the strength of his love. Despite his title, she knew that High Lord Rafel shared many of her views regarding a woman's place in society, having seen a true meritocracy in practice during the time he had served as emissary to the Endarian ruler, Queen Elan, during the Vorg War. Carol's fondest dream was that one day she would lead a movement that fully affirmed the rights of women in Tal.

The strength of her disgust for Tal's patriarchal system of government had been the chief reason that her father had only taken her to Hannington Castle once, when she was much younger. His fear that she would accidentally reveal her treasonous inclinations by reacting to life in the capital was too great a risk. That was fine with Carol. She had personal reasons for avoiding that place.

A knock on the door interrupted her reverie. Her father poked his head in the doorway. "May I come in?"

"Certainly," said Carol. "I was just looking over my books."

"Ah," he said. "If you'd been born a man, you'd be a force to reshape the world."

"Only a woman can do that."

A broad grin spread across his lined face. "If any woman could, it would be you. You have always been as strong-headed as Arn."

Carol's mood soured. Her thoughts immediately turned to Arn, who as a troubled, twelve-year-old orphan had knifed a minor lord in Hannington's central square for beating a peasant woman. At the time, the local magistrate had sentenced Arn to death, but on the day that he was scheduled to hang, Rafel had watched the boy use his last words to curse the law that allowed a lord to beat a woman senseless only because he was of noble birth and she was not. Having uttered his condemnation, Arn stood defiantly as the noose was placed around his neck and drawn tight. Standing in the square that day, Rafel had seen something in the lad that caused him to step forward to intervene. At Rafel's request, King Rodan granted Arn a pardon, but only on the condition that the high lord take the boy into his house and assume responsibility for his training and behavior.

From the first day that he had arrived at Rafel's Keep and been placed under Battle Master Gaar's harsh tutelage, the high lord had informed Arn that the stay of his death sentence only remained in effect at Gaar's pleasure. Seven-year-old Carol had observed Arn's training from afar, developing a fascination for the slender boy with the curly brown hair and brown eyes that flashed with fury. The battle master had set out to test the depths of Arn's character, rotating him among a trio of trainers in the martial arts, each seemingly determined to break the urchin's will to continue.

Whenever she got a break from her own studies, Carol had slipped away to watch this strange, raging orphan. If he failed to perform to expectation, which was generally the case, his trainer assigned him after-hours duty, lifting heavy stones from one pile to another. Often Arn would stumble to his knees in exhaustion, but he always struggled back to his feet, forcing himself to complete the assigned task no matter how he bled from his falls. Sometimes he would glance up to see Carol watching him, his eyes unreadable. And in those moments, she found herself longing to go help him, though she could not have lifted even one of the stones or defended him from the blows he received on the training grounds.

Over the months that followed, Arn grew taller, with wiry muscles that gave his slender body unnatural strength and quickness. While he became proficient with sword and staff, expertise with a bow completely eluded him. But put a foot-long knife in his hand and Arn seemed to dance with the gods themselves. Although his trainers continued to press him, their attitudes toward him gradually improved. Gaar took notice, on occasion inviting Rafel to observe the teen's training sessions.

With the recognition of Arn's growing prowess came greater privileges, including the right to accompany the high lord on mounted hunts. Over time, the lord's interest in his young protégé changed to fondness, and then to a love that mirrored that which Rafel lavished upon Carol and her younger brother, Alan. Rafel took Arn into his house and made him family.

As Carol moved into her teens, she came to think of Arn as her older brother, and then as something more. But at the age of seventeen, when she told Arn of her feelings, he gently rejected her. Carol's reaction was one of distance and rigid detachment, and Arn soon chose to leave Rafel's Keep for Hannington Castle to enter King Rodan's service.

That had been five years ago. And during those years, she learned from her father that Arn had become the assassin known as Blade. As much as she had regretted withdrawing from Arn, she had waited too long to undo her actions. And as much as her father also loved Arn, the weight of Blade's dark legend would not let him return to Rafel's Keep, even if King Gilbert would allow the departure of his top assassin.

Seeing Carol's change in expression, her father frowned. "I'm sorry, darling. I miss him, too."

He changed the subject. "I came to tell you that I must leave in the morning. Gilbert has summoned all the nobility to Hannington Castle."

Something about that statement triggered an alarm in Carol's head. "Did he say what this is about?"

"No, but he's desperate to show the lords that he can rule the kingdom as well as his father. I'm sure it's nothing to worry about. I'll be back in two weeks."

She knew the warning was unnecessary, but said it anyway. "Be careful."

Her father smiled at her, nodded, and then turned and walked from the room.

Carol lowered the chandelier, extinguished the candles, and crossed the room to her bed. Climbing under the covers, she pulled her thick blankets up to her neck. The fire cast dancing lights and shadows across the room. The sight no longer inspired the security and coziness it had only moments before.

3

Blade stared down at the body that still spasmed at his feet, spewing its life-blood onto the moonlit ground. He was not surprised that the king would put another assassin on his tail to ensure he completed his mission. To Dagon's credit, he probably would have succeeded against someone who lacked Blade's intuitive sense.

He sheathed his knife and turned away. The night air was cold, and the snow had stopped falling. A thin sliver of moon clung to the horizon in a vain attempt to cast its light through the thinning clouds before being swallowed by the night. In ten minutes, the light would be gone, unleashing Blade into darkness.

Rafel's Keep occupied the crest of a hill, surrounded on three sides by the community it protected. On the eastern side, the mighty fortress walls topped a two-hundred-foot cliff that plunged into the valley below. Difficult to attack from any side, military leaders considered this wall impregnable. Blade would test that notion.

As the horizon swallowed the last moon sliver, the black-clad figure stepped from a thicket. He paused at the base of the cliff and began climbing, guided by feel and intuition, his fingers and toes wedging into tiny crevices in the vertical rock face. A hundred feet up, he paused beneath an overhanging ledge, considered going around, and rejected the notion. This was the spot he'd studied from his hiding place, a difficult stretch protecting an easy climb to the fortress wall.

Pulling himself up into a tight ball, Blade wedged the toe of his left foot into the same crack that supported his left hand. Releasing his right, he contorted his body outward, feeling along the lower surface of the overhang until he found what he sought. A narrow crack ran vertically up into the rough surface. Sliding his right palm inside the crevice, Blade balled his fist, wedging it tight, and released his left hand and foot, allowing his body to dangle freely.

Tensing the muscles in his right arm and shoulder, Blade lifted his body and swung onto the ledge above.

When he reached the base of the fortress wall, Blade paused, letting his heart rate and breathing slow to normal. Atop the wall, another fifty feet above him, two guards moved back and forth between watchtowers, their footsteps slow and regular. They were only there because Rafel demanded that all walls be guarded, even though this section was believed to be unassailable. Boring duty, but not shirked. Gaar saw to that, and Rafel's top soldier was not one to trifle with.

The castle wall was old but solid, and presented no more of a challenge than the cliff. Blade scaled it rapidly and paused just below the top, waiting for the footsteps to fade away toward the far tower. Lifting himself so that he could observe the widely spaced torches, Blade watched the nearest guard move away from him.

Blade had arrived at one of the darkest spots on the wall, a place of flickering light and shadow, where the shroud lay thick enough to hide his black form from the guards' torch-blinded night vision. Blade launched himself up and over the top, then down into the courtyard below. At this time, a couple of hours after midnight, the courtyard was unlit. Blade moved rapidly across the area and cut behind the stables into a series of alleys behind Rafel's towering residence. Reaching the chosen spot, he paused to listen. Silence.

To his left, a sheer wall rose forty feet, leading up to Rafel's bedroom balcony. Running his hand over the tower's rough exterior wall, Blade let the sensations from his fingertips build a mental vision. He knew the old keep inside and out. Of granite block-and-mortar construction, it had occupied this spot for more than three centuries.

Blade reached up, found a fingerhold, and began pulling himself up the wall. Darkness did not slow him; his touch told his body everything it needed to know.

The balcony presented itself to him, and he grasped its lip with his left hand, once again letting himself dangle freely as he waited for his pulse and breathing to slow. He lifted himself up to peer across the railing and into the bedroom beyond. As Blade expected, the balcony doors stood open, outlined against the bedroom's yawning gloom. The high lord, his bed piled high with fur blankets, had always loved a cold sleeping chamber. Since his wife had died giving birth to their son, he had nobody to defer to on the matter of open balcony doors and chilly bedrooms.

From the room beyond, Rafel's quiet snores were the only sounds to reach Blade's ears. He waited a full minute before climbing silently over the railing and onto the balcony landing. The breeze ruffled his hair as he glided across the threshold. Drawing the black knife from its sheath, Blade moved toward the bed, hands and feet checking for unseen obstacles.

Rafel's breathing told him he had reached the bed. Blade moved without pause, clamping his left hand over the high lord's mouth as the black knife touched the older man's throat. He felt the warlord stiffen, then relax, moving immediately from sleep to complete wakefulness. Blade expected no less.

Leaning over until his lips almost touched Rafel's ear, Blade whispered, "You recognize me."

Rafel nodded his head slightly.

"Then you know why I've come."

The statement required no answer.

"The king has marked you and your family as enemies of the throne. He instructed me to bring your head, along with those of Lorness Carol and Lord Alan, back to Hannington Castle in a sack."

Blade took a slow breath. "Long ago, you saved me and gave me a new life. Tonight, I repay that debt."

He lifted his hand from Rafel's mouth and stepped back from the bed.

Rafel struggled to a sitting position. "Blade, wait . . ."

The high lord reached for the tinderbox on his bed stand, quickly striking flint to steel. As tinder and candle sputtered to life, Blade was out the window and gone.

—⚭—

Carol jumped as a rough hand awakened her. Opening her eyes, she looked up into her father's grim face.

"Get up, Carol," he said. "I've called a meeting in the grand hall."

Before she could ask what was happening, he was gone. She jumped out of bed. The fire had died down to coals, and the stone floor was cold. Carol swiftly dressed, putting on a comfortable gown and slippers. After tying her long brown hair back, she opened the heavy wooden door and made her way rapidly down the corridor, passing candles burning in their wall mounts.

She took the winding stairway at the end of the hall down to the castle's main floor. Bypassing the huge foyer, she turned left into the study and walked directly to the door on the opposite wall. A short set of stairs brought her down into a room lined with standing suits of armor. Double doors led to the grand hall.

The last to arrive, Carol entered quietly and took a seat at Rafel's right. Her eighteen-year-old brother sat to his left. Although Alan stood only six feet tall, he had a barrel chest and thick form, weighing more than two of Carol and reminding her more of a bear than a man. There were those who would call Alan ruggedly handsome, but when her brother smiled or laughed in that self-assured way of his, beauty shined.

Around the table sat Gaar; Jason, the high priest; Broderick, the commander of the high lord's rangers; Darin, the quartermaster; and Hawthorne, their wielder of magic.

Rafel pushed his chair away from the table and stood, clasping his hands behind his back. "I have bad news," he began. "King Gilbert has sentenced me to death."

The assemblage issued a collective gasp.

"What?" The question tumbled from Carol's mouth before she could stop herself.

The old warrior placed his hand on his daughter's shoulder. "I've learned from a trusted source that our young king has dispatched Blade."

Hearing the hiss of breath, Rafel held up a hand. "Even if assassination fails, King Gilbert will raise the army of Tal from the other nobles. Against those numbers, even this keep will eventually fall to the siege. Therefore, we will begin preparations to leave Tal immediately. Since we will not be returning, we'll have to modify my legion's deployment plans to accommodate our soldiers' families and any other civilian volunteering to journey with us. Darin, you're in charge of determining what gets put in the wagons and what gets left behind."

"Yes, High Lord."

Rafel paused. "How long will it take to ready the supplies and wagons we will have to take?"

"If it were only your legion, we could be ready to march within a day," said Darin. "Readying all the civilians will probably take a week."

"You've got five days," said Rafel, frowning.

"Yes, High Lord."

"I plan for us to journey west through the Borderland Range, then across the Mogev Desert to make a new home in the lands beyond. King Gilbert will wait for word that Blade has succeeded, but once he learns of our departure, he will use his wielder to try to find us. He'll also send riders to alert the border garrisons. When Blalock locates us, the king will gather a large force to chase us down."

"We have over two thousand experienced fighting men," said Gaar. "Gathering a large enough force from the widely dispersed estates of his nobles will take time."

With a nod to his battle master, Rafel continued. "We need to plan on at least as many women, children, and tradesmen accompanying the legion. At last report, we had five hundred twenty-three serviceable wagons. There's enough dried food in our war stocks for a long journey, but we'll have to replenish our food stocks and water along the way."

The high lord turned toward his high priest. "Jason, we can expect the civilians to be traumatized. I want you and your priests to provide as much spiritual comfort as you can manage. I don't want homesickness to turn into hopelessness or dissention."

"On that, High Lord," said Jason in his melodious voice, "you can rest assured."

"We will travel directly west, crossing into the borderlands just south of where the Sul River joins the Rake. Gaar, you will deploy my legion to protect the caravan as it travels. Post your own scouts. I have another job for Broderick and his rangers."

"As you command," said Gaar.

"Broderick, I want you to leave as soon as you have briefed your rangers and readied them for action. Your rangers' task is to kill anyone that tries to flee from here toward Hannington, along with any riders the king may send toward the western garrisons. Link up with us two weeks from now at the Rake River crossing. If you get there and find signs that we've already made the river crossing, follow our trail west."

"And what of the farmers or shopkeepers who wish to remain behind with their families?" asked Broderick.

"Any who desire to stay are welcome to do so," said Rafel. "But warn them that if they attempt to travel toward Hannington, they will suffer the same fate as anyone who would betray us. Also, they should know that, if they stay, King Gilbert will place them under a new lord whose rule may be quite different than mine."

"I understand."

"Broderick," said Rafel, "you are dismissed."

Broderick stood, slapped his right fist to his chest in salute, then turned and strode from the hall.

"Hawthorne," said Rafel, "tonight you must begin to place the appropriate wards to prevent the king's wielder from discovering that we are preparing to depart. Blalock is good, but you have the advantage of time. Keep him off our backs."

"That I will, High Lord," the gray-bearded wielder said.

"Lastly, if I should fall, Carol will take my place. Gaar, you've overseen the development of her leadership skills. Despite her lack of wartime experience, I have confidence that with you advising my daughter, she will make good decisions. If Carol also falls, Gaar will take command until he judges Alan ready to lead."

Alan scowled at this, but Rafel merely nodded in his direction. Carol understood Alan's dismay that their father regarded her so highly while Alan's lack of self-control disappointed the high lord. "Let's get to work."

The room cleared, and Carol returned to her chambers to pack. First she changed into sturdy riding pants, a pullover shirt, and a warm sweater. She packed several similar sets of clothes, some jackets, and boots. Going to her bookshelves, she picked out ten favorites, including *Liberty* by Thorean. Of all the works in her collection, she considered this the masterpiece. Thorean had spent his life studying the philosophy of the erudite Endarian culture, specifically the structure of the meritocracy. The Endarians chose the ruler, male or female, from among a group that the high council deemed most intellectually accomplished. And they replaced that ruler whenever another's talents surpassed hers or his. Fear of the ideas expressed within this tome had driven King Rodan to order Thorean's execution. Although the scholar's body now lay in an unmarked grave, his thoughts on individual liberty and equal rights for women under the law lived on.

But Carol's most important book had no title. A weathered leather cover with a strange symbol stamped into the binding wrapped itself around thick, yellowing pages. Hawthorne had presented it to her three years ago, a gift to his prized pupil.

Carol placed the books with her clothes, limiting herself to one trunk due to the shortage of wagon space. She toured the room, trying to determine whether she had forgotten anything. After packing some last toiletries, she closed and locked the trunk just as two servants appeared to carry her baggage down to a wagon.

When they departed, she stood alone. Her comfortable room, still filled with most of her belongings, felt empty. She looked around as a lifetime of memories flooded her. Blinking away tears, she turned and walked into the corridor that would soon no longer echo with her footfalls.

4

Gilbert looked up as the black-cowled figure strode swiftly through the throne room's double doors, the guards standing to either side of the double doors failing to notice his passage into the king's chambers.

The untested monarch shifted uneasily on the throne as Blalock loomed before him.

"Why have you summoned me, Highness?" Blalock's voice echoed throughout the chamber, seeming to come from everywhere at once and carrying with it the rumble of a midsummer storm.

Gilbert shrank before the sound, knowing that his pallid complexion had just become much more so. He did his best to keep the quaver from his voice when he spoke. "Blalock, my patience with your recent activities has reached its end."

A chuckle rumbled in the wielder's throat. "And what activities are you referring to, Highness?"

Gilbert swallowed. "I am neither deaf nor blind. I have heard the reports of strange people coming and going in my kingdom, and of caravans arriving from unknown origins to unload mysterious cargoes here in Hannington Castle, all without my knowledge. The royal guard has also reported increasing violence, both on our borders and within the kingdom itself.

"And then there's the wielders' wing of my castle. No one is allowed to enter, and strange cries echo from your corridor almost every night. I have tolerated this because you alone have been firmly behind me in my quest to put down the rebellious nobles. However, Blalock, the people are demanding action, and I shall—"

Gilbert screamed as his body fell to the stone floor before his throne. His stomach jutted forth, with his head arching backward. Blalock walked forward to stand over His Majesty's pain-racked form.

"You shall what? Your screams are useless. Your guards cannot hear them. Only you and I are privy to those beautiful sounds. Perhaps I should let them drift out over the town below. Do you realize, my dear king, that with a flick of my mind I can snap your spine, killing you or not, as I please?

"I have kept you in power because it served my purpose. I should be quite angry over this attempted intrusion into my affairs. However, this demonstration has served a purpose. Remember it, Gilbert. If you annoy me further, I will make your own guards chop you into pieces."

Through tear-filled eyes, Gilbert saw the wielder turn and walk swiftly from the room. The king gasped and sobbed on the floor. Twenty feet away, his guards continued to stare down the hallway, oblivious to all that had transpired.

—◊◊◊—

As Kragan, robed in black, stood before the hearth in his bedchamber, the sound of his door opening pulled his attention to his left. An ancient figure in robes of midnight blue entered, his long gray hair and beard merging into a mane that swept over his shoulders, draping both chest and back.

Kragan's fury at this violation of his privacy crept into his voice. "What is the meaning of this, Gregor?"

Flashes of light glittered in the ancient blue eyes that locked with Kragan's own. Veins stood out on the back of the old man's hands, hands as gnarled as the great staff they held. "I don't know what you are scheming, Blalock, but it stops here."

A sneer spread across Kragan's face. He stared at the only wielder in the kingdom who imagined he had power that surpassed Kragan's own. Though Gregor had been King Rodan's powerful ally, the old fool's imagination was about to get him killed.

"I have no idea what you're talking about, Gregor."

"Don't bandy words, Blalock. I have long advised Gilbert to rid himself of you and your poisonous words and deeds. But he will not listen to my counsel. Thus today, I take matters into my own hands."

"Meaning what?"

"You will trouble this kingdom no more."

The great staff rose in the old wielder's hands as webs of power shimmered from his body, an aura that extended to engulf Kragan's form. But as the light closed in upon its target, the aura frayed at the edges. Kragan felt no fear, yet Gregor's mastery taxed him far more than he had expected. Although the most powerful wielders could call forth elementals from each of the elemental planes, they tended to specialize. Kragan's specialty was earth magic. Gregor's was that of air.

Kragan gritted his teeth as his mind tapped the essence of the earth elemental, Dalg.

Red-veined tendrils crawled from Kragan's skin, worming their way up into the surrounding aura. The brightness around Gregor intensified to the point that Kragan had to close his eyes lest the searing light blind him. For several moments, Gregor's aura seemed poised to drive the interlopers back in upon their creator, but then, with an effort that pulled a low grunt from Kragan's throat, the wielder called forth a tremor that threatened to collapse the room's floor, walls, and ceiling.

Gregor extended the fingers of his right hand as the fire elemental Jaa'dra materialized and surged forward, seeking to enfold Kragan in its flaming arms. The entity was too slow. The floor beneath Kragan acquired the texture of mist, dropping him into the ground as an inferno roared into the space where he had just stood. Manipulating the density of the stone as if it were flowing water, Kragan pushed himself back into the room, this time behind the spot where Gregor stood.

Then, as if bursting from earthly bondage, legions of tendrils snaked up through the floor as others descended from the ceiling, slowly burrowing paths through the shimmer to the gray-bearded wielder within. As Gregor dismissed the fire elemental to focus all his mental might on the air elemental that formed his shield, Kragan smiled.

The realization of his own mortality dawned in Gregor's blue eyes, and he spoke with a voice that still carried the power of lost youth. "Blalock, even if you defeat me, the king will learn of this."

"Indeed, Gilbert will find you. But what he finds will give him little comfort."

As Kragan turned away, the old man's wail began.

5

Rafel's Keep
YOR 412, Late Winter

After four days and nights helping organize the pack-out of Rafel's Keep, Carol faced the dawn with a mixture of fatigue, trepidation, and excitement. Her thoughts turned to Arn. Despite how the memory of his rejection still hurt her, she did not believe that he would follow through on the order to assassinate her father. She could not believe it. She knew that the deep rage she had always sensed just beneath the surface of Arn's mind had its origins in the loss of his parents, but he had refused to discuss the topic and she had not pushed. During the years that he had become a part of her family, she felt that rage recede, but Arn had never completely vanquished the pain. And when he left for Hannington Castle, his estrangement from his adopted family had unleashed the killer within. In some ways, Carol felt responsible for that.

For so long she had told herself that she didn't care, that it was better to have learned of Arn's true nature earlier rather than later. Could any man who harbored such a dark side ever truly keep it contained?

Having not seen Hawthorne since last night, Carol made her way across the courtyard to the wielder's quarters, anxious to hear of his progress in establishing the wards her father had told him to erect.

When her knock drew no answer, she felt a disquieting sense of wrongness invade her mind. She opened the door and stepped inside Hawthorne's large outer chamber. He sat cross-legged in the center of a large black-and-silver rug, the intricate patterns seeming to rise from the carpet into the air.

The wielder's head hung low on his chest, a strand of spittle settling into his gray beard from the corner of his mouth, unnoticed. Hawthorne's eyes stared unseeingly at the rug's helix, directly in front of where he sat.

Quietly, Carol knelt beside her mentor and friend, concern tightening her chest. Unsure of her next action, she hesitated. Hawthorne was clearly in trouble. With a trembling hand, Carol touched him lightly on the shoulder.

The wielder's head came up, his eyes focusing on her face. He wiped his beard.

"Hawthorne, what's happening?"

The wielder glanced down at the rug and then returned his gaze to Carol, sadness etched into his features.

"Lorness, I'm failing your father. I'm failing you."

"Tell me," she said.

"I've done my best to strengthen the wards that I have placed on several of the high lord's wagons to prevent Blalock from seeing our preparations. Nevertheless, he is stronger than I imagined, chipping away at my barriers faster than I can reinforce them. And when they fall, he will know of our flight from Rafel's Keep and track us. Even though we are beyond the range of his direct spells, there are primordials that can create a broad swath of destruction in our world. The more precisely they can be targeted, the more intense the damage they can cause. I fear that Blalock may have the power to call upon one of these beings."

"How can I help?"

Hawthorne tightened his lips.

"Despite the potential I've long sensed within you, Carol, your father has forbidden me, on pain of death, from subjecting you to the ritual that would grant you access to the physical magics. Absent that, there's nothing you can do to assist me."

Carol gritted her teeth, biting back the shout of frustration that tried to crawl from her throat. She'd spent years studying under Hawthorne, mastering the arts of meditation that should have enabled her to become his prized apprentice, but her father had been adamant in denying her the opportunity.

In the Ritual of Terrors, aspirants opened their minds to the forces that governed the elements of fire, water, earth, and air. Hawthorne had said that the greater one's potential, the more powerful the elemental opponent she attracted to the confrontation. If Carol survived, the ritual opened a mental channel to that realm. Possession awaited those who failed, their minds forever trapped in torment, a tool of their supernatural masters from that day forward.

"Come with me," Carol said, rising to her feet.

"I need to continue to strengthen the wards. Even though I won't succeed, perhaps I can give us a few extra hours."

"That's not good enough. We have to go see my father."

Hawthorne hesitated, and then rose unsteadily to his feet, allowing Carol to help him.

With the wielder's left arm draped over her shoulder, Carol made her way to Rafel's command center. Her father was bent over the map-covered table with Gaar at his side. She and Hawthorne stepped up behind the men. Sensing their presence, Rafel turned, concern suddenly filling his eyes.

"Hawthorne, what's wrong?"

Gaar moved to the wielder's side, relieving Carol of the old man's weight and guiding him to a chair.

"High Lord, I'm sorry, but my magic will not hold. By this time tomorrow, Blalock will break the wards and me along with them. Then you will be defenseless against his power. I have failed you."

Carol stepped forward, her voice breaking her father's silence. "But there is a way to strengthen Hawthorne's defenses."

Rafel turned toward his daughter, his features hardening. "You will not perform the ritual. I have forbidden it."

"And I have always bowed to your command. However, this is no longer just my capricious wish to learn magic. If Hawthorne fails, our people die. We cannot prevail against all the forces the king will bring against you. Even if we succeed in fighting our way out of Tal, there is a more important reason to let me try.

"If our people see that you are protecting me, keeping your daughter safe in a gilded cage while others confront danger, they will lose all respect for me as future leader. You told Gaar that I would replace you should you fall. How can I do that? How can I face our people, knowing I could have done something to protect them but was unwilling to take the risk?"

Rafel's jaw clenched as he stared back at Carol. Then he shifted his gaze to meet the eyes of his battle master. Ever so slightly, Gaar's head nodded. When Rafel looked at her again, the anger in his gaze had transformed into pride.

"Well argued."

Rafel turned to Hawthorne. "All I ask is that you send her into this battle properly prepared."

Hawthorne rose to his feet, pushing away Gaar's hand. "High Lord, on that, you have my word."

—⁙—

Having retired to his quarters to make ready for the Ritual of Terrors, Hawthorne felt a sudden breeze sweep through the room, blowing out the two candles in the holder set in the center of his rug. For several seconds, he remained cross-legged in the dark, trying to divine the source of the draft. It had not come from the door directly in front of him but from his left. But there were no windows or doors on that side of the room.

Had he subconsciously reached out for a minor air elemental, like Tuuli, without intending to do so? Examining his thoughts just prior to the event, Hawthorne found no direct evidence to support that theory. He remembered thinking of Carol and the strength of will that he had recognized within her since she was a tiny girl. Hawthorne had always felt that she was a gathering storm, destined to reshape the world in which they lived. But such drive almost always had its roots in a deep-seated well of fear. Although he didn't know what Carol's hidden fears were, he didn't doubt their existence.

Rafel had recognized these traits within his daughter as well, which was why the high lord had forbidden Hawthorne to put Carol through the ritual until now. Her combination of willpower and fear would likely attract the attention of one of the more powerful elementals, possibly even a lord of the elemental planes. And that elemental would attempt to bolster her fears, using them to break her will and mind.

If only he had more time, Hawthorne could have brought her along more slowly, helping her to dig through the mental blocks that people erected within themselves, so that she could bring those buried fears out into the day and come to terms with them. But the power and speed with which Blalock had chipped away at Hawthorne's best wards had denied him that luxury.

Calling forth a minor fire elemental, Hawthorne relit his candles, watching as the shadows fled into corners. He was intensely aware of the presence of his own double shadow stretching out behind him and climbing the far wall. Turning his head slightly, he watched from the corner of his right eye as the twin shades moved under the direction of the dancing flames. Where those two wraiths overlapped, the darkness became absolute, as if it were a portal to the realm of the dead.

With an angry hiss, Hawthorne dismissed the vision and refocused on the flames. It would not do to let Carol pick up any of his own fears when she arrived.

—⁓—

When Carol stepped into Hawthorne's chambers, a pair of white candles burned in a holder set in the center of the rug. The wielder, now clad in flowing black robes, stood on the far side of the room holding an ancient book in his left hand. He read from the tome softly, gesturing elaborately with his right. The candle grew brighter and changed to a deep shade of green.

Having long since memorized the ritual, Carol needed no instruction. She walked forward to sit cross-legged in front of the candles. Staring into the flame, she freed her mind to wander within her body, the wielder's distant chant vibrating in her ears. Her body took on the feel of comfortable clothes, her mind floating separately from form.

Hawthorne had taught her that controlling the mind of an elemental required the person attempting to cast the spell to possess an innate psychic ability. This prerequisite was a rare trait, and not all those who possessed it desired to undergo the rigors and dangers of becoming a wielder. That made wielders of magic a rare breed.

Since Carol had been a little girl, she had often sensed what someone was about to say before they spoke. Hawthorne had recognized the trait when she was a mere five-year-old. Thus he had trained her in the wide variety of meditation techniques necessary to free the mind from its bodily tether.

The feelings of the flesh became distant vibrations. Carol concentrated on the flame, allowing herself to become one with the light. A cool mist swirled about her. The wielder's chamber was gone, an ancient temple spreading out in its place. Torches burned along the walls, sending smoky trails upward. Strange gargoyle heads carved into the native stone stared down at her. On the far wall, a door opened outward, just a crack.

Carol felt her spirit shudder as she beheld the portal into the elemental realm. She knew that the only thing she needed to fear was giving way to the terror that awaited her. Little comfort. A weight descended. She had a sudden feeling of an evil presence lurking just on the far side of that doorway.

Had her father been right? Who was she, after all, to dabble in arcane rituals of power? But wasn't that the entire point? There was no way to know whether the aspirant undergoing the ritual had the inner fortitude required until she took the test.

The mist swirled around Carol's form as a cold breeze whipped through the room, blowing out the candle she now held. Only the dim light from the torches in their sconces penetrated the gloom. The air felt heavy, like a thick, wet blanket, cold and damp.

Carol struggled to keep her thoughts positive and comfortable, even as they continually turned toward darkness and evil. This was not going well. In the ritual, what you thought took on reality.

A deep moan sounded from behind the door. Carol got up and began walking toward the portal. To her horror, she found she was no longer wearing her riding clothes. Instead, she wore a nightgown, a garment associated with quiet nights and cherished books. Almost never worn outside of her private chamber, the attire now made her feel weak, vulnerable. The revelation that this was one of her deepest fears violated her self-image in a way that she had never imagined, filling her with dread when it should have imparted fury.

She did her best to visualize herself in chain mail. The nightgown stubbornly remained. Forcing herself to stride rapidly to the door, Carol tried to achieve boldness through action.

The handle felt slimy, leaving her hand damp as she pushed the door open. It swung outward to reveal a narrow stone stairway that spiraled downward, its steps worn by the passage of many feet, the granite walls almost scraping her shoulders.

Having discarded her candle, she grabbed a torch from its sconce and started down the stone steps, cold on her bare feet. With each turn of the stairs, she checked to see what lay beyond. Six turns revealed more of the same.

The stairway ended. Carol entered a large chamber, its high ceilings supported by tall, fluted columns. In the great hearth on the far wall, a smoldering log bled its red light into the mist that swirled almost to her knees. She felt her eyes drawn to the throne facing the fireplace and to the shadowed figure held in its arms.

Carol tried to swallow. Clenching her hands into fists, she forced herself forward. The red wood of the chair had the texture of scabbed flesh. Bas-relief faces distorted in pain crowded together along the surface, faces that seemed to move as she approached.

The lorness concentrated, trying to visualize a fat little boy sitting in that awful chair. She laughed aloud at the thought, but the sound came out shrill and nervous, fading to a sad echo in the elemental chamber. The figure in the chair stood and turned toward her.

Slitted golden eyes glowed in a face of luminously evil beauty such as she had never imagined. She stared as one would peer over a precipice, frightened yet tempted to jump, as if the depths called to her. The being with a feline face and clawed hands stood over seven feet tall, muscles rippling beneath his bronze skin as he moved.

"Do you know where you are, girl?" he asked.

Carol tried to think but did not like the thoughts that came to her.

The elemental moved closer. Carol felt his hungry eyes devour her body as she watched.

"Normally I allow my servants to test themselves against the would-be wielders of magic. Sometimes they return with a new soul.

Occasionally, they are defeated. However, you are the one of whom the Endarian, Landrel, foretold, and I will have you for myself. I am Kaleal."

Again, she tried to swallow, coming no closer to success than on her last attempt. Kaleal. The Lord of the Third Deep. A primordial she could not possibly defeat. Hawthorne had not prepared her for this. Panic rose, constricting her throat. She centered, desperately picturing steel bars between herself and the primordial.

A sneer crossed the primordial's face as the bars materialized between them. He held out a hand, flicking one finger upward. A huge gust of wind hit Carol, and she lost her focus. The bars disappeared.

Kaleal's eyes narrowed.

A wave of desire assaulted Carol, leaving her squirming beneath his gaze. Her breath came in ragged gasps. A picture of the primordial's strong arms encircling her body filled her head.

Kaleal moved so close that his body lightly touched hers, fingertips softly stroking a path on the surface of her hand. As he bent his exquisite face to look directly into her eyes, Carol's knees sagged. She struck out at his cheek, but somehow her slap became a caress, her arms moving up and around the primordial's neck of their own accord. As her hands touched his smooth skin, a wave of passion surged through her body, almost robbing her of the strength to remain standing.

Kaleal moved her hands to his chest, guiding them to stroke his skin. Carol's eyes widened as she fought with every ounce of her strength to deny the feelings cascading through her body. His lips brushed her neck, and she felt her hands move over his chest of their own accord. With horror, Carol realized that he had released them. The feel of the muscles beneath his skin brought tears to her eyes as the true nature of such terrible beauty burned her soul.

She held a being that no master sculptor could hope to capture with his art, with skin so thin and smooth it reminded her of a satin sheet.

The musky smell of his sweat dizzied her, adding to the heat rapidly building inside her.

Something sparked within Carol as she struggled desperately to get hold of her feelings. This was a madness worse than death. They said that to succumb to a primordial was to be possessed.

No! Her desire was her own . . .

And her rage returned.

With a burst of will, Carol forced herself to think of her deepest longing, one that had truly torn her heart.

"Arn!"

Her scream echoed through the chamber.

Kaleal stumbled backward, putting his hands up to cover his face. When he lowered them, Arn looked down at her.

Carol felt something tickle the recesses of her mind, something hidden deep.

Arn leaned down. She kissed him, running her arms around his neck and into his curly brown hair. A wave of emotion stronger than the primordial's desire coursed through her body and soul. She loved him, and the knowledge that she had long denied wrapped her in a lifeline to which she clung.

Since she was a little girl, she had always loved Arn. Her memories rocked her: Arn taking her riding far beyond the boundaries of her father's holdings. The way he tried to explain his rejection of her advances when she had finally worked up the courage to express her desire for him. His attempted kindness through the years of their estrangement. His devotion to her father, and the high lord's love for the younger man.

Their lingering conflict no longer mattered. "I love you, Arn," she gasped, clasping him to her. "I love you."

With that admission, a new strength of will blossomed in her mind. She loved the real Arn, not this impersonation. Releasing her arms from around his neck, Carol pushed him away.

The primordial snarled, once again Kaleal. The dark slits within those golden eyes widened as his lips curled back to reveal fangs. "You reject my passion, then you shall know pain."

As the primordial reached for her, Carol's anger crystallized, sharpening her mind like a scythe. Above Kaleal, the ceiling supports gave way, crushing the primordial to the floor beneath tons of falling stone. As he tossed the rock aside in an attempt to rise, steel chains strapped him to the ground. Kaleal fought desperately to break free. The chains thickened and held. Adding power to her visualization, Carol strapped around his neck a steel collar bolted to the floor.

With Kaleal's howl of rage echoing in her head, the room dissolved, and her father's face swam into her vision, tears cutting swaths down his face as he held Carol in his arms.

Gaar's voice cut through the red haze. "Gods! She lives!"

"Carol, I thought I'd lost you." Rafel pulled her tight to his chest. "Hawthorne sent word, and I arrived to find you on the verge of death. Thank the gods of light for returning you to me."

She smiled. Her whisper was barely audible. "Don't worry. I'm just tired. I'll be fine."

Picking her up in his arms, Rafel carried Carol back to her room, lay her on her bed, covered her in a thick pile of blankets, and stood watch as sleep enfolded his daughter.

6

Carol opened her eyes as the wagon bumped over inhospitable terrain, her head resting on a sack that smelled of barley. Beside her, water splashed out the top of one of several barrels. The creak and crunch of the wheels brought her to full awareness. Outside the canvas that enclosed her wagon, a yell arose above the other noises as a driver urged his team of oxen forward.

She was still dressed in the riding clothes she had worn to Hawthorne's chambers but had to search to find her boots. Climbing forward, she pushed aside the tarp that separated the wagon bed from the seat and poked her head outside. The driver, a groom named Jake, shared the wagon seat with a teenage girl Carol recognized.

Carol squeezed up between these two. Directly overhead, the sun shone brightly in a cloudless sky.

"Good day, Lorness," Jake said, touching his right hand to his hat. "We were worried about you. You've slept clear past noon."

Carol laughed lightly. She had come through the ritual alive and, despite the narrow escape, in full possession of her faculties.

"Thank you, Jake. I'm glad to be here to see you and Lucy."

Lucy flushed prettily, obviously pleased and surprised that Carol remembered her name. She turned her attention to the girl. "Jake seems to be enjoying our new adventure. What about you, Lucy?"

The girl looked down. "I hate it. We were happy back home. Why did this have to happen?"

"I . . . I really don't know," said Carol. "All we can do is make the best of our new adventure, because there's no turning back."

Biting her trembling lower lip, Lucy dropped her eyes again, tears pooling at the corners. Carol reached out and put her hand on the girl's shoulder.

"I've always dreamed of something like this," said Jake. "I'll wager that before this is over, I'll fight vorgs and worse, too."

Lucy stared at Jake as if a rabid skunk had bitten him, making Carol smile.

Carol felt stronger than ever before. For the past five years, she had denied the love that the ritual had uncovered. She marveled at the thought, turning it over in her mind. She had often heard that the line between love and hate was blurry. But she had released her anger at Arn for the hurt he had inflicted. She had begun to fully trust herself again.

And what had the primordial said to her? Something about her being the one of prophecy. She had confronted the lord of the third deep and survived, setting something in motion that she did not yet understand.

This bit about the prophecy was something she would have to discuss with Hawthorne.

A horse trotted up to the wagon, interrupting her reverie.

"It's good to see you up and about today," her father said. "You gave me a scare last night."

"I'm fine."

"I see that I've been deceiving myself that Alan was my only wild child." Turning his horse, her father rode off down the line of wagons.

From her stomach, a low rumble caused Carol to notice just how hungry she was.

Reaching under the seat, she brought out a small basket, filled to the brim with apples, carrots, and strips of dried meat. Her other hand grabbed a waterskin. Despite these being travel rations, Carol ate ravenously. The countryside continued to roll by as she ate, the distant blue mountains showing no sign of getting any closer. She finished her meal and, growing sleepy again, drifted into slumber.

She awoke to find her head on Jake's shoulder. As the sun sank toward the cloudless horizon, she stretched and yawned. "It seems I've made a pillow of you, Jake."

"I've had worse duty."

"Look!" Lucy exclaimed with a clap of her hands. "We're going to camp beside a stream tonight. We can wash up!"

Brightening, Carol saw the line of wagons crossing a shallow stream to form a defensible double circle on the far side of the brook. The formation was more of a long ovoid than a circle. Rougher terrain required the caravan to be split into multiple, mutually supporting campsites.

As they came to a halt, Carol hopped down and walked toward where her father stood with a group of men. He broke off his discussion as he saw her approach. "Are you well rested?" he asked.

"And ready to work. What do you need me to do?"

"Hawthorne needs your help. Blalock is putting enormous pressure on his wards, and he's having difficulty keeping them in place."

"On my way."

Carol felt her father's eyes follow her as she made her way to the wielder's wagon. Poking her head inside, Carol found Hawthorne sitting, his face strained and tired. He motioned for her to sit across from him.

"Blalock is hard at work now," he said, his voice barely rising above a whisper. "I need you to do exactly as I tell you. Take my hands. Now clear your head. Allow your essence to drift inside the shell of your body. My mind will reach out to yours. You must allow me to guide you. Don't try to assist with what I'm doing. Just let your mind move in conjunction with mine. Do you understand?"

"Yes."

She centered. Having long ago mastered Hawthorne's meditation techniques, she released the connection that tethered her mind to her body. She felt the wielder's mind touch hers, felt its power. She also felt its weakness, a weakness that she unintentionally probed. Recoiling, Carol instantly regained control of her focus. Again, she opened herself, letting go of all thoughts. Once again, Hawthorne's mind made contact.

A moment later, she opened her eyes to see her mentor staring down at her. "What happened? Why did you stop?"

"We are done," he said. "We've been at it for over two hours."

Suddenly she noticed how dark it was. Except for the candlelight, she would not have been able to see Hawthorne's bearded face.

"With your help, I was able to enhance the wards so as to block Blalock indefinitely," he said. "I dare say, he must have been surprised to feel my defenses strengthen, just when he thought they were about to crumble. That will give him pause."

Over the next hour, Hawthorne instructed Carol on the precise nature of his magical defenses, imparting the knowledge required to bypass them should she ever become separated from the caravan.

Hungry, Carol excused herself. Walking toward the fire, she saw that dinner had ended. Upon seeing her approach, the head cook waved his hand.

"Jock, do you have anything left?" Carol asked. "I missed dinner."

"Follow me, Lorness, and I'll alleviate that."

He led her around one of the crackling fires to where a large black kettle, marred by dents and scratches, sat along the edge of the coals. Jacob wrapped his hand in a thick cloth, lifting the pot by its wire handle onto a flat rock. Grabbing a clean metal plate from a stack that had not yet been put away, he removed the lid, allowing the smell of fresh baked beans to waft out, making Carol's mouth water. The cook took a dipper and ladled two full scoops onto her plate.

Carol picked up a spoon. Then, sitting down on a rock near the fire, she began to eat. The beans were good, with strips of meat mixed in, giving the whole dish a zesty flavor. She finished the plate, washing down the last bite with a cup of cold stream water. Thanking Jacob, she walked back to where her tent had been set up, undressed, and crawled into her blankets, immediately falling into a sound sleep.

Her father's voice outside her wagon woke her. "Time to wake," he said. "The sun's almost up."

Carol poked her head out from under her thick blankets, breathing in the brisk morning air. A thin layer of frost covered the ground outside her tent, the cold making her reluctant to leave her covers to put on clothes. She mustered her will, threw off the blankets, and grabbed her pants, sliding into them, shivering. Next came her icy shirt, followed by her jacket. Why, oh why, hadn't she thought to tuck them under her blankets when she had crawled into bed?

Carol slipped on her socks and her boots and walked over to where the cook fires blazed. In the predawn darkness, men and women were busy tearing down tents, packing wagons, and saddling horses. The last guard shift came off duty, replaced by the outriders who scouted well ahead along the caravan's planned route.

The morning sky acquired a peachy glow as Carol finished packing and found her horse. Jake was ready to saddle it, but she shooed him away. Fastening the bridle, she saddled the animal, slapped Amira's side to make the mare expel a breath, and then hitched the girth strap tight. Lastly, she tied a rain slicker behind the cantle and swung up onto Amira's back.

It felt good to be on horseback again. Carol loved the feel of the powerful animal underneath her, of the wind cascading through her hair. She trotted forward along the wagons beginning to roll out of circular formation. A double column of soldiers stretched ahead of the lead wagon to the west. In the distance—out to the front, on both sides, and to the rear—she could see the outriders in position. Another group of soldiers sat atop their horses in a double column, waiting to follow the last wagon.

Carol saw her father at the front of the lead column. A rider behind the high lord carried his battle flag, a silver dagger on a black background. She sensed in him a tremendous excitement.

As she spurred Amira forward, watching her horse's condensing breath puff out into the frigid morning, Carol shared his feeling.

The day passed clear and bright. Although the mountains looked no closer, the snow that covered the upper portions of the range stood out with a brilliant glare. Thin, wispy clouds spread across the western horizon as the sun sank. The wagons formed a circle on a flat expanse of grassy ground, a dry camp. There would be no washing up this evening.

In the gathering twilight, tents were erected quickly, a clear indication that the group was getting more efficient at setting up camp. The cooks soon prepared dinner over open fires. They would be serving beans again tonight. Carol grabbed a plate and ate as soon as dinner was ready, anxious to commence her training despite being tired from the day's ride.

She made her way through the darkness to Hawthorne's tent and, throwing open the flap, found the wielder seated on a solid black rug that made him appear to float. Two fat candles burned in glass bowls. The smell of incense hung in the air. Hawthorne smiled up at her.

"Shall we begin?"

"I'm ready," she said, sitting to face him.

"You know about the difficulties involved in the use of the higher magics, but experiencing them is something far different. Even many of the lesser elementals will attempt to misdirect your will. They will try to cause mischief and distract you so that your casting goes awry. The higher elementals will aim to make you lose concentration so they can break your mind."

The wielder absently stroked his beard as he talked.

"You will start with the magics of the weakest elementals. Just because I said your mind is powerful, don't think that this will be easy. All elementals are cunning. Be wary, lest overconfidence becomes your worst enemy. Do you understand?"

Carol nodded, closed her eyes, and began the meditation that allowed her consciousness to wash her body. She centered, separating spirit from flesh. When she opened her eyes, she saw that Hawthorne had spread a parchment scroll before her. Without hesitation, she read the word written there.

"Wreckath!"

As she spoke the name, she mentally reached out, ensnaring the minor air elemental, Wreckath, willing it to breathe a small gust onto one of the candles. She expected to meet resistance, not enthusiastic cooperation. A strong wind struck the candle, knocking it over, lighting the rug fringe. A stream of sparks jetted into Hawthorne's beard, and Wreckath fanned them into a flame.

The wielder yelled as he flopped over and rolled on the ground, trying to smother the fire in his beard. Casting the elemental away, Carol lunged for the water pouch, uncorked it, and dumped the contents onto Hawthorne's head.

"Enough! Enough!" the wielder sputtered.

He lay back, breathing heavily. When he opened his eyes, his gaze caught Carol, who was slightly unnerved.

"What did I say about control?" the wielder muttered as he stood up, wiping water and ash from his face.

"I'm sorry. I expected it to be harder."

"And next time, it may very well be. Whether the elemental's domain is fire, water, earth, or air, casting a spell is a wrestling match. You reach out and grab the being with your mind, forcing it to manipulate a part of nature. If the being feels you overcommit, it will use your own momentum against you. If you are too tentative, the elemental will fight. You have to strive for balance. Now, let's do it again. This time, try to be more careful."

For the next two hours, Carol practiced, finally managing to control Wreckath to the wielder's satisfaction.

"That's all for tonight," said Hawthorne, rising. "We'll take it up again tomorrow evening."

Carol walked back to her tent, realizing she was beginning to associate mental exhaustion with the practice of magic. She crawled into her bedding, the thought of what lay ahead leaving uneasiness in its wake.

—⁘—

For the next several days, strange breezes whipped around the wagons, kicking up small dust clouds that danced back and forth, blowing hats off heads. Carol continually practiced, improving her control of Wreckath. As the line of wagons neared the Sul River, Carol had acquired such skill at controlling the breezes that she could tie a knot with freely hanging strings.

The people of the caravan were not overly impressed, having had lifelong familiarity with wielders, most of whom had minor abilities and demonstrated them in the towns that their carnivals passed through. Nevertheless, Carol felt proud of her accomplishments.

She had also begun working with a minor fire elemental, Golich, which had the ability to create small lights, like fireflies or that of a distant torch. This time, she was much more careful on her first attempt and managed to cast a spell without inflicting damage on Hawthorne or his tent. The elemental struggled, but she maintained firm control, creating a pair of lights and moving them around the interior of the tent together and then in opposite directions.

The Sul and Rake Rivers formed the western boundary of the kingdom of Tal. Rolling along, brown and muddy from the spring runoff, the Rake River appeared before them as the wagons topped a gradual rise. On the far side, the borderlands began. With the river not particularly wide or deep at this point, Rafel's outriders had determined that this was the best crossing site for many leagues.

On the opposite side of the Rake, the ground rose in a series of brush-covered hills that gave way to the snowcapped mountains in the distance. A broad plateau rose to the northwest. Rafel planned to stay south of the plateau country, avoiding towns like Rork, not wanting to invite trouble despite the large size of his force.

Carol rode Amira across the river in advance of the lead wagons. The water flowed swiftly but was shallow, only reaching up to the mare's belly. Climbing out beneath the leafless branches of an overhanging cottonwood tree, she trotted on up the hill, halting next to where Alan sat atop his warhorse, Charger. She loved her brother, who had been beating all of Gaar's trainers in contests of arms since he was sixteen. The only reason her father had not promoted him to captain and given him a company to command was that Alan lost himself in battle, becoming so involved in his personal fight that his leadership was diminished to the equivalent of, "Follow me!"

"Hello, sister," Alan said.

"Hello yourself, little brother." She turned to watch the line of wagons.

She talked to Alan for two hours as the wagons crossed the river. When the last one emerged on the bank to begin climbing the gradual rise, Carol urged Amira off the hill, waving a hand at Alan as she rode down to see her father.

Rafel rode alongside the rear wagon, talking with Gaar. She pulled Amira to a walk as she came up beside her father. "I want to ride out with Alan and the outriders tomorrow."

A look of concern settled on the high lord's features. "I don't like having you and Alan out at the same time. If something went wrong, I could lose you both."

"Tomorrow is our first full day in the Borderlands. It will send a signal to our people that you're not sheltering your own children from the dangers we all face."

The warlord glanced at Gaar, who nodded his approval.

"Very well, then. You can ride out with Alan's group tomorrow morning. It's rough country. Carol, I implore you, be careful."

She inclined her head and spurred her horse forward along the line of slow-moving wagons. As the day passed, the countryside through which the caravan traveled changed, the gently rolling swales giving way to rocky foothills. Rafel kept the wagons in a broad valley that wound to the west, a route necessitated by the rugged country on either side that made wagon traffic impractical. The snowcapped mountains loomed ahead, close enough now that they had begun to lose their blue tinge.

As the wagons climbed, the air grew colder, forcing Carol and the other travelers to don warm jackets by evening. With the sun sinking below the Borderland Range, they made camp next to the stream that wound its way along the valley's center. Showing his eternal vigilance, the high lord ordered guard posts manned in groups of three instead of the twos that they had maintained up until now, positioning listening posts out beyond the guard line.

Flakes whirled around the cook fires as the morning broke with a hint of snow. Wrapped in her warm coat, a bow and quiver of arrows strapped over her shoulder, Carol felt comfortable in the saddle atop Amira as the mare moved out with the rest of her team at a ground-covering saddle gait. Alan rode beside her, wrapped in his own heavy coat, his battle-ax hanging from his saddle.

The riders split into groups of four; Carol and Alan made up half of the westernmost group. The four riders traveled in a varying wedge formation with one out front, two off to either side, and one in the center. Alan was in front with Carol slightly behind and to his right.

The ground had become rocky and steep, the loose shale making the horses slip and slide although they managed to keep their footing with no spills. An hour out of camp, Alan rode up a wooded ridge followed by the others.

By now, a thin blanket of snow covered the ground and draped the tree branches. The snow, soon falling heavier, muffled the sound of their horses' hooves, cloaking their passage with an eerie silence.

7

After weeks that had yielded no success in his magical search for High Lord Rafel and his border legion, a breakthrough sent a thrill through Kragan. Rafel's son and daughter had just passed outside the wards that Hawthorne had placed to prevent Kragan from locating the caravan.

Locating Rafel's kin was one thing. Doing something about them was quite another. Although Kragan was able to sense their location, it was not as if he could scry on them across the leagues. Nor could he cast a direct spell upon them. And eventually they would once again disappear within the boundary of Hawthorne's wards.

The king's army would be no help whatsoever, as Coldain still struggled to gather a large enough force from the noble estates scattered across Tal to take on Rafel's legion. Only the high lord, as commander of the army of Tal and protector of the kingdom's western border, had a large force supplied and ready to march on short notice. Due to the frequent skirmishes along the border that he guarded, Rafel's soldiers and rangers were combat elite. To prevail against that legion would require an army several times as large.

That did not mean that Kragan was without options. The vorgish wielder, J'Laga, possessed one of Kragan's scrying vases, all filled with water Kragan had taken from the same basin. He had distributed almost all the vases to key followers in the Borderlands and beyond, with the last vase resting on a pedestal near Kragan's hearth.

To this clear crystal vase Kragan now strode. Smaller than his fist, it sat on the circular top of the black marble pedestal, the water within as still as glass. As he gazed into its interior, his mind reached out for the water elemental that he had used to fill these vases, Boaa. And as he did so, the water within the vase began to move, climbing the sides of its container, forming a lens to match that formed inside J'Laga's vase.

The image shifted, then steadied. J'Laga, dressed in buckskin, sat cross-legged within a tent, lost in his study of a manuscript, unaware that Kragan had activated their link. When Kragan spoke, the water within his vase picked up the vibrations of his voice, as did its distant counterpart.

"J'Laga."

The vorgish wielder raised his head and shifted his gaze so that he looked directly into Kragan's eyes, showing no sign of being startled. His eyes sparkled with an intelligence that was exceptional among the vorg, who were known for their cunning.

Not surprising, considering how the vorg had been created by Landrel, the ancient master of the Endarian life-shifting and time-shaping magics. Not that Landrel had intended to create the species. He had merely been trying to cure his son by stealing the life essence of a wolf and funneling it into the boy. But Landrel had delved too deeply with his cure. Although his son had not been physically altered, Landrel's grandchildren had become the first vorgs. Despite his horror at the deformity, Landrel had taken his family and fled from Endar, lest they be euthanized.

J'Laga's raspy voice pulled Kragan from his reverie. "You have a task for me, Lord?"

"There is a small human patrol a few leagues east of Far Castle. Tell Commander Charna I want them captured or killed."

"I'll inform Charna."

"And if anyone should escape, make sure it is to the west. Herd them to Far Castle."

J'Laga's lips curled just enough to reveal yellowing fangs. The vorg knew what awaited the humans within those ruins.

As Kragan released control of Boaa, the water spilled down the sides of the small vase to pool again in the bottom. Turning away, Kragan felt confident. When he declared that he had killed Rafel's only children, the warlord would return to Tal to extract his revenge. And then Coldain and the gathered army of Tal would put an end to the warlord who posed the lone threat to Kragan's plans.

8

Far Castle—Southern Borderland Range
YOR 412, Winter's End

Carol, Alan, and the two outriders continued west until late afternoon, eating dried meat and drinking water as they rode. As the sun sank toward the horizon, they swung back to meet the wagons. Alan dropped over the side of the ridge into the next canyon. Carol turned north of a rock ledge and began to descend into the canyon a short distance from where Alan had gone down. Dale and Griffith, the other two riders in the group, rode down the ridge a hundred paces to the east.

With such suddenness that Carol had no time to react, a huge vorg leapt from the thicket above and to her right, landing on Amira's neck. The mare plunged sideways, losing her footing on the shale and throwing Carol clear. She struck the ground and rolled down the slope. As she crashed into a cluster of bushes, she reached out to arrest her slide and felt long thorns rip her hands and body. Rising to her knees, Carol saw the vorg repeatedly stab Amira with a long knife. Then the vorg raced down the slope, running straight toward her. As he neared the thicket, Carol reached out with her mind, sending forth a sudden gust of wind that blew a cloud of dust into the vorg's face, leaving him clutching his eyes. Carol fired an arrow into the attacker's stomach. A look of surprise settled on his wolfish face as he slumped forward.

The air sang with the yells of the living and screams of the dying. Carol looked up to see vorgs running down the hill, clubs and swords raised for the kill. Dale and Griffith spurred their mounts toward her, slashing vorgs as they came. A spear pierced the chest of Griffith's horse and the animal fell, throwing its rider into a group of five vorgs who were upon him before he could rise, hacking with fury. Dale's horse plunged through this group, his sword sending a vorg's head spinning into the air.

Carol worked her bow as rapidly as she could fire, dropping three vorgs that rolled to rest within a dozen feet of her position. Glancing left, she saw Dale dragged from his horse, a war hammer caving in the side of his head as he hit the ground.

Eight more vorgs raced across the distance that separated them from Carol. The number dropped to seven as her arrow caught one in the face, sending him flopping across the ground. She wondered why the vorgs had not returned her fire.

Understanding dawned. They wanted her alive.

Into the midst of the vorgs a lone rider plunged, his battle-ax rising and falling as its wielder leaned recklessly forward in the saddle. Alan's ear-splitting yell echoed off the hills as he split the head of the nearest vorg, while a second vorg spun away through the air, his chest caved in like parchment by the flying hooves of Alan's warhorse. Another vorg raised his spear only to have his arm removed at the shoulder. Carol loosed her last arrow, depositing it in a vorg's back, sending him toppling into one of his comrades.

Alan's horse burst through the vorgs and into her thicket. Leaning down at a dead run, he grabbed Carol's arm, sweeping her up and onto the horse behind him. The two of them crashed through the brush and down the ridge, Carol's heart leaping into her throat. Alan had Charger running down a slope where a horse should be led, not ridden.

Wrapping both arms around his waist, Carol hung on as tree branches slapped and gouged her. Charger stumbled and lurched, but somehow managed to right himself as they hit the ravine bottom and began running up to the west.

Carol wondered why Alan was heading west, away from the wagons and soldiers. Looking back, she found her answer. Dozens of vorgs swarmed into the canyon from the east, cutting them off from the caravan.

"We have to warn Father," Alan yelled back at her.

"If you can find us a place to stop safely for ten minutes, I will try to contact Hawthorne," Carol replied.

"It'll have to wait, then."

Carol saw a dozen vorgs on horseback less than a tenth of a league behind them and coming hard. And the vorgs were not riding double.

Alan spurred Charger on, Carol's extra weight seeming to trouble the warhorse little. Together they thundered up the canyon floor, leaping over rocks and plunging through thickets. Alan reined the horse to the right, sending it up a steep trail on the north side of the canyon. Ducking left and right to avoid being swept from the saddle by overhanging limbs, Carol clung to Alan with all her strength.

As they reached the top of the ridge, the big horse was breathing hard, its sides heaving. Alan urged it along the ridgetop, heading west at a dead run. A bug slapped Carol in the face as she peered over Alan's shoulder, and the whistling wind stung her eyes.

The weight of two riders was beginning to tell on the warhorse. Carol could see that the vorgs were gaining on them. Alan rode off the top of the ridge and down a ragged slope, counting on being able to outride the vorgs in rough terrain. Horse and riders plummeted off a small ledge, landing five feet below. Charger slipped and almost fell in the snow, but managed once again to stay upright. Alan spurred the animal directly down the steep incline and then up the other side of the arroyo.

As they topped this rise, Carol could see that the maneuver had gained them some ground. The horse was now laboring hard, his breath coming in gasping pants. Sweat formed white foam where the saddle blanket ended, the animal's eyes wide and distended. Carol realized they would run Charger to death before much longer.

Rounding a bend, she saw a pinnacle looming before them. Atop its sheer rock walls, the skeletal remains of a crumbling castle perched like a vulture surveying the surrounding terrain.

As Charger reached the base of the cliff, Alan turned him along the bottom of the rock wall. She saw what he was heading for. A steep trail led up the side of the cliff, so narrow and worn from lack of use that no horse could climb the incline. Alan pulled the stallion to a stop, he and Carol swinging to the ground in unison. Slapping its rump, he sent Charger galloping off and then followed Carol up the treacherous path.

The going was hard. What had once been a good trail had fallen into ruin, large sections of the rock wall having sloughed off to plunge to the ground far below. The path rose steeply and, at the crumbled parts, narrowed to less than a foot wide.

Looking down, Carol saw the vorgs reach the trail's base. One attempted to ride up the path but plunged off, not to rise again. The remaining vorgs tied their horses to trees a short distance away and walked back toward the trail. Alan and Carol steadily worked their way up the cliff.

As day gave way to night, the two emerged at the top of the trail to confront the exposed ribs of the ancient fortress, moon shadows creeping around the rubble like specters. The castle walls had fallen in several places, forming piles of broken stone. Bare wooden timbers and supports jutted upward where roofs had been. For obvious reasons, the builders had felt no need to construct a moat.

Alan scrambled over debris from a fallen wall and Carol followed. They found themselves in a dark courtyard fifty paces across. The inner castle still stood.

"So, this is Far Castle," he said.

Carol shuddered. The legend of Far Castle whispered from her childhood memories. In ages long past, it had been the kingdom of Tal's proud western outpost. Baron Rajek, the lord of Far Castle, had gone mad, leading his vassals in revolt. Legend said that an evil wielder named Draken had clouded his lord's mind, enticing him into rebellion.

Rajek had been defeated and Far Castle thrown into ruin. But Draken, in his desperation, had performed a summoning. In doing so, he had allowed a being from the netherworld to enter his body, replacing his form with that of the creature. Unfortunately for him, the thing that was rumored to still lurk within the bowels of these ruins had consumed his mind as well.

Carol forced the old story from her thoughts. Since they had nowhere to go but inside, she and Alan made their way carefully through the main entrance, the doors having long since rotted and fallen off their hinges. What little light remained in the night sky failed to penetrate far, bringing the siblings to a halt in complete darkness.

Carol concentrated, producing the light of two weak torches. It was the best that Golich could manage. In a perfect world, she would have acquired far stronger spells before attempting to escape from vorgs into a haunted ruin. Alas, she had yet to make perfection's acquaintance.

Here, among the overturned chairs and bits of rusty armor, she saw old bones lying in piles scattered about the floor. Luminous wisps of torch-lit fog dripped from the edge of an ancient blade, still clutched in the bony grip of the dead.

Carol deeply inhaled and immediately regretted it, the smell of mold and dust so thick that breathing was a challenge. Each step sent up a cloud of decay, the specks of which swam through the dim light like a horde of tiny gnats, only the missing buzzing in her ears giving lie to the illusion.

Alan tripped over something hidden in the thick layer of dust on the floor, stumbling forward to crash into one of the fallen timbers that dangled from the collapsed roof, the impact loosing a stream of small pebbles and dirt from above. He cursed softly.

He motioned toward the rear wall. A wide passage opened directly ahead. Carol followed close behind her brother as he moved into the next room, the purpose of which had long since been lost. After several paces, the wall angled sharply to the right, to a spot where a doorway opened, revealing a stone stairway.

Alan ducked into this opening with Carol staying close on his heels, their muffled steps and rasping breath the only sounds. Steep and narrow, the gray steps descended in a progression of winding turns. Saying nothing to Alan, Carol starkly remembered the spiraling steps that had led to the primordial in her Ritual of Terrors.

Her brother took no chances, probing ahead with the shaft of the spear he had purloined from a dead warrior in the hall above. The tapping sound reminded Carol of a blind man she had seen as a little girl. She had asked her father why the man was probing the ground in front of him with the long stick.

"He is a warrior, lost in the black," Rafel said. "The tapping is his guide through a dark and dangerous place, a land where only the bravest among us have the will to survive."

She followed Alan down the ancient steps. The rusted claws of empty sconces adorned the walls, draped with cobwebs so covered with dust that they had lost all stickiness. With trepidation cloying her soul, Carol tried to see around her brother, wanting to know what lay ahead. Alan's stocky form allowed little opportunity for such glances. His grip tightened on the haft of his ax until the veins that bulged on the back of his wrist looked like they would split skin.

Footsteps clattered in the distance from behind, the sound of heavy boots and clank of armor echoing along the halls. Alan turned right, then immediately back to the left, picking his route by feel, trying to ensure that those following them did not have a direct line to their targets. Carol put her hand on his arm and pulled him into a side alcove, sending the two lights gliding on down the hall, bouncing slightly as if two people carried torches.

The group of vorgs raced past sister and brother in the alcove, going after the lights. Carol sped the ethereal torches forward at a runner's pace, allowing them to wink out as they rounded a distant corner. The sounds made by the pursuing vorgs diminished and died away.

"We have to find a secluded place where I can contact Hawthorne," she whispered.

"Come on," Alan said.

He grabbed her hand and headed down a side passage. Carol felt her way along the wall until she was sure that no one could see them. Then, once again, she called forth the fairy lights, releasing Alan's hand as they pushed back the darkness.

Despite a feeling of wrongness, Carol pressed onward, searching for somewhere they could hide for just a few minutes without worry of being discovered.

A room opened up off the hallway to their left, and Carol paused, signaling Alan to do likewise. The two phantom lights darted inside, moving around the walls as she peered around the corner, trying to get a feel for the layout of the room. The space had apparently been some sort of armory, long ago looted of everything of value, lined with racks that had once held weapons and armor, a few damaged sets of the latter still clinging to pegs or having rusted and fallen to the floor.

A lone alcove pocked one of the walls. Carol led the way toward it. Upon reaching the spot and finding nothing more than an empty closet, she moved inside and sat down to prepare for the meditation. She found that, despite its relative simplicity, the torch spell had tired her. She needed more practice.

Carol let her mind drift, searching for that center of meditation where all was calm. After a few minutes, she reached out, sending her consciousness floating out through the castle and into the night. Snow had started to fall heavily outside, and over this landscape she passed as she reactivated her mental link to Hawthorne, using her detailed knowledge of his wards to bypass them.

The camp rushed up to meet her. She saw the light of the fires and the soldiers who formed a defensive ring around the wagons. Apparently, the missing outriders had caused the caravan to take extra precautions.

Carol whisked into Hawthorne's tent and found him seated upon his patterned rug, lost in meditation. As her thoughts touched his, the wielder straightened in surprise.

"How . . . how have you done this?" Hawthorne's mental voice stuttered.

"The same way we linked minds in your wagon."

"But the distance. This should be impossible."

"Listen, please," said Carol, her desperation rising. "I need your help."

After several more seconds of contact, she broke the meditation, confident that Hawthorne would relay what had happened near Far Castle to her father.

"And?" Alan asked when she opened her eyes.

"It's done."

A renewed clamor erupted in the hallway from which they had just come.

"The vorgs are back," Alan said.

He and Carol raced into the passage and began running away from the sound. The vorgs were close. Loud yells echoed through the ruins. Alan rounded a corner to his right and stopped, motioning for her to go on. Instead, she stopped beside him. She refused to abandon her brother to fight these things alone.

As the first vorg rounded the corner, Alan's ax sent its dying body spinning into the wall. The next two vorgs tried to stop, but their trailing companions pushed them forward. Alan's whirling blade put them out of their panic.

Carol gestured with her hands, casting a light into a vorg's face, blinding him and startling the others. Into that confusion, Alan stepped, swinging his ax in a high arc. The vorg's lighted head tumbled from its body to roll on the floor, a horrible, grinning lantern. Carol shifted her concentration, calling forth a strong breeze that rolled the glowing vorg head toward one vorg after another. In panic, the warriors retreated back the way they had come.

Carol extinguished the light and sagged back against the wall. She had just done something she had not known that she could do, controlling two elementals simultaneously. Hawthorne had not told her that wielders could cast two different spells at once.

Alan lifted Carol in a bear hug that threatened her breathing. "My sister the wielder. You are amazing."

She felt herself blush at the unexpected compliment, thankful that it was too dark for him to see her cheeks.

Shrieks of terror from the direction the vorgs had disappeared drew their attention. Another sound could be heard as well, a primordial sound, deep and guttural. Carol felt the hair rise along her arms, neck, and scalp. Something was killing the vorgs.

"Come on!" said Alan.

Horrible noises echoing through dark ruins have a unique ability to lend speed to the feet of the weary, and this was no exception. Casting her fairy lights in front of Alan, Carol had no difficulty keeping up with the pace he set. He plunged deeper into the dungeon, away from whatever feasted on the vorgs.

She lost track of the turns as they raced onward. A heavy scraping sound echoed down the halls behind them as Alan plunged into a passage on the right, running down the stairs three at a time. They reached the next level, but Alan continued down, Carol close behind him. The stairs terminated in a room that spread out before the two well beyond the illumination provided by the magical orbs. Carol sent one of the lights scanning out to the left across the damp floor.

She and Alan followed about ten feet behind, past an array of disparate torture devices.

A mixture of scraping and slavering noises issued from the stairway they had just descended, sending them scurrying forward again. Carol raced along behind Alan, searching for an exit along the room's back wall. Instead, they came face-to-face with a closed iron gate. Alan grabbed a rusty key ring from a peg beside the gate and started fumbling with the lock. The noises across the room grew louder, much louder. Alan found the key that fit and turned hard. The rusty key broke off in the lock.

"Damn!" he yelled, giving the gate a savage kick that swung it open with a squeal of rusted metal.

The gate had not been locked.

Alan grabbed Carol's hand, and the two plunged through. This passage was different. Gone were the worked rock walls and square corners. The tunnel was a natural part of an ancient cave system that the builders had widened. Oddly-shaped cells had been carved into walls, some of their iron doors having rotted off their hinges and fallen to the floor.

The siblings rounded a bend to encounter another set of stairs that spilled them down into a large room. A foul stench drove the air from Carol's lungs, indicating the nearness of the thing that followed.

Alan slid to a stop at the edge of a deep pit. The floor in front of them abruptly ended. Carol glanced back, the side of the room from which they had just come seeming to move in the darkness.

"Move!" Alan yelled.

Turning left, they ran along the edge of the pit that grew ever wider, forcing them back toward the entrance. Carol sent one of the lights toward the thing chasing them. It was monstrous, with a bulk extending beyond the radius of the dim glow. The shambling pile of flesh had a lumpy appendage that she took to be a head but with no discernible face. Beneath the slimy skin, its features shifted, a large, cabbagelike bulge moving first toward her and then toward Alan.

Then Carol was lifted into the air, grabbed by Alan as he jumped off the ledge. She barely had time to suck in her breath before the plunge came to a sudden stop as he grabbed an outcropping of rock with his free hand. In the gasp that issued from his mouth, Carol could feel the pain that surged through his arm. That pain was overridden by her own as their bodies slammed against the pit's rock wall. She scrambled to attain her own grip on the stone.

Pulling herself to a secure handhold, she yelled at Alan, "I've got it. Go!"

A slurping sound from above was followed by a cloying stench as the thing slipped over the ledge, slithering down.

Carol gagged, a rush of bile filling her mouth before she forced it back down.

Alan started climbing down the rough rock wall. She did likewise. The sounds from above caused her to risk handholds she would never have attempted under normal circumstances. Alan modulated his descent, moving just fast enough to stay even with her. Carol suspected that he knew she was tiring, the exertion of the chase plus the efforts of her spell-casting having worn her down.

She was determined that she would jump into the unknown depths below rather than allow that thing to catch her. Just then, its head burst into her little circle of light. The cabbagelike appendage expanded, stretching the skin beneath and reaching out toward her. As she released her grip on the wall and pushed outward, the strange appendage grabbed her arm, pulling her back toward the fleshy mound.

With a yell, Alan leapt from his perch on the wall, swinging his ax with one hand as the other encircled her waist. Carol felt a gush of putrid liquid drench her clothes as she and her brother fell away. The rough rock of the cavern floor broke their fall almost as soon as it began. Unprepared, Carol felt the sudden stop knock the wind from her body, breaking her concentration. The elemental that she had been controlling swept into her eyes, its light blinding her.

She grabbed Golich again, forcing it outward where Alan could see, but it had obliterated her night vision. Alan grabbed her and carried her along. A loud plop behind them amped up her panic.

"The light is drifting away," Alan said. "I can't see a damned thing."

Still blinded, Carol could not see to direct Golich's activity, so she concentrated on locking the light to her own right hand. When his pace increased, she concluded that her attempt had worked.

The wind rushed past Carol's face as he ran, slavering sounds of pursuit licking her ears. She blinked her eyes. Even though her vision was slowly returning, she could not fully make out the details of her surroundings. They seemed to be in a large, natural cavern, through which Alan ducked left and right, dodging obstacles that she assumed to be stalagmites.

He was breathing heavily now, her weight another burden sapping his strength.

"Let me down," she said. "Just hang on to my hand."

As Alan complied, she stumbled, righting herself as they raced forward through a room in which she could see neither ceiling nor walls. Her light failed to illuminate the monstrosity shambling along behind them, but from the slightly diminished volume of its sounds, they appeared to have gained ground.

For the next few minutes, the two ran through the maze of stalagmites that grew from the cavern floor. Finally they reached a place where the walls angled to form a narrow passage. As they rounded a bend, Carol felt, more than saw, a cleft in the left wall. Tugging hard on his hand, she pulled Alan inside.

"Quick! Take off your socks!" she whispered.

She already had her boots off and her thick socks in her hand. Alan followed suit. She grabbed the socks from his hand and tossed them, along with hers, into the center of the passage. A breeze whisked the sweat-soaked things across the floor and down the passage, the odor giving ample evidence of their presence. Along with the fast-moving socks, she sent the fairy lights bobbing down the hall.

A nearby scraping sound sent the two crowding back into the crevice, so that the rough stone of the wall left its imprint on Carol's back. The monster passed directly in front of them. The claustrophobic space and horrible slurping sounds robbed her of breath, a feeling that grew in intensity until Carol felt she would scream. Stench bathed her, the creature so close that she could have reached out and touched it.

Then the monster was gone, continuing along the tunnel in pursuit of those socks.

Carol and Alan slipped on their boots and ducked out of the crevice, back into the main cavern. Creating just enough light for them to see where they were stepping, Carol hoped that the turns they had taken would block the glow from the slime creature's view. They loped along, heading back the way they came.

Reaching a rough wall, they paused. Was this the wall they had climbed down to enter this cavern? She had no idea. Perhaps she could enter a state of meditation and project her consciousness around the cavern until she found an exit. But that would not work. There was no light, and she could not cast a spell from within a meditative state.

Alan grabbed her arm and led her to the right, scrambling up and over a pile of boulders to a place where an old cave-in had almost blocked the passage out of the main cavern. Carol squeezed through the crack, crawling after him as swiftly as she could manage.

The rocky path added bloody scrapes to Carol's legs and shredded the knees of her pants. Luckily, the crawlway through the rubble soon gave way to a hall that enabled the siblings to stand side by side. Together, they limped onward, pushing themselves through exhaustion.

One foot in front of the other, she thought. *Just one foot in front of the other.*

Unable to maintain the effort, Carol let the lights go out. Alan stopped beside her as she sank to the ground.

"Do you feel that?" he asked.

"A breeze!"

With renewed energy, she rose and led Alan down the hall, one hand held out before her as the other traced the wall. As she rounded a bend, the pale light of the full moon framed a door-shaped opening thirty feet in front of them. Heart pounding, Carol moved toward it.

Without warning, the floor collapsed beneath her. She screamed and plunged. But as she fell, Carol caught the lip of the pit with her left hand . . . and then her right. Although her body slapped the wall hard enough to leave her gasping, she held on until Alan reached down to grab her wrist and pull her up.

"It was trapped," he said. "Probably constructed when this dungeon was built."

Carol peered over the edge, sending a light down to a bed of sharp spikes.

She patted him on the arm. "Thank you."

"Of course, sister."

Skirting the pit along a foot-wide lip, they continued down the passage at a more deliberate pace on the chance that the ancient trap builders had constructed more than one of their nasty surprises. They soon reached another iron gate, this one blocking the hall and preventing them from reaching the moonlit doorway. And this time, the gate was locked.

Alan fumbled with the key ring he'd found earlier, twisting each key in turn, careful to avoid snapping one off in the lock.

Finally one of the keys worked. The gate squealed loudly on its hinges as Alan opened and then closed it behind them. He took the time to lock the gate. "Just in case our large friend finds our trail," he explained.

He reached the opening first, coming to an abrupt halt. "Damn it!"

Stepping up beside her brother, Carol's heart sank. The doorway opened into empty space dozens of feet above the ground, halfway up the sheer rock wall that dropped away from Far Castle.

PART II

Endarians possess the innate ability to channel life energy and even time itself. But the volume that can be exchanged is determined by the wielder's talent and skill.

—From the *Scroll of Landrel*

9

Wind. Arn cursed under his breath. He hated the wind. He did not care much for winter's end because of the wind that accompanied it. Out here, just below the craggy cliffs lining the top of the hill, above the canyon that dropped away in steep, shale-covered slopes, a weird sea of currents swirled. Streams of cold air sliding down from the snow-capped peaks far above wrestled with puffs of warm air rising from the low plains to the east. The chill bumps along Arn's neck left little doubt as to the outcome of that tussle. Spring would be a long while yet in making its way into the high country.

That small but insistent voice inside his head was bothering him again. Something was not as it should be. Dense woods of juniper and scrub covered the south side of the canyon. Across the ravine, he could see the almost treeless, rocky expanse of the northern slope. Nothing moved except the trees and brush rustling in the wind. Even the normally abundant wildlife refused to graze in this biting breeze. A decaying hut nestled in the trees at the bottom of the slope was the only indication that anyone had ever been here.

Arn was twenty-seven, just over six feet tall, slender, and lithe. He kept his curly hair short—easier to take care of that way. He kept a dagger strapped to each thigh; the handles of two others protruded from sheaths in his boots. But the much larger knife that hung in a thick leather scabbard on his left hip was what drew the eye. The weapon had a black bone handle ornately decorated with intricate carvings, its wide blade extending a foot in length and angling to a sharp point.

Arn moved silently across the loose rock and shale, his long stride rapidly carrying him toward the next crest in the slope. There he paused, withdrawing the big knife that he had named Slaken from its sheath.

Slaken was his one magical possession, its very existence as ironic as his own. The dull black blade, darker than a starless night, absorbed light rays, leaching them into the handle. There they warped and twisted, dancing along the strange runes carved into its surface. The effect was fluid, as if light flowed along the narrow channels the script cut into the weapon's landscape.

Overcome with gratitude that Arn had saved the life of his only son, Rodan had granted him the right to have any one thing the king could give. What Arn had asked for had taken Gregor and the king's chief armorer five years to make: the black blade with the carved handle, a handle with so many magical inscriptions that one blended into the next.

The blade was so magical that it had no magic. It was magic twisted in upon itself so that one spell blocked another until none worked. In fact, no spell had any effect upon the knife, nor upon the person who had made the blood-bond with the weapon, and only Arn could hold the blade. Slaken gave Arn the one thing he desired most in the world— the ability to operate without the direct interference of wielders.

Arn blinked, pulling himself out of the sudden trance into which he had fallen. He did not often allow himself to study the knife, as he found the effect it had on his mind disconcerting.

Right now, on the other side of the ridgeline, something else awaited him, pulling him forward. This had all been in his dimly remembered dreams. Since that moment of shame when he had hidden inside the wood box, too afraid to look to see who had murdered his mother and father, he had felt the almost imperceptible tug of destiny. His feet sensed the path that would eventually lead to the confrontation from which he had shied as a boy. He had no evidence to back this belief; he just needed it to be true. So once again, he would yield to that pull.

—◊◊◊—

Battle has a smell. Long before the fighting started, adrenaline flooded the bodies of those who awaited its commencement, flushing the pores with sweat, both hot and cold, and in some cases loosing other bodily functions. And those smells drifted out on the breeze, detectable by those who paid attention. As Arn moved through the thick brush near the military crest of the ridge, he smelled the fighting before he saw or heard it. He quickened his pace, gliding through rocks and dense brush.

Reaching a rocky outcropping that provided a spectacular view of the deep canyon beyond, he stopped. The sound of distant screams and yells drifted up on the breeze, accompanied by the clash of metal on metal.

Spread out along the narrow canyon floor, at least a hundred vorgs pressed forward, howling in frustration as they tried to climb a fallen tree that formed a ramp into a narrow breach in the towering rock wall that terminated the box canyon. Atop that ledge, a lone shirtless warrior moved, his blond hair swirling around his shoulders as he fought, lost in the dance with his ax. Above him and to the right, a bowman fired down into the vorgs that scrambled upward over the bodies of their fallen pack mates.

The warrior advanced along the ten-foot section of the wall that held the mighty tree ramp, clearing away vorgs as fast as they could scramble to the top.

A low moan rose from the vorgs nearing the top of the ramp as the rush of their companions pressed them forward into the whirling, blood-soaked terror that awaited. The moan built in volume until it could be heard from all corners of the canyon.

For the briefest of moments, Arn paused, engulfed by a memory. He'd seen a battle like this in his dreams, a lone warrior battling along a great ramp atop the walls of a mighty fortress, in a different place, a different time.

A motion toward the rear of the battle group caught Arn's eye. An ancient vorg, long fangs curling over his lower lip, pushed his way forward, clutching a staff in his hands. Wielder. Very soon now, the blond barbarian and his friend were going to die.

Arn moved into a dead run down the steep slope, his feet touching the ground just long enough to push off as the loose shale began to slide beneath them. The vorgs at the rear never saw him coming, so intently did they focus on their trapped quarry. As he moved headlong into the throng, Arn's hands worked his knives in quick staccato thrusts into backs, kidneys, and throats, motions designed to clear a path forward. As the vorgs fell away before him, the ones behind struggled to react to his passage, their rush impeded by their startled and dying comrades.

The wielder raised his staff, his voice rising in singsong spell chant. Arn's black blade opened a new mouth below the sorcerer's chin as the last syllable turned into a gargle. A mighty rumble erupted from the staff, but the fireball missed its target, crashing into the cliffs high above the rift where the barbarian battled. The force of the explosion shook the canyon floor, stunning the surprised vorgs and causing them to whirl toward their dying wielder.

Arn did not hesitate, continuing his momentum toward the ramp, although now the crush of vorgs slowed him as they began to realize a new enemy was among them.

Suddenly a new rumble shook the ground as a rock spire gave way, high on the cliffs above. With a mighty yell, the barbarian atop the tree ramp charged into the confusion, the great ax cutting through the vorgs that blocked Arn's path. Into the gap Arn raced, running up the ramp toward the rift as rocks rained down.

Seeing the danger, the barbarian whirled, following Arn back up the ramp. On the ledge above, the archer strummed his bow, dropping the nearest vorgs as they rushed to follow.

"John!" the barbarian yelled. "Rock fall. Get into the cave."

The bowman glanced up and then leapt into the opening, narrowly avoiding a boulder that splintered on the ledge beside him. Arn reached the ledge and raced into the dark opening, feeling the barbarian close on his heels. The assassin did not pause, scrambling deeper into the darkness as the sound of falling rock behind him rose to a deafening rumble.

The ground lurched, throwing Arn to the cave's rocky floor. He scrambled forward into absolute blackness, feeling his way as dust clogged his throat. Reaching a point where the ground sloped steeply down, Arn crawled rapidly onward, stopping only when the air began to feel clear.

Leaning back against the wall, he gulped in great gasps, an effort that brought on a round of violent coughing. The sounds of the other two men coughing nearby were the only other noises heard. The rockslide had apparently stopped and, at least for the moment, the vorgs had not followed them into the cave.

The barbarian's voice echoed through the blackness. "Stuck in a damned cave, blind as a bat. Exactly what I was hoping for today."

"Quit whining," the other man responded. "If you'd followed me inside to begin with, we could have gotten away from the vorgs without a fight."

"John, I told you. I don't like caves."

Apparently remembering Arn's presence, John called out. "Stranger, you still alive?"

"I seem to be," Arn replied.

"You're one crazy fool," the barbarian said.

"You're welcome."

The barbarian laughed.

"Do you have a name, stranger?" John asked.

"My friends call me Arn."

"You'll have to excuse Ty," John said. "He's Kanjari. They're not long on manners. If you hadn't killed that wielder, things could have gotten ugly."

"Well, I'm glad it all came out so well, then."

Ty laughed again, the sound echoing away into the darkness. Arn wondered whether the barbarian was a bit insane.

Feeling around in his pack, Arn retrieved his tinderbox and a candle. Within seconds of working the flint and steel, he produced a small flame that he transferred to the wick.

"You do have your uses," Ty said, moving into the small circle of light.

The flickering flame revealed a surreal world in which the cave ceiling crept downward until it was barely six feet above the floor. Beyond that circle, the darkness pressed in like an elemental intent on snuffing out the offending illumination.

A thick coat of dust gave the men the look of savages, readying themselves for some arcane ritual. Arn stared at the Kanjari. He had only seen one other at a carnival when he was ten. The Kanjari were nomadic horse warriors, their love of fighting surpassed only by their love of horses and wide-open spaces. Although generally frowned upon by their people, some Kanjari loved showing off their skills and joined traveling carnivals.

At six and a half feet tall, Ty looked like the god of war. His ax was unique, with beautiful carvings of running horses adorning its ivory handle, their blowing manes visible through a sheen of blood. The blade formed an arc like a crescent moon and jutted out from the haft. Etched into the blade's flat sides, a majestic stallion pawed the air, eyes rolling wildly, ears laid back along its head.

John stood two inches shorter than Arn. His raven-black hair hung down to his shoulders and a beaklike nose gave the impression of a hawk. But it was the man's eyes that held Arn's attention, their irises as black as their pupils, twin pools of darkness.

"We better move on," said John, who Arn had immediately pegged as the most sensible of the pair. "I grew up in this area, and I've been through all these caves. This one has another way out."

"No," said Ty. "You're not dragging me deeper into this thing."

"Look," said John, "even if the entryway isn't blocked, there are a whole bunch of angry vorgs waiting out there to welcome us back. They're probably already searching for a way in. Our only real chance is to use the back door. It's a bit hard to get to, but I've done it before."

Arn rose to his feet. "Makes sense."

"Listen," said Ty. "Why do you think I hate caves? It's because I followed him into one before. If he says this one's a little hard, then it's damnation."

"I'm not seeing a lot of choices."

The barbarian remained silent for a moment, and then shrugged. "Just remember what I said."

Arn and Ty scrambled down the slope behind John into the crevice beyond, a crack just wide enough to squeeze through. After about three feet, the entire nature of the cavern changed. The passage allowed just enough room for them to crawl forward on hands and knees, but it was much wider than the light of the candle could show.

The experience felt like being sandwiched between two gigantic slices of rock-hard bread, except here the stone surfaces glittered with kaleidoscopic reflections. Tiny stalactites and stalagmites covered the ceiling and floor, like icicles sparkling in the candlelight. The flickering flame sent showers of shimmering lights cascading off the nearest little spears, while sparkles glinted from the floor and ceiling farther along.

The sight dazzled Arn. Everywhere he looked, strange colors danced back and forth, always changing, never repeating a previous pattern, the uncanny beauty of chaos.

While the icicles were mesmerizing, they were hard on the hands, knees, and back. Soon Arn and Ty were cut and bleeding from scores of tiny wounds. Every few feet resulted in one of the men bumping his head, catching his back, or firmly planting his shin on one of the sharp objects, which brought forth a steady stream of curses from Ty.

"I knew that son-of-a-vorg would get us into something like this," Ty muttered from somewhere behind Arn.

Meanwhile, Arn was doing his best just to keep John in sight. At last the trio came to a point where the roof of the cave moved up to about five feet, allowing them to sit and rest. Leaning back, Arn rummaged through his pack and extracted three strips of jerky, handing one to each of his companions. Together, in the damp stillness of the underworld, they enjoyed a less than hearty lunch, washing the meat down with a swallow of water.

"You'll need to take off that pack now," John said to Arn. "It gets a little tough from here on out."

"I thought we were already through the hard part!" Ty yelled. "Give me that pack, Arn. I'll push it in front of me. You just stay close to John with that candle. If he gets us stuck down in here, I want you to burn his stinkin' toes off before we die."

Arn grinned, starting to take to the Kanjari's madness. Handing his pack to Ty, he scrambled into the small opening where John had just disappeared. It could not be classified as a passage; it was little more than a horizontal crack. Arn lay on his belly and wiggled into the orifice, holding the candle out before him. Here there were no pretty formations, only a dank, musty crawlway.

Wriggling forward into the candlelight, Arn could feel the walls of the passage on all sides. As he crawled on his belly, he continually raised his head or back slightly too high, bumping one or the other on the ceiling.

The silence from behind attested to the sheer horror Ty was feeling. John paused every few minutes to allow Arn to catch up.

After an hour, the passage began to descend and narrow until the friction of the floor and ceiling pressing against Arn's body was all that kept him from sliding down. He was now convinced that they would be unable to crawl backward. If something blocked the passage ahead, they would die.

Arn heard the sound of heavy breathing behind him. He forced himself to slow his breathing to avoid the prospect of hyperventilation. The entire weight of the mountain bore down upon him as he wriggled forward. Just then, a gust of air hit him in the face and blew out the candle.

"Damn it!" Arn said.

He immediately heard laughter from behind. "I'm going to kill that bastard if it's the last thing I do," rasped Ty.

"You'll have to beat me to it. And I'm closer."

John's voice echoed through the crawl space. "If you gentlemen would stop the chatter, you could be out here with me, standing in this large cavern."

Arn squeezed forward to a point where the tunnel flattened out. Finally, by feeling around with his hand, he found a place where, by turning his head sideways, he managed to get both skull and shoulders through. John grabbed both his arms and, with a strong pull, tugged Arn out into a large cavern.

"I think I'm stuck," said Ty.

Arn felt his pack handed to him. Blind, he began fumbling through it, searching for the tinderbox, flint, and steel.

Behind him, Ty's cursing reached epic proportions.

"Just let me reach through and guide your head," said John in a gentle voice, showing slight concern. "There. Now stretch your arms straight out in front of you. Don't move your head and I'll pull you through."

A flame sputtered to life on the candle just in time for Arn to see John, with both feet against the wall, pulling on two arms. With a loud scraping noise, Ty slid out of the hole. He arose, his scraped and bloody face showing clear evidence of his ordeal, his eyes awash with relief and anger.

"John, if you ever lead me into another cave, I'm going to tie you between horses and rip you apart," Ty said, his hands braced on his knees.

"Well, if that's all the thanks I get for saving your ass, next time I'll take you the hard way," John replied, all gentleness gone.

Arn could see very little of the cavern in which they now stood. He cautiously took a few steps away from the wall to examine more of the room.

"Be careful," John said. "There's a drop-off about ten feet in front of you. This is a big cave, but it's only a small part of a much larger set of caverns. Luckily we aren't far from an exit."

"Then let's get to it," Ty growled.

John headed off along the ledge to the left. Rounding a bend, they were confronted with the sight of a natural stone bridge, arching away into the darkness.

Without hesitation, John stepped out onto the span and began to cross, Ty and Arn trailing behind. The bridge, barely five feet wide and sloping away on both sides to a deep drop, was covered in slick limestone flows that provided precious little in the way of firm footing.

Their passage across the bridge ended on a ledge that soon became the floor of another cavern. Here John turned into a narrow side passage that led to another large room. A shaft of light shone through a hole high up on a steep shale slope. The way out.

As the three men scrambled up the slope, anxious to be outside again, a sour, musty smell filled Arn's nose. Bat guano.

"I didn't think I'd ever be happy to crawl through bat crap," Ty said, "but right now, it smells pretty damned good. Of course, I've been smelling John for a while."

"As if you're a basket of ne'er lilies," John said.

As the exit loomed large, Arn felt a gust of brisk air splash his face. He inhaled deeply, letting it wash his lungs.

Arn held up a hand. "Wait here a minute."

He extinguished the candle, put it back in his pack, and led the group noiselessly to the cave's mouth, pausing to allow his eyes to adjust to daylight. The cave emerged on a hillside that sloped steeply away to the west. The clouds above had begun to acquire shades of red and orange as the sun sank below the mountains that formed the western horizon. Before him, the terrain was changing. The foothills where they had entered the cave had given way to a land of tabletop plateaus. Pine trees now mixed with junipers.

The men camped that night in a secluded glen on the edge of the mesa, their site sheltered by the rim. As the western horizon swallowed the sun, a blaze spread across the sky, consuming the thin clouds in a cauldron of scarlet and rose.

Unwilling to light a fire, Arn shared the last of his dried venison with the others. Despite the poor fare, an aura of good cheer governed the camp.

"Where are you bound for, friend?" John asked Arn after they had finished eating.

Arn reflected for a moment. Where indeed? "West."

Ty raised an eyebrow. "That's some bad country. Might want to give it some thought."

"West is as good a direction as any and better than some."

"Is somebody after you?" asked Ty.

"Why?" Arn asked.

Ty leaned back on his elbows. "You're traveling alone. Not a healthy thing in these parts."

"I'm a loner."

"Ha. Aren't we all? Take John over there. To hear him tell it, he's really only made one mistake in his life. He had the misfortune of saving my life one fine spring day last year. So now he's got my company until I can return the favor. And now, come to think of it, so have you."

"No, thanks. You two got me out of the cave. We're even."

"Nope. That was John again. I'm afraid you're stuck with me for a while. Kanjari tradition."

"You can't watch out for me and him both."

"Sure I can. We'll all travel together for a while. From what I've seen of you so far, it shouldn't take long for you to get into more trouble. Then John and I can be on our way."

Arn nodded toward John. "What if he doesn't want to go?"

"Sounds interesting," said John.

"I travel alone," Arn said, the conversation beginning to irritate him.

Ty grinned. "That's something you'll just have to get over."

"We can argue about that tomorrow," said Arn as he climbed to his feet. "I'll take first watch."

He shifted his gaze from one to the other of these unlikely companions, unable to shake the feeling that Ty had predicted his future. Turning away, Arn walked into the night.

—⁓—

Having agreed to travel together as far as the rough border town of Rork, Arn and his companions set out at dawn. By late afternoon, the group reached a secluded meadow with a small bubbling stream. After sending John out to scout the surrounding area, Arn and Ty set up camp.

Arn leaned back against a large rock and gazed out at the scene before him. The pass they would travel through tomorrow lay a short distance to the west. The mountains stretched to the north and south. He planned to travel through the pass and then turn northwest toward Rork.

The town's only permanent population consisted primarily of slave traders and tavern keepers, most of them bandits who had grown rich enough to set up operations that were even more lucrative. The other residents were made up of transient bands, both human and vorg. The only law was that enforced by the strongest gang currently in town.

Rork miraculously did not cannibalize itself. The need for a place to trade ill-gotten goods and get too drunk to stand trumped the lust to destroy.

Arn wanted to stop in the town just long enough to get supplies. As for money, he had only managed to bring a small pouch of gems and another of gold coins. If he had taken more of his wealth, it would have aroused suspicion.

Daybreak found the trio already through the pass and moving down into a lush green valley. By noon, they had crossed the expanse and three others like it. Arn stood at the top of a ridge, looking down into a box canyon, its rock walls two-hundred-foot vertical drops to the valley floor and the bottom of the canyon split by a sparkling stream that meandered back and forth through meadows of knee-deep grass. A waterfall plummeted from the top of a cliff that blocked the canyon's north end, forming a large pool.

A thin veil of mist drifted away from the waterfall, partially shrouding dozens of wild horses. Near the herd, a palomino stallion stood alone, head held high, tail and mane blowing behind the animal as it trotted back and forth. Never had Arn seen a horse so big and fine.

Ty's iron hand clapped down on Arn's shoulder, a wildness blazing in the Kanjari's blue eyes. "I will have that horse."

"And how do you propose catching it?" asked Arn.

"Are you blind? It's in a box canyon."

"I'm listening."

"You and John sneak around to the falls, and then climb down into the canyon, making a racket. I'll take care of the rest."

Before Arn could continue the argument, the tall Kanjari was gone, running toward the lower end of the canyon, his hair blowing out behind him.

"He looks like that damned stallion, doesn't he?" John asked.

Arn had to agree that they bore a striking resemblance.

As Arn and John made their way around and down the cliff, the stallion raced off down the canyon, the mares stampeding behind him.

The horse reached Ty at full speed, extending its hooves to trample the human beneath its feet. Somehow, the blow from its hooves and shoulder failed to land. At the last instant, Ty lunged sideways, leaving only his outstretched arm in front of the running animal.

The horse hit his arm, its momentum windmilling the Kanjari's body high into the air. In a miracle of strength and coordination, Ty brought his cartwheeling body to a perch atop the racing stallion.

As if its speed could blow the Kanjari off its back, the stallion raced out of the canyon, followed by the mares. Arn and John stared after them.

—⁓—

With John off hunting, Arn found what he was looking for. As the brook made its way around a high bank, a large boulder partially blocked its path, forming a deep, still pool of water. Setting his pack down, Arn extracted a small pouch, dumped its contents on the ground, and picked out a fishing hook and a ball of strong twine.

Finding a tree, Arn cut a long, supple branch to which he fastened a line and hook, using a twig for the float. After digging up a worm-filled clump of mud, he baited the hook, tossed the line out into the water, and sat down on the bank. He had just settled to the ground when the small stick disappeared under the water. Jumping up, he pulled on the pole, bending it sharply. Fearing the pole would break, Arn reached down, grabbed the string, and began pulling it in.

The fish at the other end battled fiercely, but in a few seconds Arn had it flopping around on the bank. A sense of exhilaration flooded over him. Some of his happiest memories were of his father teaching him to fish in the stream that ran behind their cottage. The triggered emotions felt fresh and new.

He picked out another worm, squishing its body slightly between his fingers. Arn did not sit down as he tossed the line out into the water. As the worm hit the water, another trout rose, splashing the surface, and disappeared. Again, the float went down, but this time Arn landed the fish with his pole.

For the rest of the day, Arn enjoyed the best fishing he had ever experienced as an adult. And as the hours passed, he felt the rage that lurked beneath the surface of his thoughts recede. Recollections of the years he had spent as a member of the Rafel family made their way into his mind. Sweetest of all had been his time spent with Carol. As they had grown older, his brotherly love for her had morphed into something different.

Carol had been seventeen when she had told him of her love. Although he was five years her senior, he had loved her, too. Yet even more than the difference in their ages, the thirst for vengeance that lurked within him had made acceptance of her love impossible.

Arn had rejected her advances with a lie, telling her that he loved her only as a sister. After that, Carol had grown cold. Cordial but distant. So he had left Rafel's Keep for Hannington Castle and, shorn of the love in which High Lord Rafel and Carol had bathed him, Arn had unleashed the fury within. In the years that followed, he had earned the nickname Blade, and the distance between him and Carol had become an uncrossable chasm.

Arn frowned and rose to his feet. A sense of unease had returned. Picking up his stringer of fish, he turned and headed back to camp.

10

Arn awoke to a new sunrise, bathed in the campfire's warmth. "Where's Ty?" he asked John.

"Where else? Riding that horse of his. Has been for the last two hours."

Arn rose to his feet and sniffed his armpit. "I'm going down to the creek to wash up."

"I was about to recommend that."

Arn walked off, wondering just how he had managed to get himself tangled up with these two. As he stripped off his garments and plunged in, the icy water interrupted his reverie. By the time Arn pulled his body from the pool, put on his clothes, and returned to camp, he found a breakfast of smoked venison awaiting him.

Just then, Ty thundered into the canyon, sitting atop the palomino as if he had been born there. Horse and rider moved in one fluid motion, blond manes blowing out behind them. Having rejoined Arn and John the previous evening, Ty had ridden out to gather the mares at first light.

"You ready to travel?" he asked as the stallion slid to a stop beside the campfire, whereupon he dismounted.

"We've been waiting on you," Arn said.

"Good. I want to herd the mares to Rork for sale. You two can cut cross-country and meet me there, day after tomorrow. I've got to take the herd the long way around."

"There are fifty-three mares in that herd," said John. "I figure they're worth eighty gold, but we'll be lucky to get thirty in Rork."

"If that much," said Arn.

Ty packed food and water, slung his ax across his back, mounted the horse, and galloped away.

After packing the rest of the dried venison, Arn and John traveled up the west side of the canyon and headed through the pass that lay beyond before turning northwest. Twilight found them setting up camp on a hill overlooking a broad valley. In the distance, a small cluster of lights in the town of Rork twinkled, the moonlight revealing fingers of forest that seemed to reach out threateningly.

Arn offered to take first watch, and John agreed. The night was cool but warmer than those of the past few weeks. Arn seated himself on a boulder and looked out at the distant town. He had been in many like it. In the outlands, law was a joke. Traders, who were just bandits grown tired of raiding, had decided to rob people more efficiently, setting up trading posts, gambling halls, taverns, and brothels. The towns that sprang up around them made undertaking a highly profitable business.

In these parts, vorgs formed the majority of the population, although human bandits were almost as common. The lands farther to the west were the stuff of rumor and myth. Few who journeyed there returned, and those who claimed to were difficult to believe, their tales so populated with evil priesthoods and summoned creatures as to defy description.

But the tales Arn found most appealing were those of vast stretches of beauteous, unclaimed land and game-filled forests. He had no right to daydream of making a new home under a different name in any such place. Men like him died the way they lived, at the pointy end of a sharp weapon. Luck was a fickle master.

As the moon sank in the west, Arn awakened John for his shift and, returning to his bedroll, fell into a dreamless sleep.

—⁀—

The morning sun over their shoulders cast long shadows as Arn and John strode into town. The few people they saw in the street lay stretched out, victims of last night's revelry.

The dirt road cut deep ruts between shabby wood buildings sporting hand-painted signs advertising their services. A short way down the street, Arn saw a large building with a sign on the front that read, WILL SLOAN'S TRADING POST. It struck him as significant that the only undertaker in town had set up shop directly across from this establishment.

Evidently the post was profitable since it featured cut-stone construction, looking more like a fortress than a store. Thin slits high up on the walls served as the closest things to windows. Twin iron-bound doors opened wide to receive any who might be able to stagger through this time of morning.

Arn entered the venue with John close behind. On the right side of the room stood a long wooden bar with a couple of dozen stools. Most of the remaining space was crowded with drinking and gaming tables. Sunlight speared through a small hole in the ceiling, fighting its way through thick lantern smoke. If the hole was a chimney, it was not working.

Across the deserted room, a small wooden stage adorned with crude drawings of naked women occupied the center of the far wall. Next to the stage, a wooden stairway led to the upper floor. Beside the stairway, a door into the trading post drew them forward.

The back of the building, almost as large as the front, was stocked with a surprising selection of dry goods, tools, utensils, and weapons.

John suddenly stopped. "What in the deep?" he said. "How is this possible?"

He grabbed Arn by the shoulder. "The bastards have my father's bow up here. It was stolen a year before my parents died. See the 'GS' carved into the grip? Stands for George Staton."

As he reached up to lift the black longbow from its place on the wall, a voice from the rear of the store brought their heads around. "Take your hands off the merchandise. If you want it, you'd better show me some gold."

Arn judged the proprietor to be in his midfifties. He was a big man with a black patch over his left eye and a ragged scar slashing a white furrow across his face from hairline to chin. He angled a crossbow in John's general direction.

"You've got stolen goods in here," said John.

"Says who?"

"Settle down," Arn said. "We're just thinking about buying this bow. How much?"

The man looked Arn up and down, apparently not liking what he saw.

"How much?" Arn repeated.

"Two gold," the man said.

"Two gold! I could buy four horses for that," said Arn.

"Go and buy them, then. You asked how much, and I told you. Take it or leave it."

"One gold," Arn said.

"One and four bits," said the trader.

"Done," John said.

Arn handed the clerk two gold pieces. The man took out a knife, cut one of the coins along the center notch, and flipped half of it to Arn.

Arn picked out a pot and some salt, and then filled a large sack with an assortment of items they would need on the road. The new bill came to four and a quarter gold, an exorbitant price even for Rork.

As the two walked out with their purchases, John laughed. "What an idiot. This bow is worth ten times that price. My father made it, and it's the finest I've ever seen."

"Well, he robbed us on the rest of it," said Arn. "And considering that your father's bow was stolen in the first place, I'd say the proprietor got the better end of the deal."

"You're right about that," said John.

"Let's find a place outside of town to stow our packs," said Arn. "I don't relish the thought of closing my eyes here in Rork."

Arn led the way out of town and up a steep rib of land off the road. Finding a shallow crawlspace that led through a thicket to a spot with enough room to stretch and sleep unobserved, they planted their packs. John lay his old bow down, slinging his father's longbow across his back. Crawling back out, Arn and John paused to remove all signs of their entry. Then, memorizing the landmarks that would enable them to find the spot again, they made their way back to town.

In their absence, Rork had awakened. A group of five vorgs crossed the street in front of them. The leader, a large she-vorg wearing a stole of human scalps over her thick shoulders, the accessory partially hidden under her straight black hair, looked at John and grinned.

"I could eat you up," she said, running her tongue over her lips as she walked in a tight circle around the two men, reaching out to grab John.

"Easy," Arn said, squeezing his companion's arm. "She's just playing."

A male vorg snarled at John. "If Commander Charna wants you, she'll take you."

"That's right," the she-vorg said. "Perhaps we'll play some later."

The vorgs walked off, their barking taunts trailing behind them.

John stared after them. And to Arn, something about the she-vorg felt distractingly familiar.

The two headed for a building they had seen on their first trip through the town. After passing three rickety wooden shacks, they entered the only neatly painted structure on the street. A sign above the door said simply, GOOD FOOD. Three large windows spilled light onto a single long table, and the men and vorgs seated around it were shoveling food into their faces. Arn and John found two empty chairs and joined them.

A serving maid set glasses of ale in front of them without the bother of asking what they wanted to drink.

"Can I get you something to eat? Today we have roast pig."

"That's what I'll have, then," said Arn.

"Same," John added.

The young woman walked into the kitchen, the door swinging open to reveal a giant of a man, easily seven feet tall and weighing four hundred pounds. The grease-splattered apron wrapped around his waist only partially concealed the ax hanging from his belt.

"Come on, daughter. Hurry with that food," he bellowed in a good-natured voice that rang out from the kitchen.

"Now I understand how that young lady gets along in a town like this," said John.

The waitress reentered the room carrying platters, one in each hand, that she set down in front of them. The dishes were piled high with thin slices of roast pork. Arn savored the first bite, letting the flavor linger on his tongue. He ate with delight until he reluctantly discovered that he could eat no more.

John and Arn paid for the meal and left the building, crossing the street to the tavern and trading post.

"A bit livelier in here," Arn noted.

"The crowd's not getting any prettier, though."

"I believe we already met the tavern beauty."

John turned to look at the she-vorg they had met on the town's streets.

Arn found an unoccupied table, wiped the beer off the top with his sleeve, sat down, and whistled for service.

Across the room, the she-vorg sat next to the stage, her hairy arm around a fair-haired bandit, the other vorgs in her circle clustered in tight conversation.

Just then, a large and boisterous group walked in through the front door. The room filled rapidly. The bar noise bubbled up as drink flowed from keg to glass to lips. Arn scanned the crowd for the cause of the early-afternoon celebration. A fat, bald man stepped up onto the stage and rang a bell, sending a hush of anticipation through the room.

"Respected buyers. Today I have a special treat for you," the fat man bellowed. "A fresh lot of slave girls, recently captured from a passing caravan. These girls have not yet felt the touch of a captor's hand."

"More likely all their captors' hands and other parts, too," yelled the she-vorg to a tremendous roar of approval from the other spectators.

Arn turned toward the stage, a barely concealed outrage lancing forth. Bandits and vorgs bought and sold slaves throughout the outlands, living loot from raided caravans or villages. The raiders generally killed the male captives, unless the likes of the she-vorg wanted them. The women were not so lucky, taken and used by their captors, then sold at auction in the next town, where their new owners used them more.

"And now for the real treat," the fat man continued.

The back door flew open, and a middle-aged woman was thrust onto the stage. Nude, with black hair and a motherly build, she showed signs of the lash on her legs and back. Her unseeing eyes stared out at the hungry crowd.

The bidding started very slow until an old man bought her for three silver pieces. For the next hour, the slaver paraded women and children onto the stage, selling them to the highest bidder. As time passed, John's face acquired a pale-green hue, and Arn worried that he might start trouble. In truth, Arn felt his own bloodlust boil up from within as he watched the ongoing atrocity.

Suddenly the fat man returned to the stage and rang a bell. "We start the bidding for this last girl at ten gold," he said with a flourish. "I present to you an Endarian princess, captured on her way east under heavy guard."

As the door opened, an intake of breath hissed through the tavern. Charna rose slowly to her feet. A one-eyed slaver led a young Endarian woman onto the stage in chains, her head held high and proud, her majesty unmistakable. Her brown face was framed by luxuriant hair that cascaded to her waist. At six feet tall, she stood a head shorter than others of her kin, who had until four centuries ago been the most populous of the races on the Endarian Continent. Since Endarians had twice a human's lifespan, Arn could not accurately judge her age.

"Twenty gold," yelled a bearded man in the back.

"Thirty," countered another near the stage.

"Fifty!"

The fat man pointed to a tall warrior in the center. "The gentleman bids fifty gold. Do I hear sixty?"

"One hundred gold!" Charna bellowed.

A low moan of disappointment passed through the crowd, but no one matched the she-vorg's offer.

Ringing the bell once again, the fat man's voice echoed through the hall. "Sold to Commander Charna for one hundred gold."

As the she-vorg walked to the stage and tossed a heavy pouch at the fat man's feet, John's hand slipped to his bow.

Arn stopped him with a hiss. "Not now."

Suddenly a big vorg jumped to his feet, his hairy hand pointing directly at Arn, a deep growl rasping his throat. "Blade!"

Hearing the dreaded name, Arn knew the time for observation had ended.

When, exactly, he had first acquired the nickname, Arn couldn't remember. A man did not become a legend without consequences. None would remember Arn Tomas Ericson, but no one would forget Blade.

The feared name echoed through the room, raining a stunned silence upon the gathering. All eyes followed the pointing hand of the yelling vorg directly to where Arn sat. Men and vorgs scrambled to clear the path between them, overturning chairs in their rush.

Arn leaned over to John and whispered, "Wait for your chance, then grab the Endarian and head for our spot. I'll be along shortly."

John started to argue and then glanced toward the Endarian. Sending his chair flying, he scrambled back into the crowd.

A clear path lay between Arn and the angry vorg.

"Blade," the vorg repeated, pulling a folded piece of paper from inside his shirt and spreading it out. A remarkable likeness of Arn adorned the wanted poster. "Lost favor with your pissant king, did you? No more killing from the shadows. I stand to claim that reward."

Standing almost as tall as Ty with a single fang curling over his lower lip, the vorg drew a long knife, swapping it from one hand to the other.

Arn remained seated, both feet propped on the table that separated him from the vorg.

The vorg swiftly threw the table aside. Arn landed on his feet before the table hit the floor, his long blade filling his hand as if it had always been there. His opponent feinted back and forth as he slowly circled Arn, who gripped Slaken for an underhand move. Arn waited, blade down, posture erect.

Noting Arn's stance, the vorg lunged forward, driving his knife toward Arn's stomach.

Arn extended his hands, crossing them right over left in front of his body, in a block that stopped the vorgish blade an inch from his chest. Arn grabbed the vorg's little finger, uncrossing his hands as he did so.

A loud snap accompanied the arm's exit from its shoulder socket. The vorg's scream followed its knife, sailing into the crowd.

Arn grabbed the vorg by the hair as Slaken ripped through the thing's throat. Wrapping his left arm and elbow around the dying bounty hunter's head, Arn gave it a vicious twist as he continued sawing with his knife until the head came free.

The cacophony that followed came to an abrupt halt as an enraged howl rang out above the noise.

"Where's my Endarian?" Charna screamed. "Find the thieves!"

Vorgs scrambled out of the building. Arn followed the crowd into the street, using the melee to slip into an alley and cross a short open space into the forest. Arn moved quickly, loping up the hill in a ground-burning stride. Staying in the dense brush, he moved silently up the ridge, crossing the slope toward the hidden camp.

Upon reaching a halfway point, Arn slowed his pace, working his way along the heavily wooded hill. Several times, he was forced to stop as vorgs prowled through the trees close to where he lay. It took him a full hour to cover less than a quarter league to the spot where John waited. Not wanting John to shoot him, Arn approached the thicket with extreme care.

"John," he whispered. "It's me."

Arn crawled through the thorny tunnel to find John sitting beside the princess with his bow across his lap. The Endarian woman sat quietly, and all Arn could see was her head, wrapped as she was in John's cloak.

"I couldn't get the chains off her," said John.

"Can she speak common?" asked Arn.

"I think so. She seems to understand me."

"Please listen to me, Highness," Arn said, softly. "If you'll hold out your hands and feet, I'll remove those chains."

Slowly, the Endarian put forth her arms. Arn found his lockpicks and went to work, quickly sending the chains falling away from her limbs. As if he had undammed a stream, the woman began to cry, burying her head in John's shoulder. After a moment's hesitation, John placed his arms around her, holding her with a tenderness that implied he would keep her safe.

Arn observed his riding companion's face. The man's strange black eyes were pools of emotion.

"We'll wait until nightfall, then go find Ty," said Arn. "Better get some rest until then."

The two hours until sunset passed slowly. Many times vorgs passed within a few paces of the trio's thicket but continued on, unaware of their presence. As darkness descended, the vorgs began to cluster in the valley, campfires springing up across the valley floor. Charna was apparently the commander of a significant band. Worse yet, many more vorgs had descended on the valley.

Arn debated courses of action. If they did not have the princess to take care of, he would sneak down into the camp and add the oddly familiar female vorg to his hit list. However, that would not stop the other vorgs from coming after them, and with the Endarian, he could not guarantee a successful escape. So they would have to sneak out, find Ty, and then use the horses to make their escape. But how were they going to ride wild horses?

In the gathering darkness, John took the princess's hand and led her out of the thicket as Arn brought up the rear. John had given her his long coat, which hung almost to her knees, and she carried his old bow. He had offered, but she had refused his boots. As Arn watched her move silently across the ground, it was evident she did not need them.

Arn took the lead, moving up the slope, followed by the other two, pausing when John put a hand on his shoulder and pointed. On a ledge up ahead stood a vorg sentry, with another seated ten feet farther along. Signaling John to take the seated one, Arn crept silently up behind the standing vorg, just another shadow in the darkness. Suddenly he lunged forward, clapping his right hand over the sentry's mouth from behind, his left hand thrusting Slaken into the small of his back.

A swish and thud toppled the other vorg, a feathered arrow sticking out the side of his head.

John strode up and pulled the arrow free, returning it to his quiver after wiping it clean. Arn searched the remaining vorg, retrieving a bow, arrows, and a small pouch of coins.

The Endarian stepped forward, grabbed the quiver, and slung it over her shoulder. John slid into a vorg's tunic, then turned and resumed his place beside the princess. Once again, Arn took the lead, avoiding the top of the ridge, staying in the roughest terrain available, reducing the likelihood that they would encounter more vorgs on their way south.

After two hours of travel, Arn could no longer see the fires surrounding Rork. Halting at a place where the valley split, one canyon angling off to the southeast and one to the west, John pointed southeast.

"I see horses."

"I don't see anything," Arn said. "You lead the way."

John descended the ridge with the Endarian at his side. Reaching the bottom, he turned up the intersecting canyon. Less than a tenth of a league in, John stopped.

"Ty, step out from behind that tree," said John. "It's us."

"Damn those weird eyes of yours," said a voice from the darkness. "What have you got there?"

"We need to talk," said John. "There's trouble brewing."

Ty stepped forward. "A girl? You brought a girl here? And an Endarian at that. Let me guess. Someone objects to this new arrangement."

Despite his griping, Ty led the way to his campsite. There was no fire, something that pleased Arn immensely. The three men and the Endarian sat down together a short distance away.

"Okay now, what have you gotten us into?" asked Ty.

"It seems likely that a couple of hundred vorgs will be on our trail by first light," John replied.

Ty dropped his head into his hands.

"We need a couple of horses to ride," Arn said.

"That's something I can handle," the Kanjari replied.

"We're not talking about wild horses," said John. "We're not carnival riders like you."

"I've taken care of that. I've been working on two good-natured mares. Even made halters and reins out of the skin of that buck that John killed. Sorry, but I didn't anticipate the extra passenger."

"I'm impressed," John said. "I take back some of the things I've been telling Arn about you."

Ty rolled his eyes. "What's her name?"

Arn watched John look at the Endarian questioningly, but the woman did not utter a response.

"I would say she's still traumatized," said John.

"Not surprising," said Arn, "considering what she's been through."

"The woman will have to ride double with you," Ty said to John. "I'll get the horses."

Arn watched as Ty disappeared into the darkness, returning shortly and leading the two mares. Grabbing the reins Ty held out for him, John slipped them over the lead mare's neck and mounted. The Endarian leapt gracefully astride behind him. The horse sidestepped nervously but settled down. Arn took the other animal's reins from Ty. He had broken a few horses to the saddle himself, which usually took several weeks. The Kanjari were rumored to be able to train horses for others in as little as a week. As Arn looked at John and the princess sitting on their mare, he did not doubt it.

As Arn took the reins, the mare laid her ears against her head and backed away from him. Ty reached out and grabbed the bridle, holding the animal still. Arn slipped the reins around the mare's neck, rubbing her with his left hand.

"Easy, girl," he said.

Leaning his weight against the horse to let it get used to the feel of him, he grabbed its mane with his left hand and swung easily up onto its back. Ty released his grip on the bridle.

Ty let out a soft whistle, and the stallion came trotting up. The Kanjari leapt onto its back, bringing it to a stop beside the others. "I'm going to run these mares down the valley. We'll trail along, losing our tracks in theirs, and then peel off at a likely spot."

Ty disappeared into the predawn darkness. In seconds, the herd of horses began to move at a steady, ground-burning trot. John and the Endarian woman trotted off toward the south.

The Kanjari moved in behind the herd, and Arn mirrored him on the other side. As the horses broke out into the main canyon, the first gray of dawn began to brighten the eastern sky.

Ty kept the herd moving, gradually increasing the pace. Arn found himself having to work to control his horse, which, despite what Ty had said, showed no familiarity with being reined. As day's light emerged, Arn glanced over his shoulder, certain that the vorgs would be on their trail by now. With the sun high enough to illuminate the top of the western ridge, Ty brought the mares to a run, kicking up a hefty dust cloud behind them, deliberately seeking to draw the vorgs' attention.

Forcing the mares into a full stampede, the group raced down the valley, then, rounding a bend, Ty plunged into a side creek and turned away from the running herd, heading upstream to the west. John and Arn followed him into the stream, walking their horses up the twisting canyon.

For the next hour, Ty led his companions upstream, staying in the water, finally quitting the streambed to climb a steep ridge, heavily wooded in a mixture of juniper, pine, and sage. Gradually the ridge gave way to flat plateaus split by steep canyons. A stiff breeze nipped at Arn's ears, a reminder that winter had not yet left the high country.

The hillside was now so steep that the horses slid with almost every step. The party was forced to duck under the tree branches to avoid being scraped off. They found a deer trail and turned, following it high up under a row of cliffs. The trail narrowed rapidly so that Arn found his left leg brushing the rock wall as his right leg hung over a drop of several hundred feet. The rocks took on a reddish hue, and large boulders lay strewn along the canyon floor below, some damming the stream into deep pools.

Ty continued along the trail, the big stallion displaying the sure-footedness of a mule. Arn's mare also felt solid, but the horse carrying John and the Endarian was in trouble. Shaking with fear, it suddenly reared, stumbling as its front feet hit the trail again, one of its hooves sliding off the side.

Ty slipped nimbly backward, sliding off his stallion's rump to grab the panicked mare's bridle. Slapping the palomino, he sent the big horse up the trail ahead. The mare steadied, and Ty led it upward around the next bend to where the trail widened. Releasing the bridle, Ty leapt astride the stallion.

Arn scanned the area behind them, and though he saw no sign of the vorgs, the memory of meeting Charna on Rork's main street flooded into his brain. This time it was accompanied by a different vision.

Once again Arn lay inside the cramped wood box, peering out through the crack at his mother's body, bound to the far wall by glowing bands as a she-vorg approached. In his mind, the she-vorg turned back toward the cloaked figure, and the memory made his blood run cold.

Charna.

He pulled his horse up beside Ty's. "I have to go back."

"Why? We've lost them."

Arn considered telling his companions the truth but gave another reason. "A group that large will have a wielder with them. They'll acquire some of the Endarian's possessions from the slave trader, and then the wielder will find her. He has to be eliminated."

"And what qualifies you to do that alone?" said Ty.

"John will explain. In the meantime, I need to know where we can reunite."

Ty hesitated. "There's a valley three days west of here with a hill shaped like a horse head at its center. You can see it for leagues. We'll wait for you there."

John reached out to clasp arms. "I know who you are, but take care."

Arn merely nodded.

Then Ty wheeled his horse and trotted off into the woods, followed by John and the Endarian. Arn sat astride his horse and watched them disappear into the dense brush. He had saved these three people, but in so doing he had entangled their lives with his. The responsibility that came with that knowledge unleashed a wave of dread.

—⚬—

The gravel crunched under his horse's feet as Arn turned back toward their pursuers, having slipped into the Blade personality he had hoped to keep suppressed.

Arn had one significant advantage. The vorgs would not expect an attack from those they were chasing. He merely needed to intercept them, identify Charna and her wielder, and then, at a time and place of his choosing, usher them into the afterlife. The kill did not worry him. Getting Charna to tell him the identity of her partner in the murder of his parents was another matter entirely.

The day came like a gray haze, creeping into view rather than bursting free of its nightly bonds. Clouds moved in to cover the sky. Arn guided his horse along the side of the ridge just below the military crest, allowing him to see well to the front without silhouetting himself against the sky. The mare needed no urging, moving with a quick yet measured pace, exactly the gait that Arn wanted, which covered ground rapidly and could be kept up for long periods without exhausting the animal.

Around noon, Arn paused at a stream to let the mare drink and to refill his waterskin from the cold water. Once the horse had its fill, he kicked it forward again. The high ridgelines gradually gave way to smaller hills and valleys. A forest of tall pine trees emerged to wrap itself around him. The going became easier, as the forest floor was relatively clear and spongy beneath the tall trees. An eerie quiet had settled upon the world.

Large flakes of snow began drifting down, coming faster and faster as wind moaned through the treetops. Arn untied his jacket from the top of his pack and put it on, along with his leather gloves. A spring blizzard was going to make its presence felt.

Arn continued east as the storm grew in strength. Snow swirled all around him, collecting on his horse's neck and on his head and shoulders. Squinting his eyes to keep the flakes from temporarily blinding him, he now relied on his unerring sense of direction to guide him. As darkness fell, more than a foot of snow already covered the ground.

Still, he pressed on, although more slowly now, a long scarf covering his face, neck, and ears, as he and the horse resembled a moving snow pile. Arn was confident that the vorgs had holed up for shelter. Miserable conditions were usually the best for an assassin's work. Discomfort made beings huddle up, dulling their senses. Few people liked being uncomfortable, but killers loved it. Weather like this helped keep them alive.

Arn moved on through the night, even though the snow continued, hard and steady, accumulating to a depth of more than two feet. The mare was tiring rapidly now. Their pace had slowed to a crawl. Snow pushed against the horse with each step, causing it to lurch forward in uneven hops. As dawn approached, Arn stopped. The mare was spent.

Arn took off his jacket. He removed his knife and cut the jacket into two halves, swung one leg over to sit sidesaddle, and began work on the leather pieces. He pulled one leg up and placed his foot inside the center of one of these pieces. Wrapping the leather up around his boot, Arn cut the material into straps and secured them to his leg. He repeated this process for the other leg so that now both legs were wrapped up to the knee in the thick leather, his boots completely covered.

Arn shivered in the cold air. His shirt and scarf did little to protect his upper body from the wind and blowing snow, but it was a necessary inconvenience. If he kept moving, he wouldn't freeze. The real danger was to his feet. Armies took most of their war casualties from foot problems, not from battle. The cold compounded this. Frostbite attacked the feet first. When they went, the soldier stopped. When the soldier stopped, he died.

Swinging his pack onto his shoulder, he slipped from the horse, removed the bridle, and, with a smack of his hand, sent it looking for shelter among the trees.

Arn placed the bridle in his pack and resumed his eastward trek. He longed to move higher on the ridge to take advantage of the easier terrain. This he resisted doing. The easy route invariably led to death. The extra exertion of slipping and sliding along the steep slope would help to keep him warm.

The sky brightened, but the snowfall continued. Arn thought back to his sleep of days before. How long had it been? Chewing on a piece of dried venison from his pack, he tried to recall. He had reached the point where sleep deprivation induced hallucinations, waking dreams that competed with reality. Arn shook his head. He had been through this many times before. He had to keep moving, fatigue his new companion.

As the day brightened, Arn moved into even rougher terrain. The scarf that wrapped his face protected his ears from the biting cold while his exertions warmed his body. The sturdy leather of the jacket was holding up well on his feet, shielded from some of the sharp edges of the rocks by the deep snow. A layer of ice had formed in his hair and eyebrows.

Toward noon, Arn reached the end of the canyon through which he had been traveling. It faded out into a set of gently rolling valleys, wooded in patches, mainly along the low ground. The wind howled out of the west, blowing the snow in sheets, forcing Arn to duck his head to protect his eyes.

Travel became harder than ever, and he guessed that he had covered not quite three leagues by evening. Arn found himself laboring forward now, forcing himself onward through strength of will. Occasionally he reached into his pack to get the water skin or to retrieve a piece of dried meat.

As night fell over the frozen land, the wind died, and Arn breathed a small sigh of relief. He was as tired as he could ever remember being. He had gone longer without sleep or rest, but the tremendous effort required to plow through the snow had taken its toll.

Suddenly he came to a halt at the edge of a clearing. Across the valley, less than a tenth of a league away, a fire blazed, and figures could be seen moving in front of a cave.

Arn went forward with renewed strength, skirting the clearing, losing himself in the thickets and briar patches that covered the low ground. As he approached the cave, Arn stopped more often, pausing to look and listen before continuing on. Several times he slipped and fell, but the deep snow deadened the sound.

Once again, Arn forced himself to slow down, approaching the mouth of the cave by way of a shallow gully. The vorgs had no guards posted outside the cave and only one at the entrance. This one's duty seemed to consist of stoking the fire and warming his backside instead of watching for attackers. So much the better.

Charna had a couple of dozen vorgs with her in the cave, all but one asleep. Arn would have liked to take out the guard with a throwing knife, then sneak in and kill the wielder and Charna silently while they slept. But his hands were now too cold to throw a knife accurately.

Arn placed Slaken in his right hand and held one of the pointed throwing daggers in his left. He lowered himself into the deep snow and began crawling toward the cave entrance. He buried himself completely, wriggling slowly forward on his belly, tilting his head to one side so that he could keep one eye out of the snow to watch the guard. As he neared the circle of firelight outside the mouth of the cave, the vorg straightened, walking forward to peer out into the darkness.

Arn burst from the snow, running full speed at the guard, who screamed as Arn drove the smaller blade into his eye socket. As Arn's shoulder propelled the vorg backward into the fire, his momentum carried him into the cave and into the midst of the scrambling band. Most were struggling to grab weapons and get to their feet. The nearest of these crumbled to the ground, blood gurgling from the gash where the vorg's throat had been. Arn drove the dagger into the back of another as he plowed forward.

The group's wielder jumped to his feet in the middle of the room, waving his arm and gesturing at the running assassin. Fire blazed from his fingers but failed to strike the intended target, instead engulfing several warriors to Arn's left.

Lunging forward, Arn reached the wielder, driving his knee up into the vorg's groin. As the sorcerer doubled over, Arn thrust Slaken through the base of the wielder's skull.

"Blade!"

Charna's enraged scream echoed through the cave. Seeing that he was almost upon her, Charna grabbed the nearest vorg and shoved him into Arn's path, impaling her soldier onto midnight steel. From the back of the cave, the vorgs' horses suddenly stampeded through their rope corral, bolting through the warrior horde and racing out into the night.

The confusion had allowed Charna to gather several of the vorgs into a fighting group that prevented Arn from reaching her. One of these lunged forward with a long spear. Arn jerked sideways and backward, crashing into another vorg as he did. Shoving his knives into the vorg's stomach, Arn drove both of them back out of the cave, plunging down the slope, coming to rest in a snowbank atop the dead body.

Sheathing both knives, Arn wrenched the dead vorg up onto his back as he ran forward, pulling a muscle in his left arm as he did so. He slid down the ridge, carrying the vorg's body on his back. He felt the *thunk* of an arrow embed itself in the corpse as he became one more shadow in the darkness.

Arn dropped the vorg and ran at full speed. He fell, struggled to his feet, and plunged forward once more. He turned hard right, angling through the trees toward the dense woods. In seconds, he was in the thick brush, hearing the vorgs' yells over his own labored breathing. As the shouts became faint, he knew that, at least for now, they had lost him.

Arn backtracked, working his way up the ridge behind the vorg cave before turning west. The vorgs no longer had their wielder, but they would not need one to follow his tracks through the snow once the sky became light.

Vorgs had the ability to see much better at night than men did, but their night vision came from an ability to see temperature differences such as body heat. Tracks in the snow at night were as invisible to vorgs as they were to humans. And these vorgs would want to find their horses first.

Arn's left arm ached with pain from a pulled muscle. Still, he pushed himself forward. Now that the excitement had stopped, he was once again exhausted.

For two hours, he moved along the side of the ridge, staying in terrain that would make horseback travel difficult. Arn guessed that it was about three hours after midnight when he turned back. Hurrying as quickly as he could back the way he had come, he stayed in the path he had already made through the snow. Since the snow was so deep, he did not need to walk backward in his own footsteps. Merely dragging his feet plowed a trail to disguise that he had doubled back. And because he had already cut a path through the snow, he made better time. Arn thus arrived close to the vorg cave with almost an hour of darkness to spare.

As he got to within less than a quarter league of the camp, Arn began searching carefully for just the right spot to leave the trail. Finally, he found what he was looking for. During his escape, he had passed under several tall pines with thick branches extending out over his path.

Arn jumped up, grabbed one of these lower branches, and swung his body up. Working his way around to the far side of the big tree, he began scaling upward. He continued climbing through the thick boughs until he was confident that he was invisible from the ground below. Then he climbed higher just to be sure. Now he had to wait until dawn.

The wait was not long. Arn was nearly frozen by daybreak. His flight from the scene had worked up a sweat that now chilled him to the bone.

The eastern sky brightened quickly, the ground below seemingly darker than ever as the sky turned gray above. Then the first rays of sunlight that Arn had seen in days struck the top of the nearby hills. To his tired eyes, the painfully bright landscape was mesmerizing.

He was in a grove of pines, about forty feet up. The branches arced downward under their snowy burden, blocking his view.

The snort of horses and the guttural yells of vorgs broke the calm. The sounds grew louder, passing directly below him, only to fade and disappear in the distance. Arn waited a short time after the sounds died away, then climbed rapidly to the ground.

He was stiff and had a hard time moving. His injured left arm made its presence known. Still, climbing down was considerably easier than climbing up. At the lowest branches, Arn glanced around. Seeing no sign of the vorgs, he leapt the eight feet to the ground and turned back along the trail toward the vorg cave.

The vorgs had left only one guard behind. Snorts and stamping from within indicated that, in addition to their own, the vorgs had recovered their dead companions' horses. That and the fire that blazed inside the cave indicated their intention to return.

Staying in the thick brush as long as possible, Arn took out one of his throwing knives and hurled it at the lone vorg. The knife slipped from his numbed fingers, sailed five feet over the vorg's head, and clattered to the ground inside the cave. Whirling toward the sound, the vorg pulled his sword.

As Arn rushed forward, the guard spun toward him but was too late. Arn's blade quickly felled the warrior.

He looked around the cave, stooping to recover his throwing knife. The surviving vorgs had stripped the dead ones and piled their bodies in the snow just outside the cave entrance. Inside, their clothes and belongings lay heaped against the far wall. The repaired rope corral held six horses. Crude vorg saddles and spiked bridles lay stacked nearby.

Arn searched through the clothes quickly but carefully, using a discarded spear to move the material around before touching them in case they had been booby-trapped. Finding no traps, he sorted through the items, separating out heavy coats, clubs, swords, and spears. The money, if there had been any, was gone.

Selecting a thick shirt and sheepskin coat from the pile, Arn removed his frozen buckskin shirt, put it in his pack, and donned the vorg garb. Warmth trumped smell. Then he noticed a strangely marked bundle leaning against the far wall. The wielder's pack.

Arn opened it carefully, using Slaken to spring the catch and lift the flap. As the flap came open, a spring snapped into the leather surface of the pack, driving forth a small needle. Arn looked at the weapon carefully. The curved needle was covered with a red, gummy substance.

Opening the flap, Arn spilled the pack's contents onto the floor. Ignoring the jars filled with strange ointments, he focused on a leatherbound tome. While he could not read the words written on the cover, he guessed it was the wielder's spell book.

Books like this were rare and expensive. Every wielder hoarded the spells he knew, writing them down. Since wielders only knew spells that they had been taught or had found on scrolls or in books, one could sell one of these tomes for a handsome price. Arn picked the book up and put it in his pack.

He then moved to the back of the cave where the vorgs had penned the horses. Selecting the strongest looking of these, he saddled it, mounted up, and drove the other horses out of the cave before him.

For several hours, Arn followed this path before exiting the flow and turning west once more, allowing himself to doze in the saddle as he rode.

Evening found him walking Ax, the name he had given the ugly horse, up a beautiful valley. Here, the snow was far less deep. The hills on either side were forested in blue spruce, but the valley floor was clear, the snow giving the scene a peaceful quiet. Again, Arn found his head nodding forward as dreams mingled with his waking thoughts, the two forming an indistinguishable blur. He rode steadily west. The vorgs were probably lost behind him, but to rest was to invite death.

Twice during the night, Arn stopped to let the horse drink from streams and paw the snow for the grass buried beneath. Then he resumed his ride, again allowing himself to doze in the saddle, conserving his strength for the task ahead. He needed to be confident he had lost the vorgs before he could reunite with his companions. Even though they no longer had their wielder, he suspected one of the vorgs was a good tracker.

"Most likely it's Charna herself," Arn said, patting the horse on the neck. "Ax, what do you say we find out just how good she is?"

Ax did not respond.

11

Southern Borderland Range
YOR 412, Winter's End

Having waited for dawn, Carol climbed to her feet beside Alan. The sunrise bathed the snow-covered landscape beyond the opening. The exit from the lower dungeon level yawned a hundred feet up on the rock promontory that was Far Castle. Carol stood beside Alan in the mouth of the opening, gazing over the edge and pondering what to do.

She looked at her brother. "Hang on to my belt while I lean out for a better look."

Alan grabbed hold. "Got you."

Carol eased up to the edge and leaned out, the sight of the drop directly below her causing her head to spin. A large pile of rock lay scattered about the base of the cliff. She imagined her belt coming unfastened, but a quick check revealed that it was still firmly attached.

She regained her composure and examined the cliff below them. Handholds were few and far between. Neither she nor Alan could make the descent. Carol was about to signal Alan to pull her back when she noticed an unusual rock formation four feet to her left.

"Walk me to the left," she told him.

He moved left, still holding her belt, as she moved with him. She placed her left hand against the wall, leaning out even farther. Someone had carved hand- and footholds into the rock wall, extending down the face of the cliff and completely hidden from view to anyone not leaning out of the passage mouth.

"There are hand- and footholds over here," Carol said. "Let go of my belt. I'm going to swing around and try to reach them."

"Be careful."

For an agonizing moment, it seemed that she would miss the rock ladder. But then she was on it. She paused, breathing heavily, her hands shaking so mightily that she worried about losing her grip.

"Are you okay?" Alan asked.

"I'm fine."

She forced herself to concentrate on the cliff directly in front of her, lowered her body, and found the next foothold. Hand over hand she descended, with Alan following just above. Her feet finally touched the ground.

Alan jumped off the ladder from five feet up and stretched his arms toward the sky.

"Far Castle, be damned!"

Carol looked around. The landscape was clear of snow except for patches in the shade of trees and on the north-facing sides of the hills. The valley they had ridden up lay masked behind a ridge to the east.

"What do you think Father is doing now?" she asked. "Will he be looking for us?"

"I doubt it," Alan said. "He'll deal with the vorgs before he sends someone for us."

The sun was not yet high in the sky, but its warmth was already making itself felt. The last of the mist that clung to the valley floor faded. The tang of pine clung to the air.

"Let's find a secure spot to make camp and wait," said Carol. "They know where we are."

It took a little over an hour to find their spot under an overhanging ledge on the ridge south of Far Castle. Alan volunteered to hunt, while Carol gathered firewood.

When Alan later emerged from the arroyo immediately to the west, holding a rabbit in each hand, she could hardly believe their good fortune. She had almost forgotten what it was like to eat. She had started a fire among twigs and branches. After packing the precious tinderbox and flint back into Alan's pack, she sat back.

When the rabbits had reached a golden brown over the fire, Carol reached out to grab the spit nearest to her. As she did, Alan's foot kicked it out of her hand and into the dirt, followed closely by the other rabbit.

"Vorgs!" Alan quietly exclaimed as he kicked dirt over the fire.

Carol quickly rose. Rounding the bend in the valley about a tenth of a league away, four vorgs approached on horseback. The leader pulled his horse to a stop and pointed up the hill toward Alan and Carol.

She grabbed Alan's shoulder. "Come on! They see us already!"

"No use running. Just wait on them."

Alan lifted his ax from its place against the rock wall. Carol glanced at her empty quiver and useless bow and drew her hunting knife instead.

The vorgs spread out and began trotting their horses up the hill toward the duo. As they reached a point about two hundred paces away, the leader suddenly yelled, wheeled his horse, and galloped across the valley, followed closely by the other vorgs.

Carol pointed along the ridgeline to their east. "Look."

Six of Rafel's rangers trotted down the slope toward them. Leading the group was Derek Scot, a young sergeant who was rapidly developing a reputation in the elite company.

"Mighty glad to see you, Derek," Alan said as the ranger dismounted.

"Lorness Carol. Lord Alan. I'm surprised at you two," Derek said. "You know better than to make a fire in country like this. You could have attracted a lot worse than those four."

"Looks like we did," said Alan, reaching over to slap Derek on the back.

"Hop up behind us, and we'll get you back to the caravan. It's a half-day's ride back to the east. Take some jerky and water."

Carol ate as she rode, her left arm wrapped firmly around Derek's waist. She found that she could not eat as much as she thought. Still, the jerky tasted better than a venison steak. The group moved off across the valley with the rangers spreading out before them as scouts, way out to each side and to the front.

She caught sight of Rafel's camp just before dusk. Never had a group of dusty wagons looked so good. As the group rode in, the high lord met them, clasping hands with Alan and then turning to sweep Carol up in his arms.

"Gaar," Rafel said, "go roust that lazy old cook, Maxwell, and get these two something to eat. I won't have my only son and daughter looking like inadequately stuffed scarecrows."

The thought of the two lost outriders dampened the joy Carol felt at her return. "I'm sorry we couldn't save Dale and Griffith," she said. "The vorgs cut them down right in front of me."

Rafel placed a hand on her shoulder. "They were fine warriors. They will be missed."

Carol and Alan shared a meal and a long discussion with their father, then Carol bid good night to the others and flopped into the back of her wagon for a much-needed sleep.

She awoke the next morning to the clanging of pots and pans. The cooks were busily readying breakfast in the darkness before the dawn. The smells of bacon and hot coffee filled Carol's nostrils as she inhaled. She shivered, as much from the pleasure of being back with friends and family as from the morning air.

Feeling around in her wagon, she found the pouch containing her prized toiletries. She made her way to the small stream that ran through the camp and set about cleaning up. The water left her gasping as she splashed it over her face and neck, seeming far too cold not to be frozen. Still, she attacked the task of washing with vigor. By the time she was satisfied, her hands ached with a dull throb that made it painful to close her fingers.

By now, most of the camp was awake and moving about. The last guard shift made its way back, the scouts having already ridden out in preparation for the caravan moving out. Carol made her way to Hawthorne's wagon.

"Why don't you ride on the seat beside me today, and you can tell me all about your adventures while we travel," he suggested to her. "Tonight, we'll begin to focus on some of the more advanced lessons. That was my intention before you and your brother got yourselves lost."

"I need to pack my wagon, Hawthorne, and then I'll return."

With that, Carol walked back and packed her things away for the day's travel. After pulling out her notebook, along with her quill and ink, she headed to Hawthorne's wagon.

As the day passed, the column began moving down out of the hills. The trees changed from pines to juniper, and then these gave way to scrub. As they crested a small rise, Carol could see a river running along the base of the hills. On the far side a vast desert stretched away to the west.

"The Mogev Desert," Hawthorne said.

"I've never heard you mention it. How are we going to get across?" she asked.

"There are watering holes for those who know where to find them," said Hawthorne.

"Have you been here before?"

"No, but I have something that will help."

Hawthorne handed her the reins and leaned back, fishing under the canvas until he found his large bag. He began digging around inside, whistling softly under his breath.

"Ah-hah. Here it is."

He pulled out a small wooden box, opening it to reveal a forked twig just larger than his thumb. He filled a cup with water and floated the twig on its surface. The pointed end swung around until it pointed directly ahead, toward the river.

"A water scryer," Hawthorne said. "It points to the closest water source."

"This is excellent. How does it work?"

"The creators of magical devices spend an extraordinary amount of time perfecting their craft and guard their secrets jealously. Most wielders never take the time to try to discover new methods, instead relying on their regular spells. That is also why magical devices are so rare and costly. They are said to be some things in this world of great power.

"To create a device with a powerful spell would mean casting the spell again and again as you searched for the right nuance, the correct permutation. As you know, the more advanced the spell, the harder it is to control an elemental. Trying to create too great a magic device would most likely end with the wielder making a mistake that allowed the elemental to possess him. Or her."

"Incredible," Carol said. "I had no idea that such arts even existed."

"They exist. Put them out of your mind for now. You must first master casting before being able to think about trying to make even the simplest magical item. What level of magic have you reached at this point? Two spells?"

"Okay. I get your point."

Although Carol had been meaning to ask Hawthorne about the growing sense of fatigue she felt, she decided against it. Her mentor was under enough pressure, repairing wards as Blalock damaged them, to be bothered with trivialities. Yet her tiredness was making the practice of spell-casting more difficult.

Toward dusk, the line of wagons pulled up alongside the river. As his people made camp, Rafel sent word that the caravan would celebrate tomorrow's coming of spring and the start of the new year with a few days of rest by the river. Meanwhile the rangers would scout for watering holes. One group would be given Hawthorne's water scryer.

Carol made her way over to the row of fires and was rewarded with steaming-hot coffee. Avoiding the handle, Carol cupped both hands around the iron cup, letting the warmth steal through her palms and up her arms. She brought the cup to her lips and sipped as Alan strode up to the fire.

"Father's called a meeting in his tent," said Alan. "He sent me to get you."

"What about?"

"He didn't say."

Carol refilled her cup and followed Alan around the campfires, dodging the scurrying cooks, to where Rafel's tent stood. Inside, Jason, Broderick, and Hawthorne sat on the tarp spread across the ground, while Gaar remained standing to Rafel's left.

Rafel motioned for Alan and Carol to sit, then began speaking.

"Jaradin Scot is missing. Four days ago, he led his ranger team on a deep reconnaissance mission to the north. They should have been back yesterday."

"I don't like it," Broderick said. "Jaradin's too damned good to be late like this. I sent an entire squad north to see what happened. They're due back tomorrow. In the meantime, I'm having a tough time trying to keep Derek in line. He's mad as a snake that I didn't send him out after his brother. But if I had sent him, he wouldn't come back until he found Jaradin."

"You did the right thing," Rafel responded. "We can't afford to lose both of the Scot boys. As good as Jaradin is, Derek's better. We're going to need him in the weeks ahead."

"I've put him in charge of one of the desert reconnaissance teams," said Broderick. "I assigned Alan to his team to keep an eye on him. They leave first thing in the morning."

"Why haven't you used Hawthorne to locate Jaradin?" Carol asked.

The wielder spoke. "I'm working so hard maintaining the block against Blalock that I haven't got the strength to cast another spell. The only reason I've been able to hang on for this long is by occasionally borrowing some of your strength. I established our mental link for this cause."

"You haven't slept since we started the journey?" asked Carol.

"I'm able to doze some and still maintain my concentration. When I'm too tired, I siphon some of your energy."

"So that's why I've felt so tired," Carol said, feeling anger that the wielder hadn't explained what he was doing earlier. Her permission should have been asked.

"It's also why I was surprised that you were able to cast your spells at all," Hawthorne continued.

The look on Rafel's face showed that he did not like the current conversation. Carol knew that he didn't understand or fully trust magic and was greatly worried that she could be destroyed by forces beyond her control.

Carol made her way back to her tent and crawled into her blankets without bothering to remove her clothes. As her head sank to the ground, sleep wrapped her in its arms.

12

Morning found Arn riding up the steep side of a narrow, rocky canyon. During the night, he had traveled into country that grew rougher by the hour but that had received far less snow than the canyon where he had encountered the vorgs.

Ax continued to move with power, seeming to have an infinite reservoir of stamina. The horse needed little guidance from his rider. Arn found that once Ax understood the general direction Arn wanted to go, he would continue that way, selecting the best route as they traveled. This left Arn free to listen and watch for danger.

Dawn came, and as the day passed, the ground over which Arn traveled grew rockier. Juniper trees beat back the pines. The sounds of Arn's passage startled several deer, sending them bounding away.

The day was the warmest in several weeks, and the snow was disappearing rapidly. Small streams rushed along canyon bottoms that would have been dry without the recent snow.

Across the way, Arn saw a herd of bighorn sheep browsing, apparently not disturbed by his presence. The large ram with the sheep watched him with sharp eyes, looking for any sign of dangerous intent. A lone eagle passed overhead, swooping down onto the opposite hillside to snatch up a rabbit in its claws.

Arn thought about the problem at hand. Charna was persistent. That meant that the vorgs were probably back on his trail. He was confident that he could lose them once the ground dried sufficiently to make tracking difficult, but that would not happen for another couple of days.

Another option was to let the horse go and lose them on foot in extremely rough terrain. Arn did not like either of these ideas. He wanted to get to Horse Head Rock as quickly as possible, so he did not have time to wait for the ground to dry. He had also grown fond of the horse he rode. Ax was the most tireless animal he had ever known.

Arn had a better plan. He surveyed the steep cliffs higher up on the hillside. Layer upon layer of rocky outcroppings jutted toward the rim.

He nudged Ax with his heels, guiding the horse up between the cliffs. There was no real trail here, and loose shale covered the ground. Ax paused to select the best footing, then plunged ahead to the next section of firm ground. Here, the cliffs closed onto a two-foot-wide ledge.

Arn guided the horse along the ledge and around a bend. To his right, a two-hundred-foot drop plunged toward the bottom of the canyon. He leaned back in the saddle and looked up. Above him the cliffs rose several hundred feet, separated one from the other by slides of loose shale. Mountain-goat country.

The path widened, climbing more steeply. Arn came to a place where the cliffs above him split into a narrow chute, extremely steep but possible to climb. He dismounted, grabbed the reins, and began scrambling up the rocky chute, pulling Ax behind him. The trail was even more treacherous than it had appeared from below.

He looked down the chute that he and Ax had just climbed. Arn smiled. This would do perfectly.

He hobbled Ax in a lush meadow atop the rim. Then, after a quick glance around to mark the spot, he returned to the gorge, making his way back to the top of the chute. Arn positioned himself on the uphill side of a loose boulder.

The vorgs came into sight just as the sun rose high enough to illuminate the bottom of the canyon. An even dozen, they rode toward him along the path that Arn had taken. Charna rode in front, bending low over the side of her bay horse, studying the ground. The vorgs followed single file up the narrow trail, their eyes nervously scanning the canyon walls.

Arn ducked back from the ledge, focusing his attention down the chute to the spot where the trail widened. The sound of horses' hooves on the stones reached his ears long before any of the vorgs came into view on the path. Charna appeared first, followed closely by three others. More horses crowded close to hers as she paused to study the ground at the base of the chute. With a look of sudden understanding, she looked up.

Arn stepped out of his hiding place and hoisted the head-shaped rock high, sending it flying into the tree branch that held a boulder in place. As the branch splintered, the rock began to roll, followed by a cascade of stones in a bounding torrent.

Charna spun her horse, knocking two other vorgs off the trail and over the cliff. She plunged back down the narrow path right into a line of her warriors. Pulling her battle-ax from its place on her saddle, she beheaded the first vorg, knocking its rearing horse over the cliff.

The rockslide hit the group of five vorgs who had crowded behind her on the wide part of the trail, sweeping them away.

Arn began running along the path back toward the rim of the canyon. As he feared, the vibrations from the landslide had dislodged other rocks higher on the canyon walls, sending them plunging down toward him. Wandering preachers gathering their congregations, they charged into the canyon. Arn feared that some of these secondary slides would overtake him, but he soon realized he was out of danger.

At the rim, he paused to survey the scene below. Except for the occasional boulder still bounding down the rock walls, most of the slide had ceased. A pall of dust hung in the air. Just then, three riders emerged at the bottom of the canyon heading, their horses galloping back to the east. Arn could not see who had survived. As badly as he wanted to make sure that Charna was dead, his exhaustion prevented him from pursuing the fleeing vorgs. It was time to return to his companions.

Arriving at the meadow where he had tied Ax, he soon had the horse saddled and his pack fastened. Mounting up, he turned back to the west. Here, the traveling proved easier. The rim of the canyon transformed into a large, flat tableland that gave way to tree-covered hills and gentle valleys.

He camped that night beside a stream that ran through a mountain meadow.

The next morning passed as Horse Head Rock grew from a distant object to tower over Arn. The base of the rock was a forested hill. An adjoining river ran to the west. He headed toward this and soon spied a camp. Ty stepped into the trail ahead.

"Arn! Is that you? Hey, John. Come look at what the dog drug home. Whew! Don't get too close, though, or the smell will knock you over."

John emerged from behind a tree and lowered his bow. Arn dismounted and led his horse to where Ty stood. His extended hand was met by a forearm grip that belied the Kanjari's scornful words.

"You weren't kidding, were you, Ty," John said, waving his hand in front of his face to shoo away the flies that circled Arn.

"I tell you what," Ty said. "We allow Arn to go off alone for a couple of days, looking fine and riding one of my good horses, and he comes back riding a damned werebeast and smelling bad enough to make a vorg gag."

"To tell you the truth," said Arn, "I forgot that you had the princess with you. I wanted to make you feel like you were still back home with your families."

A broad grin spread across Ty's bronzed face. He whacked Arn on the back with a welcoming slap that made John cough from the cloud of dust that puffed into his face.

Arn felt a wash of relief over no longer being alone.

"Where in the world did you get that coat?" John asked. "Why don't you let me take it out and shoot it?"

"No need for that, John," Ty said. "It's been dead for a long time. Just burn it."

"Okay," said Arn, "I'll go down to the river and wash, but only on the condition that you both shut up long enough to prepare something to eat. I'm starved."

"Deal," said John.

Arn left the others and walked down toward the water. Dipping in a hand he discovered that it was as icy as he had expected. He shed all his clothes and plunged in, dragging the garments in as well. He forced himself to stay submerged long enough to clean himself and his clothes thoroughly. By the end of his bath, his feet ached from the chill.

When Arn emerged to stand on the bank, he found that he felt much better than he had in days. He lay his clothes on the grass and set to work wringing the water from them. He then slipped back into his wet trousers, carrying the rest of the garments back to camp, glad to see a big campfire. A leg of deer hung suspended on a stick over the flames. The smell set his stomach to growling.

"Hungry, are you?" John asked. "Try my special recipe, then."

Arn cut himself a large slice, the juice hissing where it dripped into the fire. He ate silently, ravenously. When he finally stopped and looked around, he saw the Endarian standing by a pine tree, looking at him with a smile.

"Kim has never seen any non-vorg with such downright barbaric manners," Ty interjected. "As a matter of fact, I don't think I have, either."

"Kim, is it?" Arn asked, ignoring the rest of the comment.

"Princess Kimber," she said, walking over to join the group, wearing fresh buckskin. "It *has* been a while since I found myself in the presence of three gentlefolk. I thank you all. Since we will continue to be traveling companions for some time to come, addressing me as Princess Kimber will quickly become annoying. My friends and family call me Kim. Please do the same."

"Thank you," Arn said.

From the regal way that she carried herself and the self-confident sparkle in her eyes, Arn could see that if the princess had not fully recovered from the trauma of her enslavement, she was well on her way. He assumed that she had tanned her crisp attire, as he imagined John and Ty lacked the vision and skill to complete such a feat. He took her hand and bent to kiss it.

"Kim it is, then," said Arn. "Are you all in the mood to discuss our plan going forward?"

"I traveled through this country as we made our way southeast from Endar Pass," said Kim. "The country on the other side of those mountains is much like what we have passed through these last few days. However, it drops off gradually until it reaches a great desert."

"If there is a desert to our west," Arn said, "we'll need to locate a town where we can purchase supplies and find a guide to lead us across."

"I don't intend to go west," Kim said. "I came in search of a particular human nobleman, and I will complete my mission. When we reach a town, I will find someone to accompany me to my journey's end."

Arn and the other two men stared at the Endarian princess. She stood with her arms crossed, her head held high.

"You can't be serious!" John said, clearly just learning of Kim's intent.

"I am quite serious."

Arn watched as her remark precipitated a heated argument between Kim and John. Despite the logic John offered, she steadfastly refused to budge from her decision to complete her search.

Finally, John threw up his hands in disgust. "If you're determined to get yourself killed, then I'll go with you."

"Get a rope, Arn," said Ty. "Let's tie up these two before they injure themselves."

"Hold on," said Arn. "Kim, if the nobleman still lives in Tal, I will know of him. Whom do you seek?"

Kim's brown eyes softened as she stared at Arn. She took a deep breath. "Years ago, during the Vorg War, King Rodan of Tal sent an emissary to my mother, Queen Elan, proposing an alliance. That man's name was Jared Rafel, and over the weeks that passed as the queen gathered her army of the North, she and Lord Rafel grew close. But when Lord Rafel was recalled to take command of the army of Tal, they parted. Now my queen, my mother, has sent me to seek him out to deliver a personal message."

"What?" Shock flooded Arn's body. This Endarian princess was seeking Rafel, his adopted sire, who was likely fleeing into the west at this very moment.

"And," Kim continued, "although he does not know it, Jared Rafel is my father."

Her statement rocked Arn. Even though he had betrayed King Gilbert to warn Rafel, leaving himself a hunted fugitive, his debt remained. Now he had stumbled upon a daughter Jared Rafel did not know he had. Apparently the fates were not ready for Arn to separate his lot from that of the high lord.

An old rhyme filled Arn's mind.

Our fates intertwine
And we are granted no rest
Much as Landerthel dew
Seeps from the Krel nest
And though we do struggle
To burst from these bonds
The master, Jalsathoth
Arises and dons
His armor and weapons
And all his war things
Forward he drives us
To see what fate brings
The wise know 'tis useless
For none may e'er change
How the gods they do move us
While playing their games

Hope lit Kim's face. "You know Jared Rafel?"

"I do. But you won't find him in the east. Tal's young king has branded Rafel a traitor. The lord leads his legion into the west as we speak."

This last part was an educated guess, but Arn believed what he said.

Seeing the pain in Kim's face, he hesitated. Despite his reluctance to believe in fate, he felt its weight on his shoulders. "If you're determined to find High Lord Rafel," he said, "then I will help you."

"As will I," said John, his voice thickening.

John and Arn stared at Ty. "Okay. I guess I'm in, too. The gods only know what sort of trouble these two would lead you into without me along."

Kim's gaze wandered from one to the other, tears filling her eyes. "Thank you."

"There is no debt, Highness," John said. "While I live, my life is yours."

Ty cleared his throat. "If you two are done mooning over each other, I suggest that we get some sleep. We have a long day ahead of us tomorrow, and I want to get an early start."

John turned toward the Kanjari. "I've had it with your snide comments."

"The mush was getting so deep that Arn and I had to stand on our toes to keep our noses clear."

"I'll take first watch," Arn said, wanting no part of the empty chatter. Upon Kim's revelation, he yearned yet again for solitude. "Ty, I'll wake you at midnight."

With that, he turned and walked up the hill toward the scarlet sunset that boiled above Horse Head Rock. He reached the crest just a hundred feet from the camp, a position that presented a commanding view of the valley and their camp.

For the next several hours, he sat watching and listening as the moon rose in the east, ignoring the ache in his injured arm. As the evening waned, a strange trick of the high-country atmosphere carried scraps of conversation from the camp to Arn's ears.

"I'm not saying we can't trust him, John; I'm just pointing out that if he's Blade, he doesn't need us. To a man like that, friends are a hindrance."

"You're wrong. I sense something about him that doesn't fit his reputation."

"I'll admit we owe Arn a lot," said Ty. "But we need to go slow with him. Just think about the last couple of weeks. He helps you escape with Kim, staying behind in a whole room full of hostile vorgs, and then he shows up again, unscathed. Then he leaves to attack the vorgs that are chasing the princess. And here he is again, horribly smelly at first but still mostly unharmed. I'll stand by what I said before. Arn doesn't need anyone but himself."

"Normally, I'd agree with you. But not this time."

"Did you see Arn's face when Kim mentioned Jared Rafel?" asked Ty. "I don't like coincidences."

"Arn didn't have to risk his life to save ours. I think he's earned our trust."

"I'm only saying we should add a pinch of caution."

Arn smiled as the wind shifted and the conversation faded. In a way, both were right about him. He had never allowed himself to become so closely tied to anyone after his parents' murders, except High Lord Rafel and his family. But that was different.

Arn lost himself in the sounds of the night, from the shrill chirp of crickets to the sough of the wind in the trees. At midnight, he walked back down to camp and aroused Ty for his watch. Seconds later he was asleep, wrapped in a dead vorg's coat.

—⁊⁊⁊—

Long before dawn, the group had eaten, packed, and begun riding west across the valley. By their ongoing banter, John and Ty seemed to have found the old humor that had been somewhat missing in the days since they had rescued the Endarian princess. Even the weather seemed to reflect their improved attitudes. A noticeable warming had occurred. Flowers bloomed, not just on the valley floor but also in the higher meadows. Evening found the travelers in one of those high meadows, well away from Horse Head Rock.

For the next several days, they traveled steadily westward, first climbing into the mountains and then beginning the gradual descent toward the yet unseen desert. One morning, they caught their first glimpse of the wastelands. From the crest of a hill, Arn saw it, a vast terrain, treeless and barren, but spotted with dark splotches.

Kim responded to Arn's questioning glance. "It's only thorn brush, growing on the tops of the dunes. From here, the brush looks rather green, but up close it's as harsh as the desert itself. Every plant that grows out there has spines of one sort or another.

"The desert is filled with all types of cacti. The rocky hills are covered with the plants, giving them a silver sheen. The needles have a mild poison that hurts terribly and barbed ends that break off beneath the skin when you try to pull them out."

Ty snorted. "John, I take back what I said about you two not mooning over each other. Get her talking about the moon and stars before she gets me depressed."

Kim frowned at Ty and kicked her horse on down the hill.

Feeling his oats at this success, Ty started in on John. "I've had a yearning to hear some love songs, myself. How about singing one for us while we ride along, John?"

"I'm going to set your head to singing if you don't shut up."

"Arn, don't you think John's getting a little touchy? Here I make an innocent remark about my love of music, and he gets upset."

Apparently not wanting to hear any more, John kicked his horse and trotted ahead of the others to ride beside Kim.

A disappointed look settled on Ty's face as his tongue's targets withdrew from the onslaught. If there was one thing he hated more than having no one to argue with, it was winning the argument too quickly. He glanced over at Arn, as if wondering whether he could get on his nerves, too, but then averted his gaze.

"I think I'll scout on ahead," Ty said.

Arn gazed at the Kanjari who did not fully trust him. "That's a sound idea," he replied. "I'd hate for you to make me mad as well."

The blond barbarian merely spun his stallion and loped off.

13

***Central Banjee River—Eastern Edge of the Mogev Desert
YOR 413, Early Spring***

The hills dropped away in front of him, drawing Arn's eyes to the Banjee River, which separated the verdant land from the wasteland that lay to their west. When they reached the water's edge, the group turned north. Ty rode well out in front, occasionally disappearing, only to emerge higher on the hillside. Arn brought up the rear, trailing behind John and Kim, who rode side by side, locked deep in conversation, with John often appearing transfixed.

Arn enjoyed feeling the powerful horse move beneath him, savoring how the animal did not need to be guided or prodded. He did have to slow Ax down occasionally, causing the horse to toss his head in disgust.

Around noon of the third day's travel along the river, Ty trotted back to them. "There's a caravan camped by the river ahead."

"How many?" Arn asked.

"Maybe a hundred desert nomads. They've got camels and horses and twenty-two wagons."

"Bandits?" asked John.

"They have women and children with them. I doubt raiders would bring women and children along."

"What do you think, Arn?" asked John.

"Ty's probably right. Whether they're friendly or not is another story. But we're not going to find desert guides without taking chances."

Ty wheeled the stallion around, leading the way toward the nomad camp, which came into view as they rounded a bend in the river. Colorful tents had been set up along the far riverbank, each sporting a unique pattern like a collection of tapestries. Nomads moved back and forth between the tents and the river, women carrying pots of water or baskets of laundry on their heads. From within the camp, Arn could hear the echo of a blacksmith's hammer.

As Arn and his three companions rode their mounts into the river, a heavily armed group of eight riders loped up to the far bank to meet them.

"Hello, strangers," the leader of the waiting group yelled as they approached.

"Good morning," Ty responded, bringing his stallion to a halt.

"And what may we do for you?"

"We saw your camp and rode over to ask your advice on getting across the desert."

"Hah! My advice? Don't try it."

Loud guffaws from the man's companions supported this assertion.

Ty grinned. "Probably wise counsel. Unfortunately, that's not an option, so we need guides. We're willing to pay."

"We won't keep you sitting on your horses in the river all day. Come to our camp. We'll discuss the matter over dinner, if your friends are agreeable."

"That we are." John spoke up.

"Fine, then."

The leader turned his horse toward the tents. Ty, John, Kim, and Arn followed, with the other armed men trailing behind.

The camp consisted of a group of closely set tents flanked by two large rope corrals; one held several dozen camels, while the other contained horses. The leader signaled for the group to halt in front of the largest of the tents, its canvas dyed bright scarlet with yellow crescent moons placed at random intervals. A deep-blue pennant with another moon flapped from the center pole. Arn and the others dismounted.

The leader entered the tent, then reemerged with another man who carried himself with an air of authority. The newcomer was short but of tremendous girth.

"Welcome, travelers. I am Narush, sultan of the Mogev Desert. Queel here tells me that you come seeking guides. We may be able to be of assistance. However, before we discuss business, let me offer you the hospitality of my tent and a hearty repast. My men will ensure that your horses are fed and watered."

"We accept your hospitality," Arn answered, inclining his head slightly.

His companions duplicated his action, except for Kimber. The Endarian stared at the sultan as if she expected him to bow. It seemed to Arn that the man had to fight off an urge to do so.

After they had turned their horses over to grooms, they were ushered inside. Narush clapped his hands, and their escorts departed. All that remained were two personal guards and three serving girls. One of the guards caught Arn's attention.

The ground on the guard's side of the tent seemed to tilt toward him, such was the size of the giant. Attired in loose, flowing robes, the man towered above everyone. Even Ty's head came only to the guard's shoulder.

"I see you've noticed my bodyguard. I would like to introduce you. Kaleb, come over and shake hands with my guests."

The giant stepped forward. Arn reached out, only to have his hand engulfed in a fist the size of a ham. He found that he could not even grasp across the palm, causing his handshake to seem like a flat fish. As

Kaleb passed along the line, Arn could see from the faces of the others that they had also shared the humiliating experience, although Ty at least managed to grip the behemoth's hand. A smirk creased the corners of Kaleb's eyes as he returned to his corner.

Irritation eliminated any good feeling Arn had entertained at their welcome. Plainly Narush wanted them to know who was in charge and was not concerned with whether they liked such a display or not. This was either a negotiating ploy or the signal of something worse.

"Shall we eat?" Narush gestured toward a carpet spread upon the ground.

While Arn and his companions were distracted, serving girls had been busily spreading dishes filled with fruits, meat, bread, and cheese upon a gilded floor covering. They also distributed goblets of water and wine. As soon as the visitors had seated themselves on pillows positioned around the edge of the rug, their host began devouring his food, interspersing grunts of pleasure between his slurping and smacking. Arn glanced up to see a look of disgust cross Kim's face, while John and Ty began eating. Arn signaled to the Endarian, subtly asking her to do likewise.

He found the food delicious. The meat seemed to be goat, although he had not seen any of the animals upon entering the camp. He was unable to identify several types of fruit, but they had obviously been gathered nearby. Evidently winter didn't set in this lowland, allowing fruits to grow year-round.

Once the diners had finished eating, the host leaned back, and one of the serving girls came forward with a bowl of water, wiping the sultan's face and hands. Once these ablutions had been completed, Narush snapped his fingers, and all but the two bodyguards departed.

"Aha. Now, my young friends, we can properly discuss your business here. Tell me, where are you going, and how much are you able to pay for a guide? I do not care to be insulted by low offers."

A low growl issued from Ty's throat, and Arn saw the muscles in his right forearm tighten.

Arn responded before the Kanjari could escalate tensions. "We need to cross the desert to reach the lands to the west. What price do you ask to provide us a guide?"

"All I want is the girl."

John started to rise, but Arn's hand on his shoulder held him in place. "No deal. She is one of our group, not property."

"Any person is property, given the right circumstances. Do not slave traders abound up and down the east Banjee? However, to allay your fears, I will agree to take her as one of my wives as opposed to my slave."

"I would never stay with you in any capacity!" Kimber flashed.

"Quiet, girl! This is a conversation between men."

"I think our discussion is over, Narush. We will be going now," said Arn, rising to his feet.

"I think not."

The two guards pulled their swords.

Arn moved, his left hand lashing out, seizing the thumb on the sultan's right hand, twisting it up and back. The sultan bellowed and dropped to his knees. The point of Arn's blade pressed against Narush's throat, causing him to tilt his head up. Other guards burst into the tent to face Ty's ax, along with John's and Kim's upraised bows.

"Tell them to back off." Arn's voice was a low growl, a prod from Slaken's tip emphasizing his point.

The small voice in Arn's head screamed. Something was out of place. But what? He had control of the sultan. These people would not risk their leader for a slave. Still, his intuition told him something else.

The guards backed slowly out of the tent. Still Arn's inner sense cried out. He scanned his surroundings rapidly but could not identify what was wrong. As the last guard backed out through the entry flap, Arn forced the fat sultan to his feet, simultaneously moving behind him so that his knife hand encircled the man's throat. Forcing Narush slowly toward the door, he felt the others move in close, their weapons ready.

Then the tent collapsed.

Arn hammered Slaken's haft into the sultan's skull, knocking him unconscious. Driving the knife upward through the tent, he discovered that the canvas was interwoven with thick cords that formed a stout net. As Slaken hung in the cords, the tent was pulled down from the outside, collapsing atop the ensnared group. Over and over they were rolled, the net-tent wrapping around Arn and his companions until they could barely move. Arn realized he was not going to be able to cut his way out in time.

"Hey!" Arn yelled. "I have your sultan. Release us right now, or he is dead."

"Imbeciles," a nearby voice sounded. "Do you really think we would bring armed strangers into our sultan's tent? The man you have is merely one of the sultan's men."

"Ah, crap," Ty said. "If that doesn't ruin a perfectly good meal."

"I can't move," John said.

"None of us can," said Ty.

Arn considered killing the man that lay beneath him, but that would serve no purpose except to ensure his execution.

Many rough hands seized the net and began methodically unrolling it, slapping chains on the wrists of those inside as they rolled free. A bald guard with a shaggy mustache began frisking the companions for weapons.

As his hand moved toward Slaken, the former assassin's voice interrupted him. "I wouldn't do that. No one holds that knife but me."

"The deep, you say."

The guard slapped Arn roughly across the face as he jerked Slaken from his hand. As the man pulled away, his body went rigid, a cold black shadow sliding up his arm past the elbow. The guard stumbled backward, grabbing the knife handle with his other hand in a vain attempt to toss the weapon away. The shadow now engulfed both arms in an inky film. As obsidian spread across his chest and down his torso, the guard shrieked, a sound cut short by the disappearance of his head. Slaken landed on the ground with a *thunk*. The guard was gone.

The onlookers stared in stunned silence, then reacted en masse, kicking and beating Arn, Ty, and John. The travelers were bound securely and dragged into the presence of a young man seated on a high-backed chair inside another lavishly furnished tent. The man sported an arrogant visage. Wearing turquoise-colored robes and a white turban, he leaned back in his ornately carved chair, one leg crossed over the other.

With Arn's wrists tied to his ankles behind his back, he lay on the floor beside John and Ty. Kim was nowhere to be seen.

John cursed profusely, resulting in another beating until he quieted down.

"I am Sultan Mallock," the young man began.

"Sure you are," said John, who received several more kicks.

"You will learn to watch your tongue," said the sultan. "Then again, after tomorrow, it will not matter. You see, we are a sporting people. Rarely are we granted an opportunity for such sport as you will provide on your way from this world to the next."

Arn, Ty, and John remained silent.

"It is really quite boring to have people killed without a contest, and since there is no reason for those involved to do their best unless they have a chance to escape with their lives, tomorrow I will host one such contest. You three will pick one champion to represent all. If your champion kills mine, then you three shall go free. If my champion kills yours, the other two shall be tortured slowly to death."

"What about the girl?" asked Arn.

"In any case, she stays. Do not worry. She will be treated well, as are all my concubines."

"You vile pig!" shouted John.

A kick to the head rendered John unconscious.

"I think that one will not be in any condition to be chosen as your champion." The sultan walked to where Ty lay. "But you certainly look strong. I gather that you will be the choice."

Ty started to speak, but Arn cut him off. "I'll do the fighting."

Anger flashed across Ty's face but faded almost instantly.

The sultan looked surprised. "Now why would you not pick your strongest? Is it because you have seen Kaleb and realize even this man's strength will be no match? Or do you think that maybe you can duck through his legs?" He erupted into laughter. "Take them out!"

Guards dragged the three men out of the tent by their feet, tossing them into an iron cage mounted on the back of one of the wagons. With the clank of a heavy key turning the tumblers within a lock, the guards departed.

Arn shifted so that he could see the other two. Blood flowed from John's nose and mouth. He remained unconscious.

"I'm getting sick and tired of you acting like you're the only one who can fight," said Ty. "I'd like to take my own chances against that big brute."

"Strength isn't going to win this fight."

"And you will?"

The eyes of the two men locked as they lay on the floor of the wagon. Arn's reluctance to trust anyone but himself in a critical situation had come to the fore. The night passed slowly. Sleep came and went, hindered by the chained men's cramping muscles.

John awoke and groaned, his face swollen. "I'm going to kill these bastards if it's the last thing I do."

Arn glanced over at him.

"What in the deep is going on around here?" John asked.

"Killer over there has volunteered to fight Kaleb," Ty answered. "If he wins, we go free. If he loses, we die."

"Now I remember. The scum said he was going to keep Kim captive regardless. I won't stand for it."

"Calm down," said Arn. "We'll have our chance."

"How do you figure?" asked Ty.

"There's always a moment when you have a chance to act. We just have to choose that time. Even a bad plan executed with shock can work."

"Well, I don't see any plan, good or bad," said Ty. "They're going to have their little carnival today. Kaleb will kill you, and that's that."

"If your scenario happens, then you're right. But if I'm victorious, then at that instant there will be shock. That's the moment when you have to act if we are to rescue Kim and escape."

John shook his head. "I don't see what we can do in these chains."

"Quiet," said Ty. "They're coming."

A group of eight guards walked toward the wagon, stopping just behind it. One of these produced a key ring and unlocked the cage. Two others reached inside and dragged Arn out, letting him fall to the ground.

"How about unchaining my feet so I can walk to the arena?" said Arn.

"We intend to," said the guard who had just dropped him. "We want to give you a good chance to stretch out so you'll give Kaleb a fight."

One of the guards took out a length of rope, tied a noose, and placed it around Arn's throat. The one with the keys removed Arn's wrist and ankle chains before putting the keys back in a pants pocket and tossing the chains aside.

Arn struggled to his feet, stumbling backward against the guard as he rose. The guard slapped him across the face, the force of the blow knocking Arn against the cage.

"Watch what you're doing, clumsy fool."

Arn felt himself being grabbed by two other guards and hauled off between the rows of tents as the rest of the group trailed along.

—⁂—

Ty watched as Arn disappeared behind the nearest tent. Beside him, John rolled away from the edge of the cage and grinned.

"He did it!"

Under John's legs lay the guard's key ring.

—ᴍᴍ—

Arn found himself pulled between the rows of colorful tents into a large, roped-off swale that formed a corral. He had passed this same enclosure upon entering the camp. Now it was empty, and a crowd of men, women, and children had seated themselves on surrounding sloped benches.

Meat and other foods were roasting on spits around the outside of the arena, and the spectators were drinking heavily of wine. The crowd yelled loudly, and boos rained down as the guards dragged Arn into the arena. One of his guards removed the noose from his neck and then handed him a foot-long, bone-handled knife before leaving the arena to join the spectators.

Arn looked around. Masses of armed men cut off all routes of escape. Just then, a loud cheer went up from the crowd. Into the far end of the arena strode the giant, Kaleb, holding a short sword in his right hand.

Kaleb was bare-chested, wearing just a breechcloth around his waist. His skin gave way to a thick coat of black hair across his chest, shoulders, and back. He walked to within five feet of Arn and then halted, raising his sword in salute to the sultan. Arn did not follow his example.

"To the death!" the sultan yelled.

Another cheer rose from the crowd. The giant wheeled with incredible speed for a man his size, bringing the sword crashing down into the spot where Arn had just stood. He leapt backward just in time to avoid the blow.

Kaleb continued his assault, driving the weapon toward Arn's stomach. Arn pivoted, just avoiding the tip of the sword that would have impaled him as he lunged in with his knife. The giant parried upward with his bare arm, taking the cut but knocking Arn off his feet.

Kaleb spun, lunging to the spot where Arn had fallen, driving the sword downward with such force that the air whooshed around the double-edged blade. Arn rolled to his right, regaining his feet as Kaleb's sword struck the ground, the blade nicking his right shoulder. Sensing his advantage, Kaleb pressed his attack.

Arn stumbled, seeming to lose his balance as he backpedaled. Kaleb lunged in for the kill. Arn changed direction, driving his body forward, his knife cutting an arc on its upward path into the fleshy part of Kaleb's palm, passing all the way through the giant's sword hand. The sword spun away into the dirt.

Arn jerked down on the blade, turning his back to the giant with the intent of pulling the knife from Kaleb's hand and back into his stomach. However, the knife had lodged between bones, causing the weapon to hang momentarily. Arn jerked again and the knife came free, but the delay had been too long.

The giant's left hand seized him around the arm and waist. As Arn pulled the knife free, Kaleb grabbed Arn's wrist with his injured hand. Arn felt himself lifted off his feet while facing forward and crushed against the behemoth's body. Kaleb gripped Arn's extended right hand.

A yell of victory issued from the giant's mouth as he slowly began driving Arn's knife hand back toward his own body. Unable to drop the knife, Arn called upon every ounce of his strength. Muscles in his arms and shoulders knotted, stretching his skin. Beads of sweat rolled down his forehead and into his eyes. Arn hammered his head backward into the giant behind him, only to have it bounce harmlessly off the massive chest.

Arn tried to kick a knee or groin, but could not damage the first or reach the latter. The knife slowly advanced. The tip of the blade touched his stomach. As it did, Arn twisted. Pulling with all his strength, Arn forced the blade through his own side and into Kaleb's stomach.

With a yell of surprise and pain, the giant relaxed his grip, trying to push the knife out and away. As the grip loosened, Arn's body dropped, causing the blade to rip downward. Agony exploded through his brain as impact with the ground twisted the knife that impaled him. The giant fell across Arn's body.

Kaleb was dying but not yet dead. His huge hand reached out, grabbed Arn's throat, and squeezed. Arn's eyes bulged as his windpipe threatened to collapse. Pulling the blade from his own body, Arn ripped upward, driving the blade into the left eye socket of the huge man. With a final shudder, Kaleb went limp.

Arn pushed the heavy body off his own and staggered to his feet. A hush fell over the crowd, stunned by what they had just witnessed. Arn glanced down. A thick redness poured from the hole in his side. He felt dizzy, taking a step forward only to stumble to his knees.

A wild commotion broke out. A herd of camels and horses stampeded into the crowd, trampling people beneath their hooves and raising a dust cloud. A stallion emerged from the melee; on its back, Ty. A guard with a spear jumped in front of the Kanjari, only to be trampled beneath the hooves of the running stallion.

Through a reddish haze, Arn saw arrows sprout from the chests and backs of armed men as a distant minstrel strummed his bow. As Arn tumbled forward, he felt himself seized by a strong hand and lifted upward into an enfolding blanket of darkness. Around him, screams faded to silence.

—☗—

Ty supported Arn's limp body with his left arm. Nudging the stallion with his right knee, he sent it spinning hard left, barely breaking stride as it raced back into the confused crowd.

Five men fronted the sultan, long spears anchored against the ground, sharp tips pointing out toward the rapidly approaching horse. Behind them, Mallock struggled to maintain his grip on Kim as she bit, clawed, and kicked in an effort to free herself.

As the stallion reached the soldiers, Ty leaned forward over the horse's neck, somehow managing the feat despite holding Arn's limp body in his left arm. Swinging his great ax out in front of the animal's head, he cleanly severed spear tips from shafts. Without effective pikes to bar his progress, the palomino stallion struck the middle three soldiers with his mighty chest, sending their broken bodies cartwheeling away.

Letting go of Kim, the sultan scrambled backward. With a simultaneous touch of both heels, Ty brought the stallion to a skidding halt, rearing high in the air. A flying hoof caved in the side of the sultan's head, eliminating the man's interest in the Endarian for all time.

As Kim leapt up behind Ty, the two remaining guards rushed forward. One stumbled to his knees and then fell facedown, an arrow's shaft jutting from his back. Ty's ax met the charge of the other.

The stallion bolted forward again as Ty guided him back into the midst of the panicked nomads. A group of men with bows had formed behind him, but now held their fire for fear of hitting their own people. Ty burst out of the crowd and rounded the first line of tents, weaving through them as he rode, using the structures to cover his retreat to the river. Ahead, he could see that John had crossed the river, leading two horses behind his.

The palomino stallion galloped into the water, pounding across the shallow ford and up the far bank. Ty glanced back over his shoulder to see a large group of riders rushing past the tents. Returning his attention to the front, Ty pulled up beside John just long enough to let Kim transfer to one of the other horses. Then they were off again at full speed, Ty supporting Arn's body and John pulling Arn's horse along behind him.

They entered the trees and immediately hit the steep, shale-covered slope that ran to the top of the ridge. Ty led the way up at a full run. The others fanned out to avoid the tumbling rocks and shale that cascaded down behind him. The horses were now beginning to labor, white sweat foaming where the riders sat. The Kanjari turned between two cliffs and emerged atop the first ridge.

This turned out to be a finger of land that jutted outward along a header canyon. He turned right, following the ridgeline up to the south. The horses were blowing hard but seemed happy to stretch out into a run along the gently sloping terrain they now traversed.

The group entered a thick grove of juniper trees and turned left, thundering down into the wooded canyon. Ty pulled to a halt under an overhanging cliff and jumped from the big horse, carrying Arn with him. He put his hand over the stallion's muzzle, signaling the others to do the same with their mounts. The horse's heavy breathing seemed exceedingly loud, but the noise of horses running over the rocks above drowned out the sound. Chunks of stone clattered down the hill, landing in the canyon bottom close to where Ty and the others waited. The rumbling faded into the distance as the riders raced on up the ridge.

Ty bent down to examine the wound in Arn's side. Blood still ran from the puncture on both sides, leaving Arn as pale as death. Ty tore the assassin's shirt into two pieces, wadding them into both sides of the puncture and binding them in place with a long strip from Arn's leggings. The measure was crude but would have to do.

Leaping astride his stallion, Ty reached down as John lifted Arn's unconscious body up to him. When John and Kim had mounted their own horses, he wheeled and followed the canyon down toward the river, paralleling the ridge they had just climbed. They soon found themselves in the thick trees at the bottom of the hills. Ty turned north, staying in the dense brush until he turned up a streambed, climbing back toward the mountains to their east.

Though it was just after noon, long shadows shrouded the canyon floor. Except for the splashing of the horses in the stream and the *clip-clop* of hooves on wet rocks, only the changing call of a mockingbird broke the silence. Ty stopped in a small glade and handed Arn down to John.

"You've got thirty minutes to tend to him before we have to move on," Ty said, his tone uncharacteristically grave. "We've got to keep moving until evening to be sure we've lost them."

A worried look flitted across the Kanjari's face as he glanced down at Arn. Then he wheeled the stallion around and headed back down the canyon to keep watch.

—⁓—

John knelt beside Arn's body, dread filling him as he carefully removed the bloody bandage. Arn's face was a shiny gray, cool to the touch. As Kim washed the wound, John doused the bandages in the clear stream, searched the bank, and returned to the Endarian's side with both hands full of a fragrant green moss. He worked quickly, packing the mixture into both the entry and exit wounds before tying off the wet bandages. John stood to see Ty riding up the canyon toward them. He glanced over at Kim, her eyes clouded with worry.

"It's too dangerous to move him farther," she said to Ty as he pulled his horse to a stop. "If the bleeding starts again, he will die."

"If we stay here, he won't be the only one to die. By now, those nomads will have realized we doubled back. They'll fan out until they cross our trail, then they'll be coming for us. I'm as worried as you two are, but think about it. If Arn could talk, he'd say to leave him."

"I won't do it!" Kim hissed.

"Of course not. But we have to keep moving until nightfall. The nomads can't track after dark."

John glanced at Kim and then gently lifted Arn's limp form up to Ty, watching as the barbarian cradled the assassin's body in his arms with no more effort than if he were carrying a child. With a touch of Ty's heel, he set the palomino into a gentle walk up the streambed. Kim and John mounted their horses and followed, John leading Ax behind them.

Slivers of light glinted down through tree branches, giving way to gloomy shadows as the afternoon wore on. A waterfall forced them to leave the stream and scramble up the steep hillside to the south.

John felt his horse slip on the shale, and in his struggle to stay atop the plunging animal, lost his grip on the lead rope. Rather than running away, Ax moved up closer to Ty's stallion. Realizing that he would not have to lead Ax, John reached down and removed the rope from the black horse's halter.

The canyon flattened and widened over the next half a league. Pines covered the steep hills, but the valley floor was open and grassy. The sun sank into the west, taking with it the day's warmth.

Ty stopped at the edge of a grove of trees, kicked his leg over the stallion's neck, and slid to the ground. Kneeling, he lay Arn down in the deep grass, close to the stream that cut a path through the valley's center. As he let the limp form slip from his arms, John watched as Kim pushed Ty aside.

"He still lives but barely," Kim said as she examined him. "I need a wet cloth and ample darla root."

"What's that?" Ty asked.

"I know," John said. "I'll be right back."

The growing darkness along the stream bank left John thankful for his exceptional night vision as he frantically searched and pulled up a handful of the orange roots of darla vines. A memory resurfaced. His father, the master bowman George Staton, had taught him to shoot, while his gentle mother, Sheryl, had taught him the medicinal properties of plants.

Ironically, Sheryl had failed to detect the poisonous fungus that had infested a batch of darla root she had used to make her family's afternoon tea. John had returned from a hunt to find both his parents dead on the cottage floor.

Refusing to succumb to memory, he returned to Kim just as she finished arranging green pine branches to form a star around Arn's body.

John and Ty moved to the edge of the clearing, leaving the Endarian woman alone to conduct her ritual. The moon rose above the eastern horizon, bathing the clearing in its glow. Kim knelt on the western side of Arn's body so that the star enclosing him stood between her and the crescent moon. The faint trill of a song wafted from her lips as she lifted her head, extending her arms, palms upward, toward the source of light.

The volume of her song increased, and with it, the moonglow. A beam crawled along the pine star, sending threads of light across the grass to Arn's body. As Kim continued to sing, John trembled. The song carried a sadness unlike any he had ever felt. The words were foreign, yet surreal images of wounds being leached from the plants into the very earth that nurtured them danced unbidden through his mind, leaving behind the conviction that nothing would grow in this spot for ages to come.

The glow illuminating Arn's prone form lost its softness, draping him in shining transparent armor. Then the song stopped, and the glow faded, first from the pine branches, then from the grass within, and, finally, from Arn himself.

Kim's head bowed forward, and the sound of her sobbing pulled John to her side, his throat constricting to the point that he could barely speak.

"Is he . . .?"

"He will live," Kim said, rising to her feet. Then, without explanation, she turned and walked away into the darkness.

"Look at the ground!" John said, staring in disbelief.

"I don't see a damned thing," Ty said, his face hosting no levity.

"Every blade of grass within the star is dead. So are the branches. I felt them die."

Stepping into the star, John felt the once-healthy grass crunch beneath his feet, transferring a sense of wrongness up his legs and into his spirit. How must the Endarian have felt?

Kneeling beside Arn, John placed a hand on his face. His fever had broken. Arn's breathing sounded normal, and a strong heartbeat pulsed through his neck. Ty joined John beside their wounded companion.

After his own quick examination, Ty lifted his face.

"By the gods," Ty said. "Looks like our princess is an Endarian life-shifter."

As John's eyes looked at the dead and withered plants, he knew it to be true. And, as he again thought of his mother, the confirmation of magic he had always believed to be a fable unsettled him.

14

Central Banjee River
YOR 413, Early Spring

Arn awoke with a start, reaching for the empty sheath at his side. "My knife?"

"Don't worry," John said. "When we broke out of that cage, the first thing we did was track down our weapons and packs. Yours was lying in the dirt right where it ate the nomad. I pushed it into this pouch with a stick. I'll let you take it out."

Arn reached for the bag, although a sharp burst of pain in his side made him wince. Returning Slaken to its sheath, he sank back, exhausted. "Pursuit?"

"Ty scouted our back trail. We lost them."

Arn nodded, closed his eyes, and let sleep claim him once again. He slept that day and the next, but managed to eat and move about on the third. Darkness found him leaning back against a fallen tree near their small campfire.

Kimber's healing magic had lent speed to nature's healing, but he was extremely sore and weak. When Arn asked her to tell him about the

Endarian spell, she hesitated but then sat down on the ground across from him, her legs folded beneath her.

"To begin with," Kim said, "we Endarians practice two schools of magic, life-shifting and time-shaping, each of which draws its energies from nature. My specialty is in the field of life-shifting magic.

"Both forms of Endarian magic require that balance be maintained. Those who have mastered the art of time-shaping can create a time-mist, speeding up or slowing down time. In the simplest case, the shaper creates a block of mist where time is slowed. The difference is then funneled into another mist, where time is quickened."

"Your people can actually do this?" Arn asked.

"Those who have mastered the discipline can work wonders," she said, "but few achieve such expertise."

"What about life-shifting? How did you heal me?"

"You can think of it as life-stealing, as some of our enemies have named it. For me to heal an injured person, animal, or plant, I must sicken or kill other living things to balance the life-energy I have directed into the stricken. As I funnel the life energy from one entity to another, I feel the pain of that which I kill, just as I feel the relief of the one I save."

She pursed her lips, and Arn knew that she was reliving the memory of what she had done for him.

"I'm sorry," he said, the words spilling from his mouth of their own accord. "It must be hard."

Blinking, she lifted her eyes to meet his. "Stealing life from one thing to give it to another always is. It is why few Endarians choose this discipline. It is why those who call us life-stealers are not wrong."

With that, she rose and walked into the dark.

Throughout the night, Arn lay awake, thinking. He had now recovered to the point that he felt he would be able to ride. Rolling over, he rose painfully to his feet and walked through the trees toward the small promontory where John stood watch. The lookout occupied a small knoll that rose in the center of the valley with decent visibility in all directions. He found John sitting atop a rock outcropping, gazing over the moonlit valley.

"You sure you ought to be out climbing around on the rocks?" John asked.

"I suppose not. But none of us seem to do what we ought to."

"You know, I've been thinking that if we head north, paralleling the desert, that we're going to run into a town built along that river," John said. "Surely we will be able to hire a guide."

"Sounds reasonable," said Arn.

"When we rescued our packs, we got back that small fortune of yours and a lot of the sultan's jewels and coins as well. We took as much as we could grab before starting that little stampede."

"The biggest problem we'll have will be keeping Kim safe," Arn said. "Maybe only Ty and I should ride into town while you look after Kim out in the hills."

"That makes sense, but we can't let her start feeling like she's a burden or she'll leave," John said.

"We've got plenty of time to come up with a good reason for the two of you to wait outside of town."

For the next hour, Arn sat beside John on the rocks, talking and watching the dimly lit valley. When he found weariness stealing his body, he bid his friend good night and made his way back to camp. Wrapping himself in his blanket, he settled down on the ground and fell into a deep sleep.

The search for a town with guides who could lead them across the desert progressed with mind-numbing slowness, leaving Kim brimming with frustration. Arn forced himself to hike for as long as he could each day, and steadily, his strength improved. The necessity of hunting for food slowed their northward progress through the mountains, and the search that they had hoped would take weeks became months. Summer waned, and the colors of fall worked their way into the high-country foliage.

John had grown comfortable enough with Kim to tease her occasionally. Arn noticed that Kim had gradually adopted some of the informal language that her human companions used. And the casual touches that lingered on John's arm came with increasing regularity.

As for Ty, Arn could see that the barbarian was in rare form. There was a big new world spread out before him, just waiting to be explored. He had the horse of his dreams, his ax, and good friends to abuse with his wit.

Ty was the first to catch a glimpse of the city, several weeks after their flight from the nomad camp. The Kanjari had been riding well out to the front but now returned at a gallop, sliding to a halt in front of the others.

"Looks like we've found more of a town than we were bargaining for," Ty said.

"Let's take a look," said Arn.

Ty wheeled the stallion around with a nudge of his knee and plunged forward along the narrow trail. The others followed at a somewhat slower pace. As they topped the ridge, Arn saw that Ty had not exaggerated.

The walled metropolis lay a half-day's ride ahead and stretched away on both sides of the Banjee River. It was bigger than any city Arn had ever seen, dwarfing Tal's capital. The thick outer wall featured a massive iron gate lowered across the mouth of the tunnel leading inside.

"I don't get it," said Arn. "I should have heard of a city of this size. We're within a few weeks' travel of Tal's northwestern border."

"Maybe the Borderland Range cut the city off from the east, forcing all the trade routes away from Tal," Ty said.

"That can't be it," said Arn.

"Well, believe it or not," said Ty, "there it sits."

A low moan of dismay to Arn's left reminded him that Kim hadn't spoken since they had topped the ridge. The Endarian's eyes had taken on a smokiness, as if she stared through the mists of time of which she'd spoken to Arn. Her lips parted, but she remained silent. Then she blinked and turned to face them.

"What we are seeing cannot be real."

"Why?" asked Arn. "What is that place?"

Kim turned to gaze out over the scene once more, spending more moments in silence before responding. "That is Lagoth. Four hundred years ago, during the Rift War, an army of Endarians and humans destroyed this city and killed its master, a despotic wielder named Kragan. The spells that killed Kragan and consumed Lagoth also created the Mogev Desert. The power of that casting split the world."

"Nonsense," Ty said. "If the world had split, we wouldn't be standing here looking at the not-destroyed city."

John shot the Kanjari a sharp glance, and Kim continued. "What you say is both true and false."

She extended her hand, sweeping it across the distant vista to the west and north. "The desolate land you see before you has only been thus for a short time by Endarian standards. As I said, a group of mighty wielders, some human, some Endarian, cast the most powerful spell in memory in the final hours of the battle that raged here. That casting obliterated Kragan and the horrific city-state he ruled. Neither he nor Lagoth's ruins have ever been seen again."

"Until now," said John.

"This changes everything," she said. "I must return to Endar Pass and warn my mother that Lagoth still exists. And if it exists, then it is quite likely that its master yet lives as well."

"Wait just a minute," said Arn. "Why hasn't anyone ever reported seeing the city? If we can stumble upon it, why has no one else?"

"The elders did not lie. More than four hundred years ago, two great armies spread out across a grassy plain to the west of that city.

Hundreds of thousands of Endarians and men faced off against an array of deep-spawned creatures—vorgs, mulgos, and worse.

"Amid the slaughter on that battlefield, wielders of great power contested, and they unleashed the horrible casting that ended the rising terror of Kragan. Nothing within hundreds of leagues would survive the spell they unleashed. The greatest time-shapers in all of Endarian history sacrificed themselves and the warriors who fought alongside them."

Tears streaked Kim's cheeks, glittering in the sunlight. "It cost Endar almost half our population, all killed by their own time-shapers."

The magnitude of the revelation staggered Arn.

Ty leaned in closer, his attention now fully occupied. "What about the splitting of the world?"

"Enormous seas lie far to the east and west of Tal," said Kim. "Seas that stretch beyond the horizon, seas that took sailing ships many weeks to cross. Sailing ships used to cross the water, bringing people and goods to and from faraway lands.

"They were the lands that spawned Kragan, and from the mysteries of those lands, the wielder drew most of his arcane powers. The elders created a wreath of time-slowing mist off the continent's shores and funneled all the excess time into the area around Lagoth, aging it thousands of years in moments. Since that day no ships have passed through the mists."

Arn rubbed his chin with his right hand. "You didn't answer my question. Why hasn't anyone stumbled across this city in the last four hundred years? Didn't your elders send scouts to confirm its destruction?"

"Certainly," said Kim. "Most of those never returned. The few who did reported not being able to find their way to the spot where the city supposedly lay, such were the changes in the land.

"Eventually, the elders stopped trying to find its remains. They assumed that the destructive nature of the magic had obliterated Lagoth, killing any who ventured too near the location of the city's ruins."

Ty stepped up onto a boulder to look out to the northwest. "Well, those ruins look to be in pretty good shape to me."

Kim nodded. "But to answer Arn's question about why the elders resorted to such desperate means to kill Kragan, I will have to defer to the elders themselves. You will meet some of them when we get to Endar Pass. That discussion centers upon an ancient prophecy that I am not at liberty to discuss here."

Ty stared at the princess.

"I am sad to be bound by laws that you do not understand, laws that keep me from giving you the knowledge that you want and need. But I cannot."

Ty looked into Kim's eyes, and the heat drained from his face. "I guess I can live with that. I don't have to like it, though."

"I agree with Kim," Arn said. "Getting word of this place back to Endar is of paramount importance."

"What about Tal?" asked John.

"To the deep with Tal," Arn said. "The king and his damned wielder can look after those people. Since we're here, and since no one else has apparently seen this city and lived to tell about it, I think I need to go down and take a look."

"I don't think that's wise," said Kim.

"Princess, I acknowledge that there is great risk. If I have not returned in three days, then the rest of you head for Endar Pass. I'll follow if I can. If not, it won't make any difference."

"It makes a difference to me," said Kim.

"Don't worry. I'll keep him safe," said Ty.

"You're not going," said Arn.

"Either with you or by myself after you leave, I'm going. And there's nothing in all the lands that can stop me."

Arn sighed, shook his head, and then turned toward the other two. Perhaps life was easier when the Kanjari wanted to keep his distance.

"Kim, you and John, please listen. If Ty and I haven't returned in three days, leave us. News must get back to Queen Elan."

John nodded and extended his hand, which Arn clasped. Kim leaned in and kissed him softly on the cheek. A sudden bear hug engulfed all three of them as Ty wrapped his big arms around their shoulders and squeezed.

"Let's get going," Ty said, "before all these sad farewells have me bawling like an infant."

Following the Kanjari, Arn swung into his saddle and nudged Ax with the heels of his boots, sending the brute cantering downhill after the palomino stallion, heeding the call of a dead city.

15

As they continued traveling westward, Carol did almost nothing but work on new spells. Among the elementals that she had learned to call upon was Lwellen, an air elemental that was the lightning master. And she surprised Hawthorne by mastering the mystic bolt spell, not because the fire elemental, Tirra, was particularly strong, but because it was very cunning. The word *slippery* came to mind. If it managed to distract her, even for a moment, Tirra could send a blazing shard into something or someone she did not want to hit. She eventually wished to throw at least ten bolts before exhausting herself mentally.

This morning she decided to check up on Alan. Retiring to a quiet spot by the river, Carol brought herself into the meditative state necessary for projection. Seconds later she cast herself out of her body, feeling the river flee away to the east.

Below her, she found nothing but a vast, terrible wasteland. What a pity, she realized, that she had to have someplace or someone she knew to focus upon in order to project like this. Otherwise she would have been able to search for the watering holes herself.

In seconds she saw Derek's small squad, spread out in a wedge formation across the sand, the horses plodding laboriously forward. As her immaterial self came to a stop directly above Alan, she could see him pull out the small water-scrying stick and place it in a cup. Adding a little water from his canteen, Alan stared downward.

"The damned thing is pointing back the way we came," her brother exclaimed. "It's pointing back toward the river. Leave it to a wielder to come up with a worthless piece of junk like this."

He began banging on the side of the cup, trying to get the stick to point to the next watering hole.

Carol could hardly believe her ears. Of course it would point to the river as long as that was the closest water source. She just hoped that Alan had enough sense to figure that out and keep checking the scryer.

"Put away the toy, Lord," said Derek. "We don't need such nonsense to find what we seek. Magic is only a tool for those who can't handle the trials of life."

Carol fell off the log she was on, landing on her butt in the mud.

Her father waved at her as she arrived back in camp. "Been out enjoying the sun?"

"Men!" was all she said as she stormed on by.

The next day Carol forgot about her irritation at Alan and Derek and set about learning a spell that Hawthorne called "earthen shield." This spell encased the magic-user's hand in a thick shell of rock for as long as she could maintain concentration. Anything she struck with her hand during this time suffered damage as if it had been hit with a hammer. For the next several days, a variety of items around the camp took a beating until Carol was banished to trying her skills on rocks and logs along the riverbank.

Yet all these spells took their toll via mental fatigue. Hawthorne raved about the fact that she managed to practice new spells even though he was drawing upon her strength more heavily than ever in order to maintain his wards.

At her request, he had shown Carol the technique for creating the wards. The trick was to bind an object to an air elemental that had the capability of creating a lensing effect in the shape the wielder desired. He then used a more powerful earth elemental to bind the lesser being in place. All things within the lens became invisible to magical detection, and even the minds within the bubble were blocked from discovery. Hawthorne had bound the air elemental Mij to the several wagons with earthen bonds, and it was these bindings that Blalock attacked, forcing Hawthorne to periodically repair them.

Carol was sleeping more—in effect, sleeping for two—and eventually reached a point where she was too tired to practice her spells. She tried again to project in order to find out how Derek and Alan were faring, but found she was unable to maintain the required level of concentration.

On the evening of the thirteenth day since Rafel had sent the ranger patrols searching for water, one of the squads returned. The men were nearly dead from lack of water and needed rest before making their report. The next morning, they revealed that they had been unable to locate any watering holes. Over the next week, other squads trickled back in with the same story. Then they quit coming.

Carol slept most of the day, now, and Hawthorne appeared more haggard and thin.

"We need to be moving on soon," Carol heard him tell her father one evening, the wielder's eyes appearing sunken in his head. "I do not know how much longer I can maintain the cloak against Blalock. When it fails, I would rather have more distance between us. While he cannot magically transport himself here, I do not think it would take him and his men long to catch up with us."

"You mean him and the king's men, don't you?" Rafel asked.

"Maybe, maybe not," Hawthorne responded.

"Whatever you mean, we can't move until we have a route. I don't intend to cause everyone in the caravan to die of thirst in that desert. I would rather die fighting."

Carol had to agree. They had already lost a half dozen wagons to accidents that killed thirteen people, most of the deaths occurring when a mudslide swept into the left flank of the caravan during a rainstorm.

Three days later Derek's squad returned. Upon reaching camp, Derek and Alan turned their horses over to grooms to be cared for and went to meet with Rafel. Carol heard that they had arrived and went to join them. As she approached the spot where they stood with her father and Broderick, she heard Derek speak.

"We found a route, or rather we found three watering holes heading in the direction we want to go. The first one is about a week's travel by wagon from here. We would have never found it, but for the wielder's little gadget."

"How's that?" Rafel asked.

"We were traveling along, checking the thing every day. For the first few days it just pointed back toward the river. Then on the morning of the fourth day the scryer pointed off to the southwest. For two more days we followed the device. When we checked the water scryer on the sixth day, it pointed back toward the river again. Alan almost threw the damned thing away, but we decided to backtrack and see if perhaps we had passed the watering hole.

"After traveling several hours and watching the scryer closely, it suddenly changed direction, again pointing to the southwest. We turned around once more, and the device immediately switched back toward the river. It was then that we figured that perhaps there was an underground stream.

"We started digging. About ten feet down we hit damp sand. Another three feet and we had a little well. After that we headed west once more and managed to locate two other places with water. Both of these were at the surface and did not require much effort to find."

"Great news," said Rafel. "Broderick, get everyone packed up and ready to depart. We're leaving within the hour. And I want to make sure we get those other three missing squads back in. If they're dead, then I want their bones. I will not leave my people to rot in this deep-spawned desert. Also, I've reconsidered my order preventing Derek from looking for his brother. Alan and the rest of the squad can guide us back to the watering holes."

A relieved look of gratitude spread across Derek's face. "Thank you, High Lord. I will leave immediately." With that, he turned on his heel and strode away.

Carol walked back to her tent and began packing her things. Men and women began bustling around the camp, and the clank of things being loaded echoed in the air. She had finished rolling and strapping her tent when Jake arrived to help her toss it on the back of the wagon. Shortly after that he disappeared, only to return carrying another tent and followed closely by Lucy.

"Gaar's been too busy to start my training like he promised," said Jake. "So I've been assigned to help the cooks, if you can believe that."

The look of disgust on Jake's face amused Carol. "Don't worry, young warrior. I'm sure you'll get more excitement than you bargained for by the time this journey is over."

Carol noticed that she had more energy today. Evidently something had distracted Blalock from his search, allowing Hawthorne to catch a little rest. At least he wasn't drawing on her strength at the moment. Her strength. That thought pulled forth the memory of what Kaleal had said about her role as an agent in Landrel's prophecy.

What did fate have in store for her?

Her father's caravan was so far from Tal by now that Blalock's pursuit made no sense. King Gilbert should be glad that Rafel and his legion had fled the kingdom. Blalock's persistence meant that the king continued to consider her father a threat, despite the distance that separated them.

Hawthorne had said that Rafel had presented Landrel's scroll to the Endarian queen at the start of the Vorg War. That had been five years before Carol was born. Was there a connection, or was she merely grasping at smoke?

Since such line of thinking rapidly went nowhere, Carol decided to get in some practice with her spells as they rode. She conjured a small dust devil that swirled along after the wagon, occasionally passing it, only to circle back around.

"Would you look at that?" Lucy said. "I've never seen a dust devil hold together that long. If I didn't know better, I would swear it was following our wagon."

"Well, let's see if I can get rid of it," Carol said.

Holding her concentration, she diverted most of her willpower into the magic bolt spell. She extended her hands, and five silvery streaks darted out into the swirling tower of sand before ensnaring the lightning master, Lwellen. She manipulated the elementals in an intricate dance, such that lightning seemed to sprout from the dust devil like arms stretched out in supplication to the heavens. Then, she allowed the whole thing to dissipate with a booming crash of thunder.

Lucy screamed as she dived into the back of the wagon.

Sight of the distressed girl wrung a twinge of guilt from Carol's conscience. "I'm very sorry, Lucy. I should have warned you that I would be practicing some of my spells. I forgot that Jake has seen me practice, but you haven't."

"You scared me out of five years of life," the girl said, slowly crawling out of the wagon.

"I never figured that driving a wagon would be this entertaining," Jake ventured as he turned his attention back to the team of oxen. Before Lucy could respond, he flapped the reins and let out a yell. "Hyaaaa . . ."

Ignoring his yells, the oxen kept to their steady, plodding pace.

The wagons traveled through the desert uneventfully. The dunes ranged in size from smaller than a wagon to larger than a house. In between the dunes, the sand was relatively hard-packed, enabling the wagons to roll without much difficulty. The sand was intermittently covered by a thick mass of thorny plants, offering thin branches covered with long, sharp spikes. Cactus and wide, spiny grasses were abundant. Someone came up with the idea of burning the needles off the cactus, enabling the hungry animals to eat the plants, and although this helped, the horses and oxen got steadily thinner.

The days were getting hotter, so Rafel ordered the caravan to travel in the mornings and evenings. During the midday hours, his people rested, crawling under the wagons to escape the beating sun. The water barrels were still holding out well, but the high lord enforced strict conservation.

At the rest stop on the sixteenth day of desert travel, Derek returned with Jaradin and his team. Carol went to meet them as soon as she learned of their arrival. She reached her father's wagon just as Alan and Gaar approached. Rafel's advisors, along with Derek and Jaradin, were already there.

"I don't know why you sent Derek out at all," Jaradin said. "The day I need my little brother to look after me is the day I end all endeavors and haul out the rocking chair."

"What delayed you?" Broderick asked.

"That is a tale that takes some telling. We were three days' ride to the north, getting ready to head back, when we sighted a nomad caravan moving south along the river. We decided to ride down and learn more. I left two of my team behind to watch for signs of trouble, with instructions to head back and tell you if we couldn't get out.

"When we rode into the camp, they were pretty jumpy about strangers but gradually settled down when they saw that we had friendly intentions. It seems they had run across a group with bad intentions, a couple of barbarians, an Endarian, and a knife fighter. I couldn't get a lot of details about how the fight got started, but apparently, there was a contest between the knife fighter and their champion. What had them rattled was that the knife fighter managed to kill their man."

"Why is that?" Rafel asked.

"That was our question, too," Jaradin said. "So they took us to a wagon that was carrying their man's body to their burial ground. Once we saw him we understood. The man was a giant, eight feet tall and the strongest-looking human I've ever seen. The nomads said the dead fighter was as fast as he was strong. He'd evidently killed more than a hundred people, so you can start to get an idea why they were so shocked to see his life bleed away into the dirt."

"Did they give you a description of the one who killed him?" Gaar asked.

"They did better than that. They gave me this."

Jaradin unfolded a paper, spreading it against the side of Rafel's wagon so they could all see.

Carol gasped. The shock that registered on the faces of the others showed that they did not catch the sound. There, on a wanted poster, beneath the offer of a thousand gold for proof of the man's death, was Arn's picture, right above the name "BLADE."

"That can't be." Carol's voice was barely a whisper, but it roused her father out of his shock.

Rafel turned, placing a strong hand on her shoulder as he looked into her eyes. "I'm sorry, sweetheart. Arn isn't after us. It was he that warned me of the king's edict. I tried, unsuccessfully, to convince him to come with us."

"That explains it, then." Broderick slapped his palm onto the wagon. "Blade must have stumbled into those nomads by accident. No wonder their hero got himself killed."

"What about Arn?" Carol asked.

"I don't think we need to worry about Blade anymore. The nomads seemed sure that he had inflicted a mortal wound on himself to get the giant," Jaradin replied. "Just to be safe, however, we rode another couple of days to the north to the place where the fight had occurred. Then we picked up the old trail left by Blade's bunch.

"We followed it north for three more days. There was no sign of Blade's body, but the pattern of their camps indicated that he was badly hurt. A strange circle of dead plants appeared at one of the sites. Weird thing. None of us had seen anything like it. If Blade's not dead, then he's headed north."

"You don't need to worry about Blade," Rafel said. "He's like my second son. He would never hurt me. And I refuse to believe that he's dead. He has cheated the Dread Lord all his life, and I have no reason to believe that has changed."

Carol stumbled away from the others in a daze. She barely realized when she reached her wagon. Ignoring Jake's and Lucy's concerned inquiries, Carol climbed into the back and sat, hugging her knees, among the crates and barrels.

Arn dead. The thought struck her like a stone. She had been so occupied with the caravan's flight these last few weeks that she'd easily kept herself from thinking about him. But that had only been because the thought of his death never occurred to her. Blade had always seemed invulnerable to the death that he doled out. After all the tales about him surviving impossible situations, could he have succumbed to fate at last?

Carol moved her head violently, trying desperately to banish the terrible thought. Her throat constricted as she wiped away tears with the back of her hand. *No. Arn is not dead. I won't believe it.* Suddenly an idea came to her. She could project out-of-body and will herself to him. For the first time, she would take an astral look at the man she loved.

Carol soon gained full enough control of her emotions to achieve the desired state of meditation. She reached out with her mind, feeling for the presence that was Arn, a presence that would give her something to focus on.

But she felt nothing.

He simply was not there, as if he'd been sucked through a hole in the universe. That feeling of total absence broke her meditation.

He was dead. There was no other explanation for the complete void that she felt. Even through the barrier that she and Hawthorne had erected, a user of magic could feel a known person's presence. Only the sense of direction would be lacking. But this nothingness could only mean one thing. Arn was dead.

A low wail escaped Carol's lips. Immediately, Jake jumped onto the wagon and raised the flap to look inside.

"Lorness, are you all right?" he asked.

"Just leave me alone!" Carol snapped. "I just want to be alone."

The handsome youth drew back as if he'd been bitten. The canvas flap dropped once more, leaving her in the hot semidarkness.

—m—

Carol was unable to shake the severe depression into which she had fallen. She submerged herself in the practice of magic to such an extent that Hawthorne became worried. She ignored the hot trek through the desert, and Jake and Lucy avoided Carol as she withdrew. To gain some semblance of privacy for her magic, Carol often created a wall of fog around the area where she was practicing.

All else became secondary to the development of her skills. She picked up two additional spells that she quickly mastered. These enabled her to ensnare enemies in thick mud and send forth a freezing wind. She found herself becoming more irritable, resenting any interruptions and taking that resentment out on the offender with a verbal barrage. Even her irrepressible brother started to maintain a certain distance.

Her father had tried talking to Carol, eventually resorting to a severe scolding that was unflinching in its honesty. But she continued to dig deeper into an emotional well. Due to the disturbing effects that Carol's practice of magic and devolving attitude was having on morale, and because she ignored his demands to cease such behavior, Rafel ordered her wagon placed last in line. This was fine with Carol.

She sat on the back of the wagon, her feet dangling down. Her leather breeches, like the rest of her clothes, were covered in dust kicked into the air from the long caravan. Her hair was tangled and dirty. The stringent water conservation had made baths an unaffordable luxury, and Carol had lost interest in brushing out her tresses.

Her brown eyes had taken on a gray cast, her face drawn and taut. Sleep came with great difficulty, for Arn's face haunted her dreams. She found herself tempted to try increasingly difficult spells, using a mixture of subtle and extreme variations, the elemental entities she directed baffled by her newfound harshness. Of late she had even been drawn toward calling upon the primordial, Kaleal. After all, what did it really matter anymore whether or not she controlled him or went mad? Perhaps she was there already.

Carol directed her will out into the dunes behind the wagon, grabbing a breeze and whipping it into a raging whirl. A dark wall of sand formed in the air, laced with jagged branches of lightning as a wall of fog crawled out before the manifestation.

Carol closed her eyes, sending out a blast of cold air that struck the fog, the resulting condensed snow immediately sucked into the whirling torrent behind it. The wind howled, and the crash of thunder close at hand caused the oxen to break into a nervous trot. The elements were far more effective than Jake's voice.

A horse separated from the main line and pulled back to fall in beside Carol's wagon. Jake brought the team to a halt at a command from Alan, who pulled his warhorse up beside the wagon. Alan swung from his saddle and climbed onto the seat beside Lucy, causing the terrified girl to shriek. He ignored her and climbed into the back.

Alan placed his broad hand on Carol's shoulder.

"Carol, stop it. Stop it now!" her brother commanded.

For a few seconds, Carol was barely aware of him. Then, ever so slowly, the unnatural storm abated, replaced by the still, dry heat of the desert. She turned to stare, glassy-eyed, into Alan's face.

"I have left you to yourself and to your practice with the hope that you would work your way through this malaise," Alan said. "But you've quit fighting and given up. That's not what I would've expected of the sister who once told me that it was her duty to learn magic so that she could bring a new political order to the world. So maybe, before you kill yourself, you should be the one to burn this." Alan grabbed her hand and thrust a book onto her palm. "It seems that you no longer value it."

He then turned, went to the front of the wagon, and leapt back on his horse, wheeling away with a flick of his reins.

Carol looked numbly at the battered leather binding. As she gazed down at Thorean's *Liberty*, she bent her head and wept. Rolling back under the canvas, she hugged the old volume, her body curled up in a ball.

—⚹—

On the wagon seat, Jake leaned over to Lucy.

"Lorness Carol will get better now. Lord Alan has seen to it."

PART III

A word of caution to any who would wield the magic of exchange: Should your channel's capacity be exceeded, the shortfall shall be drawn from the wielder.

—From the *Scroll of Landrel*

16

Lagoth—Northwest Mogev Desert
YOR 413, Late Summer

The city spread out majestically before them. Arn and Ty sat astride their mounts along a ridge a little more than half a league from the outer walls. The southern wall was perhaps fifty feet high and quite wide but had no gates. Armored guards atop the wall paced back and forth between towers that jutted skyward. All along the perimeter, the top of the wall was perforated with crenels for pouring hot oil or shooting arrows down upon enemies.

To the west, the river passed underneath the outer wall through a domed arch. The arch extended out from the wall on the outside, forming a tunnel into the city with sides thick enough to house a network of pathways. The occupants had made no attempt to conceal that this was an obvious trap.

The desert lay beyond the city's western wall, while the eastern wall wound up into the foothills before wrapping around to the north. This left plenty of room for the city and its castle atop the hill in the city center.

Arn and Ty kept to the higher ridges as they worked their way northward, maintaining cover within thick woods. Several times they were forced to detour up into the mountains to avoid armed patrols, which were made up of a mixture of humans and vorgs. As opposed to the bandits Arn had encountered in and around Rork, these warriors wore chain mail battle armor and looked to be part of larger units.

The sight of the vorgs pulled forth a reminder of Charna. He shunted aside the thought and refocused. The two riders continued to work their way through the rough country, reaching the northern edge of the wall as evening fell.

A wide road stretched away from the city to the north and west, exiting the wall beneath a great portcullis. The guard force here was quite heavy, and the sight of an additional military encampment outside the walls surprised Arn.

Tens of thousands of soldiers were gathering on the northern outskirts of the city. Lights from hundreds of fires twinkled in the twilight. From their vantage point on the hill, Arn and Ty could see the city lighting up as well.

"What do you make of that?" Ty asked.

"I haven't heard of an army that size being gathered since the Vorg War, and that was thirty years ago."

"It's a safe bet that this little sight would set off a general panic in Tal," Ty said. "How in the deep are we going to get in there?"

"They've got so many soldiers coming and going that it'll be easy to get inside the walls. All we need are the uniforms," Arn said.

The duo turned back toward the higher mountains, traveling into rougher terrain. Within an hour, they found a sheltered draw with good grass and water that would take a great deal of luck for a patrol to find. Ty turned the palomino loose, while Arn hobbled Ax for grazing and watering. Arn slung his pack over his shoulder and set out toward the city with Ty striding along beside him.

The soldiers were confident of their security, for the posted guards were none too alert. Ty and Arn moved past them easily in the darkness, crawling along and using low ground to avoid being silhouetted against the sky. Arn led the way past the outer tents, selecting a small one about twenty feet inside the perimeter. He raised his hand, motioning for Ty to guard his back.

Arn paused at the flap, listening to the sounds of breathing from within. He could make out the steady breathing of two humans, and the slower, rumbling breaths of three vorgs. He drew Slaken, the oiled black blade sliding noiselessly from its sheath, and slipped into the tent. The occupants lay sprawled on the ground with little room between them, their packs and arms stacked against the tent's sides. Arn paused to let his eyes adjust to the darkness, then stepped over the first vorg. So swiftly did the knife tip slide into the vorg's brain, just behind his ear, the soldier didn't even flinch.

Arn moved around the tent, repeating the process for each of the sleeping occupants. He then wiped Slaken on one of the vorgs' shirts and returned it to its sheath. From the smell of them, all the dead soldiers were wearing their only set of clothes and washing hadn't been a priority. Arn stripped the clothes from one of the men and from the largest vorg. He then stacked two chain shirts on top of the pile and ducked outside to where the Kanjari stood guard. He gave this armload to Ty and slipped back into the tent.

Arn stripped the remaining bodies, piling clothes and armor and wrapping them in a blanket. He rummaged through the rest of the tent, finding two pouches of coins. Placing these into the blanket, Arn hefted the bundle onto his back and stepped out into the night. Creeping back the way they had come, Arn and Ty departed from the line of tents and, finding a clump of dense brush, set about changing into their new clothes.

The armor and clothes fitted the two as well as they'd fitted the previous owners, but that didn't mean the attire was ideal. The chain shirts were third-rate. In fact, all the armor was rusty and in need of the most basic maintenance. Still, Arn had worn worse.

He watched as Ty braided his golden locks into twin forks that he ran inside the chain mail shirt. This change in appearance complimented the vorgish armor he wore, making him look like just another barbarian conscript.

After they had tossed the unused clothes and armor under bushes and secured their own clothes in a hollow log a considerable distance away, Arn picked up his pack. Then he and Ty began working their way toward another section of the camp on the side closest to the city. As dawn broke, they drifted into the crowds of soldiers and ruffians coming and going.

A line of robed and hooded slaves lugged barrels and boxes out of the city to the encampment. Green-skinned mulgos cracked whips in the air over these unfortunate souls, laughing when they found an excuse to cut cloth and flesh with the barbed metal tips. Arn had only seen two of the seven-foot-tall amphibian humanoids before arriving in Lagoth. Not particularly surprising. Mulgos preferred damp caves with no light, the very places that the nomadic vorgs and Kanjari hated.

Arn nudged Ty to signal him to move on and ignore the sights. One surprised look could get them both spotted as outsiders. After one mistake, Arn was pleased to see how quickly Ty picked up the mannerisms of the milling throng.

The two men took on the look of soldiers who had been given a last liberty before the coming march. There seemed to be a good many others in that same situation, and all were moving into the city. Those warriors coming out were in worse shape, many supported by their comrades.

The road was wide and heavily rutted by the wheels of wagons and carts. The city's outer wall towered before the disguised duo, thick and forbidding. As they passed under the portcullis, Arn made note of the number of guards and their state of alertness. This group seemed to be better disciplined than the others he had seen, standing stiffly at attention atop the wall, gazing out on the camp beyond.

The road passed through a hole in the wall that was more of a tunnel than a gate. Arn could not make anything out in these cavernous holes except deep shadow. An additional portcullis hung from the far end of the tunnel, forming another potential blockade to anyone attempting to enter the city with hostile intent. Arn and Ty fell in behind a group of soldiers that appeared to be in search of entertainment.

Inside the innermost of the city's walls, stone houses crowded up against one another on either side of a narrow street that angled between rows of shops. The streets surprised him. Neatly cobbled, they all showed evidence of meticulous and ongoing maintenance.

The soldiers ahead turned into a narrow alleyway between windowless two-story buildings. The alley curved east and then south, eventually ending at a set of stone steps leading downward. The soldiers descended these, oblivious to the two strangers who followed.

Three knocks on a wooden door at the bottom caused a small barred window in the upper portion of the door to be opened.

The door swung inward to admit the group, now ten where there had been eight. The room in which Arn and Ty found themselves resembled a cave more than a tavern. The stench of bad liquor, bat guano, sweat, vomit, and urine was intense enough to make the assassin's eyes water.

As his eyes got accustomed to the dim lighting, he could see that there was more than one room in the venue, all of them carved into the solid bedrock of the foundation.

The walls were barren, save for lanterns hung on hooks. The room in which they now stood was circular, and two arched openings led to other round chambers.

Tables of assorted sizes and shapes filled the rooms. Many of the occupants appeared to be sleeping with heads resting in pools of spilled drinks. The other inhabitants were either trying to achieve the same blissful state of unconsciousness or directing their attentions to the steady stream of women who made their way through the jumble of bodies and tables, offering drinks or themselves to those who remained alert enough to understand the proposition.

Arn walked to a table that served as a bed for three vorgs, calmly dumping two of them from their chairs. Ty took a seat across from Arn, booting the other sleeper to the floor in the process. A slender woman stepped over the body of one of the former occupants as she carried a tray of mugs. Ty reached up and grabbed two of these by their bronze handles, passing one across the table to Arn, who flipped the woman a copper piece that she caught in the air.

The woman turned on her heel and moved off into the crowd.

"These folk are into some heavy drinking," Ty muttered. "Doesn't look like they're enjoying themselves much, though."

"They're drinking like there's no tomorrow," Arn replied.

He pretended to concentrate on his ale while he surveyed the room. The place didn't have a tavern atmosphere. Taverns usually had a mixture of revelers and sorrowful folk. This one held the stink of impending hardship and death, the smell of war.

But what bothered Arn most was the lack of talk. Even the vorgs were strangely silent. He had come here to learn something about this city and the huge army forming outside the gates, but the task was going to be harder than just listening to idle chitchat at the local pubs.

Something about the women bothered him, too, something subtle, something just beyond his objective consciousness. The old nagging itch of his intuition had come to life once more. As Arn watched them move around the room, serving drinks and trying to please the patrons, understanding dawned that the women were enslaved as well. Their skin was white, unnaturally so—not albino but more like that of longtime invalids who had not been exposed to the sun in years.

The eyes of many of the slaves were dark, reminding him of John's eyes, where the pupils were hard to locate. The servers avoided the lit areas, averting their eyes whenever they had to approach the lamps.

Arn placed a hand on Ty's shoulder. "Let's get out of here and find a tavern with some life to it."

"Now you're talking sense," said Ty.

Arn led Ty back to the main street and then turned down another alley. Traffic was heavier than before, with columns of slaves who numbered in the hundreds, perhaps thousands. They headed out toward the war camp fully laden and returned empty-handed. Most of the slaves wore cheap robes and hoods pulled up to shade their eyes. What skin Arn had observed on the prisoners had the same abnormal whiteness that he had witnessed on others inside the pub.

Arn and Ty drifted in with the crowd, intent on following a slave line deeper into the city. As Arn worked his way through the bustling throng, he noticed some slaves in the line who did not exhibit the same pale coloring, and they also had some dark Endarians among them.

As they passed deeper into the city, the number of people on the street dwindled, making it more difficult to follow the procession unobserved. Arn decided that he would have to wait for nightfall to investigate further.

Arn found another pub in which to pass the day unnoticed. The venue, a full-fledged tavern, was on a main street and much larger than the first place he and Ty had visited. The noon crowd was large and growing rowdier by the moment, the air filled with the aroma of mulled wine and barbecuing meat.

As they pushed their way toward the center of the room, Arn caught glimpses of a vorg turning the handle on a large roasting spit. The wild boar's skin gradually acquired a golden-brown crispness as its body turned above the bed of hot coals.

The place was loud and raucous with laughter and drunken good cheer. Arn led Ty to a small corner table and signaled to a serving girl for two ales. And thus they passed the afternoon and evening, with Arn sipping his ale and Ty drinking enough for both of them.

As night fell outside, Arn leaned in close, lowering his voice so only Ty could hear his words. "I'm going to venture out into the city. I need you to stay here and keep your ears open. See what you can learn."

"If you're expecting me to argue with that plan," said Ty, "then you've missed the wagon."

"Keep your ears open. If I'm not here by morning, make for our camp, get John and Kim, and head for Endar. I'll catch up."

As Arn rose to his feet, he looked down at his friend in the shabby vorgish armor. "Try not to drink too much."

Ty raised his mug in salute. "Try not to get yourself killed."

17

Lagoth
YOR 413, Late Summer

To the east, towering thunderclouds hurled lightning at the mountains below. These flashes and the low rumble of thunder stood in sharp contrast to the stars that spread out across the western sky. A wind brought the first drops of rain over the city walls as the tattered flags atop the towers beat out a warning of the impending storm.

Except for the steady stream of slaves, the main road was empty. At many houses, lone slaves waited outside the doors, having come off shift. Having taken the place of one of these whom he'd left tied up in an alley, Arn pulled his hood more tightly around his face as he awaited the oncoming mulgo overseer and a line of slaves.

The hooded slaves kept their heads tilted downward as if hoping to escape the gaze of their masters. They shuffled along, single file, toward a broad plaza and the pyramid-shaped building at its center. Gargoyle statues crouched on their haunches on either side of a gaping doorway, each holding a torch in its hand.

Arn observed all as he followed the slave in front of him. Once through the doorway, slaves descended a wide set of steps that led downward. For long minutes, they continued forward and down, their passage marked only by the mulgos who stood guard along the way.

At the bottom of the steps, Arn entered a circular chamber from which four passages exited. The column entered the third from the right and began descending once more. The long march continued down dimly lit passages carved from solid rock, turning to the right here, to the left there, but always downward.

The path emerged onto a rope bridge that extended across a chasm. Far below, a faint ribbon of glowing lava wound away into the distance. These sights were quickly blotted from view as the slaves entered the passage found in the opposite wall.

The way continued straight ahead for a short time before the procession turned once more to the left.

As the line in front of him rounded the sharp bend, Arn drew a throwing dagger and hurled it into the overseer's throat, sending him slumping to the floor before he could raise his whip. Drawing Slaken, Arn shifted his attention back to the line of slaves, taken aback by their lack of reaction. The slaves proceeded forward as if nothing unusual had happened until they disappeared around another bend in the passage.

Retrieving his dagger, Arn shrugged off the slave cloak. Lifting the dead mulgo, he carried him back down the hallway to the chasm, where he dropped the overseer and the cloak over the side.

Footsteps emanated from the hallway he had just left. Arn leapt into the tunnel beyond. At the first side passage, he ducked inside, just out of sight, and waited. The sounds grew loud enough that he could distinguish between the long shuffling gait of mulgos and the nimble padding of slaves. The crack of a whip echoed through the corridors, and the footsteps dwindled into the distance.

Arn stepped out into the main passage and moved silently down the hall, following the route taken by the mulgos and their captives. His long strides soon brought him within hearing of the shuffling footsteps ahead. Arn slowed, maintaining a safe distance between himself and the slaves and mulgos while keeping close enough to observe in which direction they turned. The sound suddenly changed, the footsteps taking on a muffled tone. Arn paused, tilting his head to listen. The footsteps had lost the echo that pervaded the tunnels.

He continued forward more slowly. As he rounded a bend in the passage, Arn saw what had caused the change in sound. The slaves had moved out onto a highway through a monstrous cavern. The road crossed the chamber between towering stalagmites and carefully cultivated rows of mushrooms.

The mushrooms were gigantic, the average height of a man, some rising much taller. Thousands of smaller mushrooms also grew. The entire scene was bathed in a green glow emitted from lichen on the cavern walls and ceiling.

Arn let the line of slaves dwindle into the distance before moving out into the cavern. He ducked into the mushroom grove, the excellent concealment allowing him to push the pace. He intended to follow the slaves to wherever they were kept and then sneak in and find out more. However, the sight of a crossroad leading to a narrow trail that ran up the wall far to his right distracted him. The trail worked its way upward to a black doorway above.

Arn filed the spot in his mind as something that he wanted to investigate later and continued after the procession. Reaching the end of the mushroom grove, he paused. To his front, a man-made wall rose twenty feet from the cavern floor, stretching across the entire cavern's width, only broken where the slave road passed through a gate.

A space of perhaps fifty paces lay between himself and the wall to the slave compound. Between it and him, a forest of stalagmites rose from the floor. The wall itself didn't seem designed to act as an effective barrier.

There were no guard towers, no barbed wire, nor any other measures Arn typically associated with the forcible imprisonment of men.

Beside the main gate, he saw a narrow opening with a drop-down port-cullis just wide enough for one man to fit through at a time.

What in the deep? Did they have the prisoners so cowed that they didn't have to worry about them escaping?

The slaves he had been following came to a stop before the chute. Two mulgo guards came out through the main gate to meet them.

Arn returned to his study of the wall, which extended to the left and right, coming to an end on the far-right side of the cavern but passing out of sight in the dimness to the left. Moving along the row of mushrooms, he put more distance between himself and the gate. He ducked through the stalagmites and up to the wall.

He began to climb, pausing at the top to ensure that no guards were in position to see him. He gazed upon hundreds of large cages in which slaves slept on the stone floor, their cloaks serving as their only blankets. Some of the cages butted up against the wall to which he clung, but the rest formed a huge grid, stretching out from the wall. Within this grid, randomly placed buildings rose toward the cavern ceiling.

Arn swung his legs over the top of the wall and stepped silently down onto the bars topping the cage below. Moving across, he lowered himself to the ground on the far side. None of the imprisoned stirred.

He moved down the row of cages that lay against the cavern wall, traveling several hundred feet before stopping. All the cages in this section held males. Most housed up to a dozen men who slept sprawled on the ground. Scattered coughs could be heard interspersed with low moans and snores. Not wanting to risk awakening one of the slaves in these groups, Arn moved on. The lack of roving guards continued to puzzle him.

As he approached a building, Arn caught a glimpse of a light shining from beneath a door. This was followed by another shaft of light darting out into the cavern as a different door opened and closed. Arn ducked low behind a cage as a line of slaves was herded down the central road, perhaps a hundred paces in front of him. The slaves disappeared between the buildings and were gone.

Turning to his right, he headed farther back among the cages. He found a cage with three men, one of whom was Endarian. The lock on the cage was a simple tumbler. Arn pulled his lockpicks from the pouch at his waist. Applying pressure on the lock with his left hand to deaden the sound, he manipulated the picks with his right. The lock popped open.

Arn tested the gate slowly and, hearing no squeak, opened it just enough to pass his body through. He moved to the Endarian's side and placed a hand over his mouth.

The Endarian jumped slightly, his eyes opening wide, but stilled when he felt Slaken against his throat.

"Be quiet!" Arn whispered. "I don't want to kill you. I'm a friend, but I can't have you making a lot of noise."

The Endarian recovered his composure quickly, nodding his head to indicate that he understood. Arn lowered his knife and removed his hand from the man's mouth. The man moved to a sitting position with his legs crossed. He was tall, with finely carved features that bespoke nobility despite the lash marks on his body.

"You'd be doing me a favor if you killed me now," the Endarian said in a voice that barely carried to Arn's ears. "Why are you here?"

"I'm here to find out what is going on within this city. Perhaps you could enlighten me."

"It would do no good. All you've accomplished is to get yourself caught, too. No enemy of Kragan's who has seen Lagoth ever leaves."

"Why not?"

"Look around you. Do not be fooled by the small number of slaves you see here. We are but the new-captures. They keep us here until we have come to accept our lot or die. There is a vast city below this level, a city of slaves that is larger than the city above. It is where the slaves of Kragan have lived for thousands of years.

"It is where they are bred to provide food and service for their masters. Some are raised to work, and some are raised to be eaten. The workers who are no longer useful also find their way to the butcher's block. We new-captures are the fresh blood that is continually brought in to strengthen the herd. After we are properly prepared, we will be incorporated into the city below, assuming we survive that long."

"Why don't you try to escape?" Arn asked.

"The spell Kragan cast over this city robs anyone not aligned with him of the will to leave. Just the opposite, we will fight anyone who tries to take us away from here. The fact that you haven't already succumbed is surprising, but you will. In the last four hundred years, everyone who has cast his or her eyes on this city has fallen prey to the spell that hangs over it. Those who do not serve Kragan are trapped, with no hope of ever leaving."

"How did you get captured?" Arn asked.

"I was scouting when I discovered that Lagoth still exists. I should have returned immediately to Endar Pass to report it, but I felt a need to check it out more closely, as did the others who were with me. We crept into the city, thinking to observe and then sneak out, all under cover of darkness. Once inside, we could not make ourselves leave, despite knowing that we should. So we remained until we were spotted. We fought but were overcome. It surprised us that they did not attempt to kill us, though we killed several of them. But they prize slaves more than corpses."

"What about the army camped outside the city?"

"I do not know its purpose. It cannot mean good things for the lands of Endarians and men. Kragan is a wielder of terrible power who has long desired world dominion. Outside of this city, most believe him long dead. It saddens me to know he yet lives."

Arn leaned forward in anticipation. "Is Kragan in the city?"

"I do not know."

"Get up. I'll take you out with me."

"No. I cannot go. You will not make it out, either. I have heard that only when someone escapes Lagoth will the spell be broken. Since that is exactly what the spell prevents, it does not seem likely to happen."

"What's your name?" Arn asked.

The Endarian merely shook his head. Then he lay back down and rolled onto his side.

Arn slipped out through the gate and relocked it. Heading back in the direction from which he had come, he moved more swiftly than before. He soon reached the outer wall and climbed down to the ground on the far side.

He passed through the mushrooms on a different route than the one he'd taken on his way into the cavern. As he approached the point where he'd seen the strange doorway high up on the cavern wall, he turned toward it. Ahead, the trail ended in a set of black lava steps.

He paused at the edge of the mushroom field. As Arn lay beneath the giant agaric, he relaxed his body, taking the opportunity to rest and watch. An hour passed before he moved again. He saw no sign of activity in the area, and he felt confident that no one was near enough to observe him climbing the steps.

Arn moved. He passed across the open space quickly but paused at the base of the stairs to study the cooled lava path that showed little sign of usage. Bounding up to the opening above, he ducked inside. Arn found himself in a dark hall. There was no torchlight here. Instead, a dim red light glowed from the far end of the tunnel, too diffuse to illuminate the interior of the passage but bright enough to beckon him forward.

The passage opened into a cavern. The black walls were pocked with holes from which lava flowed, winding downward to form a glowing stream that moved through the center of the room. There the stream split to form a fiery circle.

In the center, a breathtaking statue rose fifty feet into the air. Carved from smooth white marble, a woman faced the far wall, bands of red extruding from the stone floor to bind her hands and ankles. Centered on her bare left shoulder, a red brand marred the statue's perfection. Arn stared at the image, fascinated. It formed the shape of a fire elemental surrounded by flames so realistic that even from a distance they seemed to dance in the shimmering heat.

Shifting his gaze back to the path beneath his feet, Arn knelt and ran his finger across the smooth black stone. As he turned his hand palm-up in the dull-red glow that filled this chamber, he could see that his fingers were covered in thick dust. He was the only being to have ventured into this chamber in many years. A suspicion was building in his mind. This chamber was forbidden.

Arn rose to look forward once more. A narrow trail led across an obsidian ramp that arched over the molten river, then around to the front of the statue. As he walked the path, a blast of hot air singed his lungs and scorched his eyebrows, a sharp contrast to the cool, damp cavern from which he had come. He hurried to the far side of the ramp.

Once across the lava flow, Arn again noted that the black floor showed no sign of being worn by the passage of feet. Moving to the base of the statue, he extended his hand to feel the ankle. It was smooth, the workmanship exquisite. From the wear on the stone around it, Arn judged that the statue had been bound to the floor for hundreds, perhaps thousands of years.

He moved back out onto the path and walked around to the front of the statue. Here steps only wide enough for one led up onto a raised viewing platform where a lone throne faced the alabaster figure. Turning to gaze in that direction, he felt his breath catch in his throat.

"Gods of the deep."

Arn found himself staring into the perfect likeness of Carol's face.

It was as if someone had hammered a fist into his gut, the shock of the statue's features dropping Arn onto the throne. His temples throbbed, and his vision narrowed until all he could see was that face he had given up ever seeing again. But how could Kragan have created this so long ago? And why?

Arn stood up and forced himself to breathe again. His eyes studied the abomination. It was Carol as he had last seen her, every detail correct except for one—the brand on her shoulder.

The heat waves rising from the flowing lava made her seem to quiver as she stared back at him, as if she were struggling against her bonds in an attempt to rise. This did not seem like a mere statue. This had the feel of an idol.

Arn reluctantly pulled his gaze from the statue and took a more thorough look around the chamber. No. These black walls that wept magma and the molten river that radiated heat weren't part of some chamber of worship. This place radiated hatred and fear.

A new conclusion formed in his head with certainty.

Kragan had hunted Carol through all the centuries that this idol had stood here, and he was hunting her still. Without realizing that he had drawn the weapon from its sheath, Arn tightened his grip on Slaken's haft.

18

In his chambers, far beneath Hannington Castle, Kragan felt himself come alert as the wards he had placed on the statue beneath Lagoth blared their warning in his mind. That someone had dared violate his forbidden chamber set his teeth on edge. Focusing his attention on the statue of the prophesied she-wielder within the cavern, he looked out through its warded eyes at his obsidian throne and at the man who stood staring back at him.

Blade.

Of course it was. The knowledge that the assassin had taken his unique skill for destruction into Lagoth filled Kragan with rage. Blade had violated Kragan's personal throne room, and in so doing had sealed his fate. The knife Blade wore would protect him from the spell that Kragan had cast on Lagoth four centuries ago, but this time the assassin had made a mistake that would cost him his life.

Breaking his mental link to the statue, Kragan walked to the crystal scrying vase atop its chest-high pedestal, snared the water elemental, and watched as the water crawled from the bottom of the vase to its sides. A water lens formed within just as another formed in its sister vase in Lagoth. Bohdan, the vorg wielder that Kragan had left in charge of Lagoth until his return, appeared within the vase. Despite an obvious attempt to keep his expression neutral, the vorg's short canine muzzle wrinkled to expose unusually long fangs. Kragan interpreted the look as more of a grimace than a snarl.

Bohdan's bow confirmed that impression. "How may I serve you, Master Kragan?"

"A man has entered my forbidden chamber. I want you to kill him."

"Who is it?"

"The assassin you know of as Blade, the one whose image I distributed months ago."

Kragan's jaw clenched hard enough to send a sharp pain shooting through his molars before he continued. "Blade bears an artifact that prevents any spells from directly affecting him. Otherwise I would have killed him long ago. Because of that artifact's warding, you will need to send soldiers into the caverns and tunnels beneath Lagoth to find him. As of a moment ago, he was still inside my throne room."

"I will give the command."

Kragan broke his link with Bohdan and reconnected with the eyes of the Lagoth idol. But this time, Blade was gone.

19

Arn moved rapidly along the passageways, his mind focused on the task at hand. Right turn, left, past two, right, right, past five, left, stairs down, right. He worked backward along the list of directions, always turning opposite to the direction he had memorized. The mental gymnastics formed a familiar singsong pattern.

He did not pause as the guard at the exit yelled at him. His knife caught the surprised mulgo in the throat as he began uncoiling his whip. Arn reached down and plucked the dagger from the guard's throat even as its seven-foot body writhed on the floor. Two long strides carried him out the door.

The sky was jet-black, and the cobbled street was damp and slick from recent rain. Arn darted across the main thoroughfare and into an alley. The sight of the ancient statue of Carol had staggered him, putting a tremor in his hands that he'd only experienced in her presence. Old memories came flooding back, along with repressed desire and longing.

Arn tensed his muscles, working to drive the wave of emotions from his brain. It was ridiculous to feel this way. Even if Carol still shared the love he secretly felt for her, the match could never be. He was Blade. And Blade had enemies who would seek out and destroy anyone he cared about. And thus he often worked diligently to appear as if he cared for no one.

And Carol no longer felt about him the way that he felt about her. That much was a certainty. From the day that he'd spurned her advances, a chill had hung in the air between them. This was as Arn had intended, yet he hated that he had driven her away. This side of him, the man whom the people of Tal had named Blade, was too violent to deserve her love, but he could not help wishing that he might someday prove himself worthy.

A fool's hope.

With a deep breath, Arn shifted his thoughts to the present. He had to return to Ty and get his companions away from Lagoth before they succumbed to Kragan's spell.

Arn headed down the alley, reaching a dead end. After climbing the wall, he moved across the tiled roof and descended into a narrow street on the opposite side of a row of connected dwellings. Resuming his eastward course, he worked his way steadily toward the pub where he had left Ty. He reached the main street near the pub just as the sun was beginning to lighten the eastern sky.

Yells broke the predawn silence as a group of vorgs raced down the avenue to the west. Pausing to wipe the grime from his face and hands, Arn descended the steps leading to the pub entrance. Hopefully he would pass for just another filthy soldier.

The place was empty except for three serving girls.

"Excuse me," Arn said, speaking to the trio. "Last night there was a big blond warrior in here. Did you happen to notice when he left?"

The startled women backed away from him as he stepped toward them.

"Well, have you seen him or not?"

He continued to wait for a response until the only dark-haired girl in the trio stepped forward.

"He left," she said.

"I can see that," Arn replied. "When did he leave?"

"Just a little while ago. The vorg commander, Jerlack, became suspicious during a card game and accused the barbarian of being an outsider. It happened right over there."

The girl pointed to one of the alcoves to Arn's right.

Arn walked in that direction, passing through a doorway into another room. The furniture lay strewn about in pieces. Several bodies lay crumpled upon the floor in similar states of disrepair. Bolting back into the main room, Arn grabbed the dark-haired girl as she tried to make a run for the door.

"Where did the barbarian go? Did the soldiers take him?"

"There was a fight. He killed several soldiers and ran out into the street. Everyone was yelling, and guards came running from the main gate. I saw him turn back toward the center of the city."

"Spawn of the deep!"

Racing out the door, he hit the end of the alley and sprinted back toward the central square. The yells he had heard were not about the mulgo he had killed. The soldiers were instead chasing Ty.

The streets teemed with people who had come out of their houses to see the commotion. Groups of armed men trotted down the streets, waving weapons and yelling. Arn passed several of these, his legs churning in time with his heart as he cursed himself for leaving the big barbarian alone.

The street widened at the main square. To Arn's right, soldiers crowded around the entrance to an alley already packed with armed men and vorgs. Yells echoed through the square, the din making it impossible to distinguish exactly what was being said.

Arn dived into the crowd, shoving his way toward the alley. The confusion aided him as he was just one of many attempting to work their way forward. The mood of the soldiers surrounding him changed. Here, a sprinkling of fear leavened the mob's rage. In the alley beyond, soldiers crowded together, leaving a circle of open space before a narrow stone doorway that stood empty save for a pile of bodies that lay scattered in and around the opening.

A group of three vorgs suddenly lunged at the door with spears stretched out before them. Light glittered off the crescent-shaped ax blade as it shattered the spear shafts and took a vorg's leg off at the knee. A boot caught the second vorg in the midsection, hurling him back into the crowd. The third vorg lunged forward with a sword. The ax swung again, cleaving the sword and splitting the vorg's head. Ty ducked back from the doorway as several crossbow bolts whizzed through the opening.

Arn pushed his way out of the crowd just to the left of the alley and to a doorway through which an oil lamp flickered. Ducking inside, Arn grabbed the lamp from the mantle and smashed it against the floor, engulfing the couch in flames.

Accompanied by a woman's screams, he ran through the doorway and back into the alley, yelling as he went. "Help! Fire! My house is on fire!"

The shrieks of the woman added to the melee as she ran into the street behind Arn. He elbowed his way back into the crowd as the woman struggled to make those nearest to her understand that a man had just set fire to her house. A leather-clad soldier grabbed him by the throat but released his grip as Arn shoved his blade into the fellow's stomach, then spun to slice the throats of the two soldiers closest to him.

He rushed forward, breaking through the ring of soldiers around the doorway and into Ty's hiding place. Making his way across the threshold, Arn jerked his body sideways, feeling the wind from Ty's ax on his face as it split the air.

"Ty, it's me!"

"Damn, man, I could've killed you," Ty said, gasping.

Another charge from outside interrupted their conversation. This time a large group came at the door that was only wide enough to fit two at a time, jamming up as they hit the entrance, stumbling over the dead bodies outside. Ty swung his ax, again severing a leg on one of the soldiers. A scream rent the air as the fellow fell, tripping two of those behind him.

The vorgs in front tried to stop, but were pushed forward by those behind them. The dull *thunk* of Ty's ax took on a steady rhythm. Arn moved in and out, filling the gaps between ax strokes with a foot-long blade that darted past the swords and shields of those pressing toward them. Once more the soldiers retreated, and Arn and Ty jumped to the side to avoid the hail of arrows.

"I've got a plan," Arn said.

He pulled several of the bodies farther into the small alcove, out of the line of fire from the crossbows, and began removing armor and clothes, creating a pile. Taking Slaken, Arn slit the throat of each of the vorgs and let the blood drain. He then created a series of incisions on the corpses, deftly removing organs and wads of fat and adding them to the growing pile.

"Gods," said Ty, "you're sick."

"Maybe so, but right now, this is our only way out. You watch the door in case they rush it again. They're probably happy enough to just let us roast. I imagine this building is going pretty good right about now."

Ty poked his head out and back in as a swarm of arrows clattered against the back wall.

"Judging by the smoke, I'd say they won't have too long to wait."

Wiping Slaken and returning it to its sheath, Arn spread a large shirt flat on the floor and rolled the mess around until he had it piled atop the fabric. He grabbed a lamp from the wall, removed the top, and poured the oil over the putrid pile.

Taking his tinderbox from his pouch, he struck a spark and soon had a small flame catching the oily wick. Arn grabbed the shirt, lifting the pile in a bundle and handing it to Ty. Arn then lit the oily mess.

He nodded toward the alley and Ty swung the bundle around in an arc, floating it out the doorway to land with a slurp on the ground a few feet out in the alley. Another bunch of arrows thudded into the wall. The bundle was burning steadily now, a grease fire that gave off a heavy, suffocating smoke that rapidly filled the narrow alley. This, combined with the smoke from the already-burning building, quickly made vision difficult. Three vorgs ran forward to kick at the pile, but this only caused the fat to mix with the burning oil, intensifying flame and smoke. The gagging vorgs quickly retreated.

"We're going to rush the mob," Arn said. "Stay with me, and we'll shock our way through to the open. Then run for the pyramid in the middle of the square."

With a knife in each hand, Arn ducked low, took a deep breath, and rushed out into smoke so thick that he was on top of the soldiers almost before he saw them. Ducking underneath a raised mace, Arn's shoulder caught the man in the stomach, driving him backward into the crowd. Arn plunged both knives into his sides, slashing outward to his left as the man dropped away.

He was aware of Ty to his right, moving in tandem to clear a path through the crowd. The surprised soldiers before them backpedaled under the onslaught.

Arn and Ty burst out into the central square as the crowd behind began to recover, surging after the duo.

"Run!" Arn yelled, suiting actions to words.

They flew to the pyramid's entrance as if they had wings. Two mulgos, brandishing spiked clubs, bounded down the steps to meet them. Arn released two daggers as he ran, one after the other, pausing only long enough to reach down and pluck them from the eyes of their targets.

Ty took the lead and plunged into the slave tunnels.

"Go straight!" Arn yelled from behind.

Arn could hear the panting of the vorgs behind him. While he and Ty could temporarily sprint faster, no human could outlast a running vorg. Their hope lay in getting to the rope bridge.

"Next left!" Arn yelled as he caught up with Ty.

The dimly lit passage began to throb with the unaccustomed noise of the pursuit. Yells and pants from behind indicated that they did not have a large lead.

"Right and then down!"

The sound of Ty gasping for air as they ran rang loud in Arn's ears. The long fight and two days without sleep had taken a toll on the Kanjari.

"Now, two lefts!"

They sprinted along the twisting tunnels, gradually pulling away from the sounds of those who pursued them, aided by the twists that caused the vorgs to miss an occasional turn and backtrack. Just then the two reached the bridge.

Arn crossed behind Ty. As soon as they reached the other side, they began work on the supports. Ty cut the side ropes with two swipes of his ax, but the main support ropes proved to be harder to sever. Hundreds of tough strands, interwoven back and forth, crossed the entire width of the bridge.

As Ty chopped with his ax on one side, Arn worked with Slaken on the other. Yells signaled the arrival of the vorgs. Three of them charged out onto the bridge and managed to get halfway across before Ty severed the last of the cords, sending them plunging into the abyss.

Two of the others fired their crossbows as Arn and Ty leapt into the hallway beyond, one of the bolts spattering Arn with a spray of blood as it passed through Ty's left hand. Ducking around the corner, Arn felt his own blood pulsing through his veins and his heart pounding. Sweat stung his eyes. He glanced over at Ty, who set his ax aside and stripped off the vorg shirt. The Kanjari's chest was marked by several wounds. His hair was completely matted, and there was a gash down his right cheek.

"You look like crap," Arn said.

"I'm not the only one, that's for sure. Did you know that one corner of your ear is gone? You look like a pointed-ear demon."

Arn put a hand to the left side of his head. A twinge of pain verified Ty's pronouncement. But it was the barbarian's comment that cut him to the quick. A part of him was a demon.

Arn paused to judge the activity on the far side of the chasm. The yells of impatient soldiers mingled with the curses of the workers who struggled to extend a siege ladder across the chasm. Once they had that in place, they could pull up the dangling bridge and reconnect the severed end to its moorings. And since they now had dozens of archers positioned to provide covering fire from the far side, Arn and Ty couldn't step out to eliminate the workers.

"Well, this is an outstanding debacle we've managed to create," Ty muttered.

"You haven't heard the worst yet."

Ty sighed. "Out with it, then."

"Apparently, there's a spell on the city that prevents any outsider who has seen it from leaving. That's what made you run to the center of the city, I believe. The only chance we had for breathing room was to run deeper in. It also explains why nobody knows about this place. Everyone who has seen Lagoth has been killed or captured and enslaved. There's a whole slave city built underground, and they don't even have to worry about escape attempts or uprisings."

"Why tell me that?" said Ty. "I was perfectly happy just thinking that I was going to die fighting my way out of here, and now you hit me with this? We might as well go throw ourselves off the precipice before we get captured and turned into two more of those poor devils whom they herd around."

"I have something else in mind," Arn said. And then he was on the move again.

Ty hefted his ax and jogged after Arn down the dimly lit passage. From Ty's lack of response, Arn gathered that the Kanjari was not anxious to hear about his plan.

20

Lagoth
YOR 413, Late Summer

Arn kept his pace to a jog as he led Ty along the passages that led toward the mushroom cavern and slave pens. They needed to find a concealed place to hide from the soldiers who would flood into the maze once the bridge's reconstruction was finished. All he needed was a bit of luck.

The sound of running feet from around the bend that lay ahead killed that hope. Rather than try to run back the way they came, Arn sprinted forward, throwing daggers in his hands. To Arn's right, Ty matched him stride for stride.

The platoon of two dozen mulgos rounded the corner twenty paces in front of them, two of the leaders sprouting glittering daggers beneath their chins. These tumbled to the ground, tripping a handful of those who followed. Then Arn and Ty were on them. Having refilled his hands with his black blade and one of his boot-sheathed daggers, Arn ducked beneath a swinging mace and opened the gut of another mulgo. Ty's ax sang through the air, spraying green blood and gore on the second wave of guards.

To Arn's left, a mulgo cast a net toward him, a clumsy attempt that he easily sidestepped to drive a foot of black steel between the soldier's ribs. Without bothering to watch the scaly green body hit the ground, Arn pressed forward, eliminating the advantage that the mulgos' longer weapons provided. His knives flashed in short thrusts that produced slurping *thunks*. The wails of those who faced the whirling blade of the Kanjari gave way to moans of dread from those in the ranks behind the dying. The remaining mulgo turned and ran.

In the pale-green illumination from the lichen on the walls, Arn saw that Ty had acquired another shallow cut across his upper chest.

As Arn resumed his previous course down the passage, Ty jogged along beside him. Arn did not pause when the way opened into the cavern that housed the mushroom groves. Entering the forest on the right side of the road, he breathed a sigh of relief at the easy concealment. He turned to Ty and pulled Slaken from its scabbard.

"You've seen what happens when anyone besides me touches this knife. It consumes them. What I haven't ever told anyone is what this knife really does. The spells on the haft nullify magic. If I have this blade on my person, either wearing it or holding it, no spell of any type can directly affect me."

"So, if you're free to walk out of here," said Ty, "why don't you just go, then?"

"If I wanted to leave you here, I would have done so long before. When I first took possession of this knife, I had to endure a blood ritual. I cut my hand and grasped the knife's haft, letting my heart pump my blood into the handle. Thus, the blade came to recognize me."

Arn took a deep breath, his eyes locking with the blue eyes of the Kanjari warrior as he continued. "It's possible that if I slice both our hands and we hold them together so that our blood intermingles, the knife might accept us both. Or it might kill us both. Or it might just kill you. I don't know. If this works, then both of us can hang onto the weapon and try to escape from the city. If the process only kills you, then I will strive to escape and honor you as warrior and friend."

"I knew I wasn't going to like this plan," Ty said. "Looks like you're the one who has to cut himself. My hand's already done."

Arn glanced down at the bloody hole in Ty's left hand.

"I guess that'll do," he said.

"Wait a moment," said Ty, stripping off his chain mail armor and shirt. He unbraided his hair. "If I'm going to die, I'll die like a Kanjari."

Arn sliced an inch-long cut in his hand. Holding his palm upturned, he let a small pool of blood form in his hand, then reached out to grasp Ty's palm.

They left their hands together, palms touching. Slaken needed to access blood pumping from a beating heart, or in this case, two hearts. Taking a deep breath, Arn thrust the knife's haft between their hands.

Pain lanced up Arn's arm, bringing with it a wave of dizziness that almost caused him to lose his grip on the blade. Through watery eyes he saw a black haze spread over their joined hands and creep up their arms as the anguish grew worse.

Ty retched but maintained his grip on the handle. The darkness continued crawling toward their shoulders, pulsing in rhythm with their hearts. Then, just as Arn thought he could bear the pain no longer, the darkness reversed, pouring back into Slaken's handle like smoke sucked into a pipe.

Arn and Ty stared at each other across the point of the blade.

"Holy Karak!" Ty groaned.

Sweat rolled down Arn's face. Picking up the vorgish shirt that Ty had discarded, he guided the tip of their jointly held blade to cut a long strip. Carefully binding their hands to the ensorcelled knife, he was hopeful that it would help stop the bleeding.

"I think either one of us can hold the knife now," Arn said. "At least we can both hold it at the same time, and that's what we're going to have to do until we get out of the spell's range."

"What if the spell reaches out to the ends of the lands?"

"Then we're doomed, but it's not likely. The range must be limited. We'll just have to find out how far."

The two men stood next to each other, Arn gripping Slaken's handle with his right hand while Ty held on with his left. They moved to the opening into the hall beyond the small cavern.

"How in the deep are we going to fight like this?" Ty asked.

Arn remained silent.

After making their way back out into the mushroom groves, they moved as close to the slave road as possible while maintaining cover. Arn and Ty began working their way back toward the main tunnel, stopping often to listen. After an hour of cautious movement, they turned into a side tunnel.

"We need to find a guide," said Arn.

He stuck his head around the corner to peer down the hallway. The green moss light failed to reveal any sign of guards on watch. He nodded to Ty, and they stepped out into the main passage. They turned to the right, Arn guiding their steps by pulling on Slaken when he wanted Ty to turn. In this way, they managed to cleanly negotiate the passages.

The tunnels wound away before them, twisting and turning, leading inexorably down. The sound of gruff voices brought Arn and Ty up short. Arn nodded, and they began to move cautiously forward. As they approached the last bend, the duo stopped to listen.

Arn leaned forward just enough to look around the corner. About twenty feet from where he and Ty stood, two mulgo and five vorg guards stood watch at a tunnel intersection. As part of an expanding search pattern, the post made sense—block off the intersections to herd their quarry into an inevitable corner. Arn ducked back behind the wall as one of the mulgos on the near side of the passage turned toward him.

Ty leaned forward to peer around the corner, paused several seconds, and then leaned back to look at Arn, his hand making a slicing motion across his throat. Arn nodded.

The two men moved at the same time, bounding around the corner and down the hall. Arn threw the dagger he held in his left hand as he ran. It hurtled across the corridor, catching the surprised mulgo on the opposite side in the stomach. The guard lurched backward, falling in a writhing heap on the ground.

The two mulgos on the near side were first to turn toward them. Ty's boot caught one of them in the midsection, sending the warrior flying into the wall with bone-shattering force. The second mulgo lunged at Arn, grasping with long, clawed fingers. Air rushed from its nostrils as Arn's knee crashed into its groin. Arn pulled the second of his four daggers free from its sheath and brought its haft arcing up into the base of the mulgo's skull.

The vorg guards scrambled forward, pulling weapons as they came. Ty met the first one with the downstroke of his ax. The force of the blow jerked Arn sideways, causing him to stumble. The nearest vorg dived at his legs, knocking Arn to the floor. Somehow, he managed to maintain his grip on the knife that both he and Ty held. As he hit the ground, Arn cut the vorg's throat with the dagger in his left hand.

Arn rolled back to his feet, and Ty lunged again, dragging him along behind. Ty's ax struck the shield of the nearest vorg, denting it deeply and driving its holder to his knees. Three others charged forward, trampling their comrade in their efforts to get at the barbarian.

Arn pulled hard on Ty's arm, whipping his own body around in an arc that swept the legs from under the nearest of the vorgs. He lashed out with his black blade but missed as Ty pulled him to his right. The crescent ax blade bit into hide, and another of the guards flopped onto the floor.

Arn managed to regain his feet just as one of the downed guards scrambled away, only to be smashed back to the floor as Ty slammed his ax into the running vorg's back. His follow-through jerked Arn sideways, smashing him into the wall as Ty spun to face the last guard. The vorg moved forward cautiously, whirling a flail in front of him. Arn's dagger whistled through the air. The battle was over.

"I can tell you one thing right now," Arn said, retrieving his dagger. "We're going to have to work out a better method of fighting together."

"But I thought we did pretty well."

"That's because you weren't getting thrown around like a rag doll," said Arn.

"You need more meat on those bones."

"Let's go get my other throwing dagger."

On the far side of the passage, Arn pulled one of his blades free and, with Ty, moved to the spot where the unconscious mulgo lay. Working as rapidly as possible with one free hand, Arn cut long strips of cloth from the garments of a fallen vorg, he and Ty cooperating to bind the mulgo's hands securely behind its back.

Arn frisked the soldier, finding only a handful of copper coins. He and Ty moved from one body to the next, rapidly searching for anything useful. Except for a fifty-foot coil of rope, the search failed to reveal any other items of value.

Ty slung his ax across his back, and the two men walked back to the unconscious mulgo. Ty bent down, grabbed the creature by his belt, and tossed the soldier's two-hundred-pound frame over one shoulder.

"Where to?" Ty asked.

"This way."

Arn led the way down the passage until they came back to the large mushroom cavern. Glancing around to ensure the way was clear, they turned into the grove. Once they were out of sight of the main road, he signaled for Ty to drop the mulgo.

"I think you may have hit him a little too hard to be of any use to us," said Ty. "He may sleep for days."

"I'll bring him around."

Arn knelt over the body, pressing his thumb into the nerve junction behind the mulgo's right ear. A muffled moan escaped through the gag as the guard's body jerked. Arn changed the pressure slightly, and the mulgo's eyes popped open, Ty's boot on his throat.

Arn leaned down close to the soldier's ear.

The mulgo flopped but quickly stilled as Ty increased the pressure on his throat.

Arn drew one of his throwing daggers, pressing it against the mulgo's neck behind the ear, barely drawing blood.

"Are you ready to cooperate?" Arn asked.

The mulgo nodded his head in affirmation.

"Good."

Ty tied the end of the rope to the mulgo's bound hands, wrapping it up and around his neck to form a lead line, maintaining a firm grip on the remaining coils with his free hand. Then he pulled the mulgo to his feet.

"Lie to me, and I'll know it," said Arn. "Is there another way out of these caverns that comes out beyond the city walls?"

The mulgo nodded.

"You're going to take us there. No tricks."

Again, the mulgo inclined its head.

Once these preparations were completed, the group began moving, the mulgo in the lead. The soldier led them across the field of mushrooms in the opposite direction of the entrance to the chamber where Arn had seen Carol's statue. For a half hour, they traversed the massive cavern, careful to stay within the concealment the agaric grove provided. The cultivated fields came to an abrupt end as the walls closed in once more. Stalagmites clustered close together on the floor, and pools of clear water began to appear in small crevices.

Arn scooped more of the glowing moss from the wall, spreading it on the rag binding their hands as they walked. They paused often to listen, but the cave had taken on an eerie silence, broken only by the drips of water that fertilized the limestone forest through which they traveled. The mulgo turned away from the center of the cavern and led them up along a narrow ledge to their left. This forced them into single file. The ledge continued to narrow until it was just over a foot wide. The floor of the cavern took on a surreal shimmer, the faint green glow causing it to appear to move in the distance as Arn's eyes had difficulty maintaining focus.

The group eventually reached a cleft in the cavern's ceiling. The crack widened into a passage devoid of the stalactites and other wet cave formations found in the caverns below. A musty smell pervaded the place. The only light came from the moss-covered rag wrapped around Slaken, illuminating a five-foot radius.

The group trudged through the tunnel for hours as it widened and narrowed like the undulations of a caterpillar. At last the passage opened into a great cavern. They were back amid towering stalagmites, the cave walls hidden somewhere beyond the moss torch's feeble light. The trail led onward over piles of rock and shale, only to descend on the far side. It was impossible to tell whether the trail tended upward or downward. Time lost its meaning.

Arn felt his body weakening. Illusory movement caught the corner of his vision. He had felt this way often enough in the past. The only solution was to take added precautions against letting his guard down. He moved so he could also place a hand on the mulgo. Any sudden action on the part of the creature would serve to revive him. The tension in the mulgo's muscles indicated that he did not like this new development.

Gradually, Arn became aware that the trail was rising. Moving away from the stalagmites, they began working their way steadily upward. The climb steepened, the air thinning as they progressed. Arn's breathing deepened, and he felt his heart pump more rapidly with the exertion. The effort revived him, sharpening his senses.

At last they came to a steep pile of shale. The glow of the moss on the rag had begun to fade, cutting their visibility in half, but Arn noticed a different texture to the stone. Some of the corners were more rounded, giving a weathered impression. Just then a swirl of fresh air hit him in the face, cool with a hint of pine. Glancing up, he found he could see stars overhead.

"We're out!" Ty breathed. "Damned if I've ever seen anything so beautiful."

Arn shoved Slaken's blade into the mulgo's skull just behind the ear. He stiffened, then dropped to the ground. After retrieving knife and rope, the two men began climbing the last section of shale that led outside. They emerged into a clearing on the side of a mountain with no illumination from the moon. The black outline of pine trees blotted the stars on the horizon. Arn removed the moss-covered rag from the knife that they both gripped and buried it beneath a rock. That done, the two men strode deeper into the woods and away from the endless cavern.

21

Borderland Range—Northeast of Lagoth
YOR 413, Late Summer

Arn took the night's first guard shift. He did not know exactly how late it was, but he guessed the time to be around midnight. They both needed sleep, but Ty was worse off, having lost a fair amount of blood. Taking one of the strips of rope, he bound Ty's left hand and his right hand to Slaken. It would not do to nod off and lose a grip on the blade while still in the area of the spell's influence. By the time Arn finished the task, Ty was fast asleep, his breathing rhythmic and deep.

The thicket Arn had selected for their camp was dense and full of thorns, but it provided good security. No wandering vorg or mulgo would likely venture close to where he and Ty had stopped. From within the interwoven, shroudlike bushes, Arn could not see the sky at all.

In the distance a wolf howled, a lonely wail that lingered in the night. The sounds of crickets chirping grew in volume as the insects became accustomed to the proximity of the two new occupants of their thicket.

For half the night, Arn sat and listened, losing himself in the sensations of the wild. No thought, just feeling. At last he reached over and shook Ty. The barbarian sat up, rubbing his face with his free hand.

"You ready for your turn on watch?" Arn asked.

"As ready as I'm going to be. Gods, what I'd give for just a couple of days of eating and sleeping and nothing else."

Sleep claimed Arn as his head touched the ground. He awoke to find the sun coming up and his knife-bound hand asleep. Sitting up, he began massaging his palm, spreading a tingling sensation out to his fingers. He stretched and yawned.

"Good morning," said Ty. "I was just about to wake you up. Let's see if John and Kim are still where we left them. We're going to have to hustle, or they'll go down to the city to look for us."

"Right."

Ty led the way out of the thicket, pausing at the edge. Arn came up beside him. They were standing at the edge of a clearing surrounded by stately pines. The mountains towered up before them, and a small ravine led down to their right. The scene looked familiar.

As they crested the next rise, Ty's palomino spotted them first, trotting up to the Kanjari and letting the barbarian scratch behind its ears with his free hand. The men soon tracked down Ax, who was merrily munching on the abundant grass in the center of a nearby meadow. With Arn riding double behind Ty and Ax following along without requiring to be led, they began working their way up toward the crest of the ridge. The trek through the cavern had brought them into the mountains to the east of the city.

"We ought to reach the camp within the hour," said Ty.

"That spell will be working on John and Kim's minds. They won't leave voluntarily."

"We'll just grab and hogtie them until we get out of its range," said Ty.

"The question is how to grab them both at the same time, stuck together like we are."

"Easy," said Ty. "Follow my lead."

Their destination was even closer than they thought. At the top of the next ridge, Arn spotted the cliff that marked the spot above the camp. Sliding down from the horse's back, Ty leaned a good portion of his weight on Arn's right shoulder.

"Don't get carried away," said Arn. "I'm not one of your wild horses."

"Just trying to make this look realistic."

Suddenly two forms appeared, running up the hill toward them. John and the Endarian princess reached them at the same time, concern etched on their faces.

"What in the deep happened to you two?" John asked. "I've seen better looking vorgs."

"Here, help me with Ty," Arn gasped. "The damned barbarian weighs a ton. Kim, I could use a little hand myself, if you don't mind."

John grabbed Ty by the other arm as Kim moved in to help support Arn.

"Now!" Arn said as he grabbed Kim with his left arm.

"What in the deep?" John yelled as Ty lifted him clear of the ground.

Arn struggled to control Kim's writhing form, taken aback by how strong she was. She lashed out with her feet, missing Arn, but catching Ty on the shin. The whole group went down in a pile.

Arn managed to get one of Kim's arms behind her back, ignoring the pain in his arm where she effortlessly tore off a hunk of skin. Ty yelled an obscenity as he forced John's face into the dirt while locking his friend down with his legs. Arn wrapped his own legs around Kim's torso, pinning her arms to her side. Reaching in his pocket, he withdrew the short pieces of rope and after several failed attempts, managed to tie her hands together. He then reached over and helped Ty secure John's hands behind his back.

"What in the deep is wrong with you two?" John said. "Have you gone crazy?"

"We'll explain it to you as we travel," said Ty. "Just believe me when I say that this was necessary for now."

"I'm going to kill you both. Look. You've made Kim cry."

Arn looked down at the woman. Tears of rage and disbelief rolled down her face. For the first time in weeks, he saw fear in her eyes. Arn's heart fell, seeing Kim's look of betrayal over this assault by two men she regarded as friends. Weighed down by remorse, he leaned over and finished securing the two captives by tying their feet, allowing them to take short steps without being able to run away.

Together he and Ty pulled them to their feet, maintaining a grasp on the ropes. In this manner, they pushed and tugged John and Kim down to the camp, where they sat them down. John and Kim stared up at the duo with angry faces.

"I'm waiting," said John.

For the next half hour, Arn talked, omitting only the fact that he knew the face of the idol in the depths of Lagoth. As the tale reached its conclusion, Arn was relieved to see a smile come back to Kim's face.

"But why did you need to tackle us? Why didn't you just tell us the story?" asked John.

"Because this form of sorcery is subtle. According to the Endarian I met beneath Lagoth, it's triggered when an enemy decides to leave. We couldn't be sure that the spell wouldn't cause you to run away from us once we started telling you about our discovery."

"We're not trying to run away now, so you can let us loose."

"I'm sorry," said Arn. "We can't take that chance. Not until we're sure that we're out of the spell's range. Most likely that will be after we cross to the east side of the mountains."

"You aren't serious."

"John, do I look like I'm not serious?"

For the next hour, as Ty and Arn packed and tied John and Kim to their mounts, John continued to argue and complain. The necessity of both Arn and Ty maintaining a grip on Slaken's haft further complicated the situation. Kim remained quiet, appearing strained yet focused.

Arn rode double behind Ty on the palomino, keeping a grip on the lead rope that pulled the train of horses. As they climbed into the mountains, John's arguments grew louder and more vicious, finally reaching the point where an exasperated Arn and Ty gagged him. Beads of sweat stood out on Kim's brow, her eyes set in a look of concentration, but she remained silent of her own accord.

As the day wore on and the group moved up into the higher mountains, John's struggles grew more desperate. He strained against his ropes, kicking his mount and forcing the line of horses into a gallop along the steep slope. Only the meticulous horsemanship of Ty prevented the tiny herd from stampeding over a cliff as he reached out and snared John's horse by the bridle, pulling it to a sliding halt.

Arn glanced back at John and Kim. John's saddle had twisted so that he hung off his horse at a crazy angle. His eyes were wild, and he continued to struggle, although some of his earlier vigor had subsided. Kim breathed heavily, still quiet.

"I'm going to make sure that lunatic can't move to shoo a fly!" Ty said.

They slipped off the stallion's back and soon had John trussed up and slung like a sack of feed across the saddle. As Ty had promised, movement was out of the question.

Arn turned to Kim. "Are you all right?"

The princess nodded her head. He studied her face closely. Her eyes had a faraway look and lines of concentration had etched themselves into her forehead. Although she was clearly struggling against the effects of the spell, Arn was impressed with the continuous strength of will she displayed.

Satisfied that she was indeed all right for the present, Arn and Ty moved on to check all the horses. Aside from a scrape across the shoulder of John's horse, the animals seemed okay. Arn and Ty mounted up once again and began leading the pack train along its previous route.

In the late afternoon, tall thunderheads raced in from the west. The sun's rays glinted off their tops, streaming through cracks in the clouds to paint streaks across the sky. Dark curtains of rain fell on the desert to the west, although the sky was still bright blue overhead. Thunder echoed through the canyon as the storm closed in on the riders. Ty led the way higher up along the mountainside, away from the ravines that could quickly fill with raging water.

"Keep your eye out for a cave!" Ty yelled to make himself heard over the gathering storm.

Arn looked but saw no sign of shelter on the steep slope. The air had become still and humid. Lightning soon knifed down, darting here and there, weaving the curtain of rain on a monstrous, primordial loom.

The wind came, softly at first, then in a rush that made the canyon howl. The tops of the pines bent before the assault, swaying back as the gust died out. But another gust followed, this one wet with fat drops of rain. The rain worked its way up the slopes behind the travelers as the clouds blotted out the last vestiges of sunlight. A darkness like night descended.

A flash of lightning lit the trail ahead, pine trees offering the only shelter in sight. Ty headed toward them. Thunder ripped the air, rain pouring down in torrents that made it hard to breathe.

The sharp crack of thunder followed a blinding flash directly in front of them. Kim's horse reared and bolted forward, but the rope tied to the two adjacent horses halted its run. Fifty feet away, the tallest of the pines had split down the middle. A tower of flame shot skyward, hissing like an angry serpent as it battled the rain.

Ty slipped off the big horse, and Arn mirrored him.

"We're going to have to stand here in the open, holding onto the horses and calming them until the storm passes," Ty said as he grabbed the bridle of John's horse, talking to the animal in a soothing tone.

Arn reached over and pulled Kim's horse to where he stood beside Ty, following the barbarian's example. Ax ignored all the commotion, taking advantage of the break to chomp on the tall grass that grew on the hillside. The palomino stallion trotted around the cluster of horses a couple of times and then stood still several paces away, gazing out through the falling rain toward the burning tree.

Arn reached up to place his left hand on Kim's. The soaked Endarian princess sat straight in the saddle, fortitude in her eyes as she looked down at him.

As Arn stared up at the princess, he felt the rain run down the back of his neck and through his clothes. The wind had taken on a chill. The night was going to be long.

—⚭—

As the line of horses crested the ridge and began its descent down the opposite side, Arn saw the bright light of a new dawn paint the nearby valley, revealing pine slopes that gave way to deep grass, wild flowers, and a stream. The palomino stallion tossed its head and snorted, pawing the ground impatiently as the two riders on his back paused to survey the scene. A narrow trail dropped off between rows of cliffs, widening as it led out into the valley.

"We'll get off here and lead the horses down," Ty said. "I want to keep a hand on John's horse's bridle until we get out of these cliffs."

"Good," said Arn. "I could use the walk."

The two men slid off the stallion. Ty reached up and grabbed the bridle of the first horse in the line, turning down the path as he did. Ahead of him, the stallion moved down the hill, quickly reaching the valley floor below before stopping to chomp on the lush grass. Arn and

Ty followed more slowly, ensuring that the other horses passed safely down the steepest part of the trail.

Reaching the bottom, they began walking at a brisk pace toward the valley. Despite their increased speed, John's horse was not satisfied, nudging Ty in the back with its muzzle. Suddenly, a merry peal of laughter broke the stillness of the valley. Arn and Ty looked back to see a refreshed Kim no longer fighting the effects of being spellbound.

"It's good to see that you're back with us," Arn said.

"We passed out of the spell's range as we descended into this valley," Kim said. "You can untie us now."

Ty untied his hand and released his hold on Arn's knife. "She's right. I don't feel a thing."

Arn sheathed Slaken and moved to cut the ropes that secured Kim to the saddle before lifting her down from the horse's back. She leaned against him for several seconds as she worked to restore circulation to her limbs. Meanwhile, Ty cut John free.

As soon as the gag came away from John's mouth, a stream of foul language poured forth. The outburst quickly subsided as he noticed Kim's disapproving glare. John plopped off the horse's back and into the grass, struggling to rise but unable to make his legs respond.

"You crazy fools have paralyzed me!" he yelled.

"Settle down," said Arn. "Your legs are still at rest. Rub them, and the feeling will return."

John set to work, vigorously rubbing his legs with both hands. He calmed down as Kim knelt beside him and placed a reassuring hand on his shoulder. He looked over at the princess, both embarrassed and grateful.

Ty sat down on the grass. "Oh, that feels good. I had forgotten what it was like to relax. Man, I could eat a cow, hide and all."

Arn looked down at the barbarian. Blood and dirt matted his long blond hair. Ty was so tired that his eyes stayed closed for a couple of seconds each time he blinked.

"Kim, I'd like you to take a look at the wound in Ty's hand. I'm afraid it might be getting infected."

A concerned look swept across the Endarian's face as she crossed over to where Ty sat. "Let me see that hand," she said, taking it gently in her own.

She studied the wound carefully for several moments and then directed Ty to accompany her to the stream. Arn followed, as did John, having recovered the use of his legs. Emanating from snowy mountains, the stream was a small one that ran swiftly over the rocks.

Arn watched the Endarian princess closely. Without resorting to any of her life-shifting magic, she scrubbed the filthy scabs from the puncture wound thoroughly, causing it to bleed freely once again. Then, selecting a thick cushion of soft, green moss, she packed both sides of the hole and bound the wound with a length of buckskin she had taken from her bag.

Arn turned the horses loose to drink and knelt to do the same. The water was clear and cold, with the wonderful taste of a mountain stream.

He drank long and deep, pausing to wash his face and clean his wounds. The sharp twinge from the side of his head reminded him that a corner of his ear was gone. He put his hand to the injury, washing away the built-up scab. The cold water revived him, bringing his hunger to a raw edge.

"John, what have we to eat?"

John sheepishly stared at Arn. "Kim and I ate the last of the supplies just before you two showed up."

"John!" Kim's voice brought his head around.

"Oh, all right. There's some dried meat left in one of the packs. After the way you two have behaved, I wish we'd eaten it all."

John walked over to remove a pack from Ax's back.

"You should be thanking us," said Arn. "If we hadn't tied you down, you would have probably killed yourself like you tried to back at the gorge."

John glanced up from rummaging in the pack. "What are you talking about?"

"He's talking about you going crazy and trying to run your horse off the cliff," said Ty, who had propped himself up on an elbow by the stream, "pulling Kim and all the other horses along with you. Your memory isn't very good for someone who wants to complain about the way he's been treated."

Kim rose to her feet. "John, for once Ty is telling the truth."

A smug look settled on the barbarian's face.

She raised an eyebrow and continued, "For perhaps the first time since I have known Ty, he has managed to make an accurate statement."

Ty shook his head dismissively.

John began to pace. Suddenly he stopped and clapped his hands together. "Damn. I've always wondered what it was like to be on the receiving end of a spell. Up until now I figured such stories only came from feeble-minded people with a limited understanding of magic."

"You being spellbound doesn't really disprove that theory," said Ty.

John's response was interrupted by Arn elbowing him away from the pack that contained the food. In short order, he had the dried meat out and passed some around. Ty ate ravenously as Kim continued treating his injured left hand. Arn ate more slowly, ensuring that he chewed the food well before swallowing. A person's stomach tended to treat its owner unkindly if unchewed food was gulped down after a long period of fasting.

When he finished, Arn rose to his feet. "I'll take first watch. John, how about relieving me in three hours?"

"Oh, no you don't," John said. "I'm taking the first watch. I don't want someone on guard who's so tired he'd probably fall asleep and miss attackers. You and Ty should rest. Kim will relieve me in a few hours."

Arn looked over at John and smiled. "It's good to see that you're back with us."

As Arn started to remove the saddle from Ax's back, the words of the imprisoned Endarian replayed themselves in his mind.

They say that to break the spell, someone would have to escape the city. Since that is exactly what the spell prevents, it does not seem likely to happen.

"Damn it," said Arn as he pulled the cinch tight once again.

"What?" John asked, turning back toward him.

"I just remembered something one of the prisoners in Lagoth said. I need to ride back and take one last look at the city."

"But . . ."

"But nothing. My knife will keep the spell from affecting me. I'll be back by morning."

Without waiting for comment, Arn mounted and spurred Ax up the hillside back toward the west.

Darkness swallowed him long before Ax reached the top of the high ridge that yielded the view of the metropolis he and Ty had just fought their way out of. As he crested the ridge, the sight that confronted him took his breath away.

Large sections of Lagoth were in flames. From this vantage point, he could make out little of what was going on, but from the pattern of fires, he knew what must be happening. The spell had been broken. What must it have felt like for hundreds of thousands of slaves to suddenly experience free will? Most had been raised without ever experiencing freedom. But the new-captures were a different story, with Arn immediately thinking of the imprisoned Endarian he had spoken to. They would have risen up, overwhelming the thin guard force in the caverns beneath the city. Most likely they knew where all the weapons caches were located and had organized groups to storm them.

Chaos. Whether the bulk of the slaves had rushed out, or most had cowered below ground, Arn could not be sure. But many thousands must have made a run for it. And in that confusion, despite the huge army camped outside the gates, and despite the tremendous numbers that would be killed or recaptured, thousands more would manage to make their escape.

The scene was both horrible and beautiful to behold. The knowledge that some of the slaves would find their way back to family and friends, where previously they had maintained no hope of such reunions, eased the cost in lives.

The added knowledge that Kragan, if he still existed, would be seething with anger brought a smile to Arn's lips.

22

Kragan wailed, the sound echoing through his private chambers with such volume that it brought Tarok charging into the room. With a fierce look and a wave of his hand, Kragan dismissed the eight-foot-tall grun who was his personal servant and bodyguard. He was in no mood for company of any sort.

After learning that the thousand-vorg search party that Bohdan had sent into the warrens beneath Lagoth had failed to find Blade or his Kanjari accomplice, the wielder had scoured the surrounding hills with dozens of mounted patrols. Nothing. Once again Kragan's followers had failed to capture or kill the assassin.

Worse, Blade's escape had broken the spell that Kragan had placed over Lagoth to protect it from discovery, and in so doing, had generated a slave rebellion that had burned down a quarter of the city. Even though Bohdan had eventually managed to regain control of Lagoth and its slave population, as many as three thousand had escaped, many Endarian. So even if Kragan journeyed to the city to restore the spell, the word of Lagoth's survival, and thus his own, would spread across the continent.

Kragan forced himself to take a calming breath. He did not want to be calm. He wanted to burn the statue into slag. Despite this setback, Kragan's army was almost fully assembled outside of Lagoth. As allies of Kragan, they would have been immune to the spell if it had still been in effect. Now such considerations were irrelevant.

King Gilbert had sent Earl Coldain and the bulk of the army of Tal to hunt down Rafel. Kragan's army would thus overwhelm the forces that remained here. His vorgs and men merely awaited the order that would launch them on an unstoppable arc eastward through Tal. Then, having added a host of new conscripts and slaves, the horde would sweep northwest into Endar. And if Coldain failed to find and destroy Rafel and his legion, Kragan would divert his priestly allies, the protectors, and their fanatical followers in the far west to finish the job. It would not do to leave alive a powerful warlord whose past involved a close alliance with the Endarian queen.

The vision of his twin armies converging upon Endar Pass from east and west finally brought Kragan a wave of satisfaction.

23

Borderland Range—Northeast of Lagoth
YOR 413, Late Summer

By the time Arn arrived back at the campsite, the sun was rising, illuminating the mountaintops in a peach-colored glow.

"Glad to see you're still alive," said John. "How about a nice cold breakfast of dried and salted meat?"

Somehow the prospect didn't seem as appealing as it had just the day before.

Ty groaned and sat up. "Oh, man. I think I'm going to retire and settle down to fish all day." He rubbed his face with both hands.

Over the course of a breakfast that tasted better than it had sounded, Arn relayed what he had seen the past night.

"At least some of those held must have escaped," said Kim, hope shining in her face.

"Most likely," said Arn. "And at least for now, the spell over the city is broken. That means Kragan's people will have to put a large number of guards to work handling the rest of the slaves. Maybe that will disrupt preparations for whatever the army outside the city is getting ready to do."

"Then we must resume our journey," said Kim. "I must return to Endar Pass and let my mother know about Lagoth."

"I don't care where we go, so long as it's away from that hole," said Ty.

Arn had to agree.

Within a few minutes the group was packed up, mounted, and moving into the mountains to the north. At the next camp, an opportunity to replenish their meat supplies presented itself in the form of a grazing buck. John brought it down with a single shot from his bow. The group decided to spend some time in this spot curing the meat into strips that would serve them well in the lean days that lay ahead.

Their camp sat in a small canyon, sheltered in a shallow cave from which an icy spring bubbled out of the rear wall, forming a stream that cut its shallow path down the hillside to the canyon bottom. The enclosure had the added benefit of being an excellent lookout position that provided a field of vision in three directions.

They stayed in the canyon for another day, preparing meat and allowing Ty to recover from a fever. Upon leaving the restful place, they turned north, moving along the side of the ridges and dropping down into deep canyons. For a week, they made good time.

Gradually, the terrain began to slope downward until eventually the quartet reached a broad, grassy plain, broken intermittently by tree-lined rivers. Here, vorg scouting parties forced the group to travel more carefully. They avoided the warriors by traveling primarily at night and making camps in dense thickets. Despite the monotony of their diet, they were thankful that they had taken the time to cure the meat.

On the evening of the eighth day out, John spotted a dust cloud off to the west.

"What do you make of that, Arn?"

Arn studied the cloud for several moments. The sun was sinking rapidly, illuminating the dust in a dark shade of pink.

"That's an army on the march, for sure. They'll probably be stopping at night. Still, with vorgs, there's no telling. We'd best make some time tonight so we don't run into their scouts tomorrow."

"There's only one army I know of that could kick up that much dust," said Ty.

"The scouting parties we've been seeing have been ranging out to the east," said John.

Kim looked puzzled. "With all the confusion in the city, how could they have begun marching so quickly?"

"The revolt may have hastened their departure," Arn said. "Most likely they assigned a contingent to deal with the uprising while the commanders ordered the army to move out."

"Heading around the mountains to the north and then east? Why east?" Kim asked.

"Right toward Tal," said Arn. He shook his head. "That's King Gilbert's problem. He and his pet wielder can deal with it."

"You don't sound too concerned about your former home," said Ty.

"Actually, the only two I don't give a damn about are Gilbert and his wielder. Gilbert has run off or killed most of the old warlords. But this onslaught . . . it's too bad for the good people of Tal."

Arn wheeled his horse around and began trotting across the plain to the north. Dropping into silence, the others fell in beside him.

24

Southwestern Edge of Mogev Desert
YOR 413, Late Summer

Alan's words and *Liberty* had given Carol the will to carry on. And she would do so with good cheer. Anything less would disappoint the man she loved, should he look in on her from the afterlife.

Even the cooling desert air seemed to exude new meaning. The dawn was still two hours away, but already the lead wagons were beginning to roll. The whoops of the drivers and the cracks of whips blended with the rattle of the soldiers' armor. Carol was still surprised by how cold the morning air could be in the desert, only to give way to the heat of midday. Hawthorne said it was late summer, but the mornings already felt like autumn.

The caravan had adopted a routine that consisted of traveling for about four hours in the morning, resting until the sun began to set, and traveling another four hours before camping for the night. The scryer had proven itself repeatedly, often locating water that lay just beneath the surface. Without it, even Rafel's vaunted rangers could not have gotten the wagons through the drylands. Nonetheless, the caravan had still lost five people. Three rangers from one team had died of thirst trying to locate the first watering holes. Derek had found their bodies and brought them back. Rafel ordered them buried at the watering hole, with Jason and his priests performing the ceremony of the passing. Afterward, Hawthorne placed wards on the graves to keep the animals away.

The other two deaths had come from illness. A fever had infected many in the caravan two weeks back. Dana, a cook, and Bill, one of their nine carpenters, had succumbed. The consensus among all the leaders was that the travelers had been extremely lucky to have not suffered even greater losses.

Food was becoming as much a problem as water. They had eaten all the dried meat. The meals now consisted almost entirely of beans, a diet beginning to frustrate most. The worst thing about existing solely on beans was that they did not allow you to forget them between meals.

The line of wagons came to a stop earlier than usual. Carol jumped from the seat and made her way down the line toward where Rafel was talking to a ranger. The conversation ended before Carol arrived, and the ranger wheeled his bay horse around and rode away at a trot.

"What is it, Father?" Carol asked.

"The rangers have found the other side of this wasteland. About three days from here by wagon, mountains rise to the west. Another day's travel beyond that, and there are streams and game, the like of which we've never seen. And more good news: the rangers brought in several deer to supplement tonight's dinner."

A cheer from the nearest wagon indicated that his words had drifted. Within minutes, the rest of the caravan reacted to the news, and a joyous shouting broke out all around. Despite the enthusiasm, Rafel refused to change the established travel schedule.

"I'm not about to squander our strength now when we're likely to need it later," Carol heard her father tell one of the wagon drivers. "When a group of idiots puts you in charge of a caravan, then you can try things your way. Until then, you'll do as I say."

No one else was foolish enough to be overheard griping about the high lord's decision.

The two days that followed passed slowly. Carol found herself longing for the sight of trees, streams, and wildlife. She had loved hunting and fishing since she was a little girl and prided herself in being able to outshoot her father's archers. But most of her time she spent off by herself, practicing her magic. As he had done with Wreckath, Hawthorne had admonished her for what he perceived as overconfidence with Jaa'dra, so she took time to reassure herself of her mastery over that particular elemental.

They camped that night at the desert's edge, the mountains rising like a wall before them. The scrub brush growing on the hillsides gave way to juniper as the caravan moved higher up. A good-size stream wound its way down through the valley ahead, backdropped by white peaks reaching toward the heavens like the outstretched hands of worshippers in prayer.

The mood in the camp was one of elation. Once again, the rangers brought in a bountiful supply of venison and reported no sign of danger to the caravan. Nevertheless, Rafel ordered a double guard posted. Carol, accompanied by Alan, made her way through the twilight to each of these positions, dropping off a portion of venison. They were rewarded by the grateful expressions on the guards' faces.

The siblings hurried over to the campfires to get a little dinner for themselves. Rafel dictated that all sergeants and officers ate after the soldiers and their families. This rule applied to his children as well, and Carol regarded it as one of the crucial factors that had enabled the warlord to keep the morale of his men high. These musings died away as Carol's fork sank into the tender venison steak.

"Gods, this is good," Carol mumbled over her fork.

"I don't know, sister, I'm kind of partial to beans, myself," Alan replied, managing to keep his face composed.

Just then, Jake walked up and sat down cross-legged beside them. The boy's eyes shone with hero worship as he looked up at Alan. "Do you two mind if I eat with you?"

"Are you just now eating?" Carol asked. "What happened? Did you miss the dinner call?"

"No, I just wanted to let the soldiers and their families eat first. I figure it's about time that I started taking on a little responsibility."

"How would you like to ride out beside me tomorrow?" said Alan. "I'm sure we could get somebody else to drive your wagon."

"Do you mean it, Lord?"

"Of course. It's time you started working on becoming a soldier."

"You bet I'll ride with you!"

"Well, finish your dinner," Carol said. "If you plan on riding with Alan, you'll need all your strength."

The boy wolfed down his dinner and excused himself, clearly anxious to tell Lucy all about this happy turn of events.

Carol volunteered to drive for Jake the next day. As she climbed onto the wagon seat beside Lucy in the cool predawn air, she noted that even the team seemed anxious to get started. The trail quickly became rougher as the wagons passed into the wide valley ahead. The caravan wound its way steadily westward and upward, and although the day was warm, the stifling heat of the desert was a thing of the past, leading Rafel to order the caravan to press on until dark. As they stopped for the night, Carol caught her first glimpse of the pine trees on the slopes above. After eating dinner and settling down in her tent, she stayed awake late into the night, listening to the lonesome howls of wolves.

The next morning, Carol asked Hawthorne why he had not been drawing upon her strength for some time. She was surprised to learn that the wards he had put in place were now holding without further reinforcement.

"With this much distance separating us, Blalock has to search a wider area, thus dispersing his powers."

Carol nodded. With half of Tal, the outlands, and the desert between them, Blalock could not harm her people if he did not know their precise location.

"I think I'm ready to try controlling a higher-level elemental than any you've thus far allowed," said Carol.

"You are coming along remarkably well in your spellcraft," said Hawthorne. "And you are almost ready. I want you to increase the complexity of your practice before we move on."

"How so?"

"The elementals of the next rank don't just have more powerful wills for you to overcome. They are highly intelligent, crafty, and will use any distraction to their advantage. In preparation for dealing with these entities, I want you to provide your own distractions. Cast spells while you are fully occupied with difficult tasks. Get comfortable with that, and I will judge you ready."

Carol nodded, turned, and walked over to where her father was eating. The warlord stood erect in the flaring light of the campfire, metal plate in one hand, shoveling food into his mouth with the other. He finished wolfing down breakfast as she approached.

"I'm going to ride out with one of the hunting parties today," she informed him.

"I figured," he said. "Derek and Jaradin are hunting today. You'll probably have to hurry to get ready if you want to go with them."

"Storm is saddled and ready to go," Carol said as she kissed her father's cheek. "You're in need of a shave if you want me to keep kissing that face."

"But I'm not in need of a nursemaid."

Reacting with an indignant "hmmph," Carol turned and walked to the wagon where she had tied Storm. As much as she missed Amira, and as much as it pained her to think of how the mare had died under the knives of vorgs, she was rapidly developing a strong attachment to this new mount her father had given her.

Pulling the reins loose, she swung lightly up onto the dapple-gray horse, the mare moving as she hit the saddle. Carol wheeled the animal around, leaning out of the saddle to grab her bow and quiver from their place on the wagon, and then trotted off toward the rope corral where her father had indicated that Derek and Jaradin were positioned. She found them just finishing getting their horses saddled.

"You've got me for company today," Carol informed Derek.

The two rangers exchanged quick glances.

"We were actually planning on riding pretty hard today, Lorness," Derek began. "It might be better if you waited for a little more relaxing hunt."

"You do as you damned well please," Carol said. "It'll be a snowy summer day when I can't outride the two of you."

With a prod from her heels, the mare erupted into motion, taking the wielder-in-training up the moonlit valley at an easy lope.

"Looks like we're nursemaids today," Carol heard Derek say before she raced out of earshot.

She soon slowed to a trot, and the two rangers fell in beside her. An uncomfortable silence settled over the group. Despite her annoyance, Carol soon found herself enjoying the ride. The nip in the morning air brought a glaze of moisture to her eyes as she looked back over her shoulder at the light beginning to color the eastern sky.

The three riders soon began climbing the northern ridgeline. The slope was steep and rocky, with few trees. Carol's and Jaradin's mounts had been raised in the rugged foothills of western Tal and had little difficulty with the climb. However, Derek was riding a plains-bred horse, and the bay was panicking in the unfamiliar terrain. Whenever the shale slid beneath its hooves, the horse reared and pitched, forcing Derek to work to avoid being pinned.

Despite the problems the horse was causing him, the ranger remained calm, gently coaxing the animal with his voice and rubbing its neck with his right hand as he rode. By the time the group climbed to the top of the ridge, his efforts seemed to be paying off.

As they topped the crest, Carol found herself gazing out over the most majestic scenery she had ever seen. The sun had risen just high enough to illuminate ridge after ridge, covered in pine and spruce, working their way upward toward the white mountain peaks in the distance. Fog flowed down the slopes and into the valleys, partially obscuring a nearby lake.

Behind her, a glorious sunrise colored the base of the clouds hanging above the desert. Far below, she could make out the moving line of wagons. Her eyes followed Jaradin's pointing hand to several spots along the opposite rim where scouts were located. Soldiers strategically positioned themselves in a wedge well forward of the caravan, while the majority rode in a file forward and back of the wagons. Startled by a movement to her right, Carol turned to see a flock of wild turkeys emerge from the woodland's edge fifty feet away. The two rangers sat astride their horses alongside her, also lost in the splendor of this wild place.

Carol and the two rangers followed a deer trail down a rugged slope. As they approached a clearing, Derek brought his horse to a sudden stop, signaling for the others to pull up alongside him as he pointed out a small herd of deer.

Carol, Derek, and Jaradin all raised their bows at the same time, sending arrows whistling through the still morning air, each finding its target, dropping three big bucks and sending the rest of the deer bounding away into the forest.

As they all dismounted, a loud bawl from Derek's left caused his horse to shy away. As the horse scrambled backward, Derek struggled to hold on to the reins.

The horse reared, pawed the air, and brought its hooves smashing down into a thicket. A squall rang out as a frightened bear cub tumbled from a low branch of a pine to land with a thump near Derek.

"Look out!" Jaradin yelled.

To Derek's right, an angry brown bear burst from the woods, plowing into his rearing horse. A swipe from its paw knocked the animal into Derek, sending him rolling across the ground. With an ear-splitting growl, the mother bear continued her charge toward the fallen ranger.

A silvery aura shimmered in the air around Carol's upraised right arm as she ran between Derek and the mama bear. Her magical block stopped the great paw from striking its target, but the blow sent Carol tumbling across the ground. She came up with a mouthful of grass and mud in time to hear a swish and see two of Jaradin's arrows sprout from the maddened animal.

With a bellow, the bear turned to charge him. Carol's mind cracked like a whip, sending ten glittering streaks flying through the air, striking the bear in the side and sending it rolling across the ground. As the stunned animal tried to resume its charge, Derek grabbed hold of its back. The ranger's long knife rose and fell, finding the bear's heart. The beast fell to the earth, unmoving.

As Carol struggled to her feet, pain shot through her shoulder, evidently a sprain since she saw no sign of bleeding. Though blood ran down the left side of Derek's face, the wound did not appear to be serious. Of the three, only Jaradin had escaped injury.

"Is everyone all right?" Carol asked.

Derek met her gaze, and it seemed that he might utter a thank-you for her helping to save his life. But the moment passed, and he didn't.

"Everyone except this poor little fellow," Derek said as he knelt over the small cub.

"Is he dead?" Carol felt her throat constrict. The poor little cub hadn't asked for this. Just pure bad luck, all the way around.

"No. He just knocked himself out falling out of the tree," Derek said as he examined the little bear. "Nothing seems to be broken, but he'll never survive out here without his mother."

"We can't leave him to die!" said Carol.

The dark-haired ranger gently bent down and picked the cub up in his arms. "I'll take him with me. I killed his mother. That makes him my responsibility."

The trip back to the caravan was long and slow. The mama bear had killed Derek's horse. They had strapped a deer to the backs of each of the other two horses but had been forced to leave the other buck behind. Derek immobilized the young bear and slung it in a makeshift pack upon his back. The group reached the camp just after dark.

Carol spent the evening telling the tale to her father and Alan, the latter cursing roundly for having missed all the excitement. Then, having answered as many questions as she cared to, she dragged her tired, aching body to the spot where Jake had erected her tent. As she passed the cook fires, she spotted Derek's lithe form leaning against one of the wagons, his face illuminated in the fire's glow. Catching her eye, the ranger raised one hand in a gesture of salute, then turned and disappeared into the darkness.

As she watched Derek go, a feeling of satisfaction filled Carol's soul. His small act of approval meant more to her than she would have cared to admit.

25

Southern Glacier Mountains
YOR 413, Early Autumn

The caravan wound its way through the foothills, climbing steadily toward the pine-covered slopes of the high altitudes. Around noon of the fourteenth day, they crested a ridge to look down over a high-country scene. A fast-moving mountain stream cut a path through a grassy valley to a point where a beaver dam spread the flow out, forming a large pond.

Deer grazed carelessly in the tall grass around its edges, occasionally pausing to drink from the water. Pine forests ran down the surrounding hillsides. The high-mountain pass toward which the caravan headed was so close now that Carol could make out patches of bare ground showing through the snow. To think how the desert several thousand feet below still clung to its warmth made Carol marvel at all the snow in the high country ahead.

Rafel decided that everyone needed a rest and the wagons and equipment needed maintenance. The caravan would stop here for a couple of weeks. Welcome news. Drivers parked the wagons in large, concentric circles in the center of the valley. The people made camp close to the stream, and above the beaver pond, a heavy guard was posted along the surrounding ridges. Broderick ordered the rangers to begin scouting the way ahead as well as mapping the surrounding lands to their north and south.

Hawthorne utilized the peaceful surroundings to begin teaching Carol a new spell. This time the entity to contend with was Jaa'dra, one of the greater elementals that controlled fire. Carol found Jaa'dra to be much more difficult to control than any of the elementals that she had contacted so far.

Even Lwellen, the lightning master, was more tractable. With the lightning spell, Carol found that she could make Lwellen form a great attractive charge in the ground where she wanted bolts to strike. Even though this burst of energy sometimes flowed outward, the bolt would generally strike within ten feet of her desired target.

The problem with the fire elemental was that his will was stronger than Lwellen's, and he relied on a combination of subtle and direct assaults. Even though Carol could precisely control where the fire started, the blaze often spread in unforeseen directions. Controlling the spell was very much like fighting a grass fire.

Due to his familiarity with the intricacies of the spell, Hawthorne had Carol practice well away from the wagons, on a small island in a shallow portion of the beaver pond. Carol devoted all her energies to mastering this challenging new spell, and within a week, she was able to control the elemental to such an extent that she could write her name in flames. To reward her efforts, Hawthorne gave Carol time off from her practice to enjoy her surroundings.

Carol awoke well before dawn the next morning, dressed, and began walking up the valley along the stream. By the time the sun cast its first light upon the glacier-covered peak, she had rounded a bend and passed out of sight of the wagons.

She saw a waterfall, plunging off a twenty-foot-high cliff into a clear natural pond. As she approached the cliff, she spied several handholds that enabled her to climb along its face. She found the stones slippery with the mist from the falls, but with enough holds to make passage possible.

She climbed along the stones, ducked under an overhang, and found a place to sit behind the falling water. The cool spray on her face made her shiver but felt invigorating nonetheless. Her thoughts turned to the months since they had fled Rafel's Keep. How different her life would be if she had never been forced to leave. For one thing, her father would have never allowed Hawthorne to put her through the Ritual of Terrors. And she would never have learned to master the magic that she intended to use to breathe life into Thorean's vision.

She was beginning to think that even the knowledge of Arn's death had helped her hone her abilities, albeit in an almost suicidal frenzy of spell-casting. Now all the practice was yielding desired fruit. Despite how Hawthorne had warned her of the dangers Jaa'dra presented, it had proved no match for her. After all, she had directly confronted the primordial who ruled the elemental planes and, through sheer force of will, had emerged victorious.

Kaleal's statement that she was the one foretold by Landrel now began to seem possible. And if she truly were destined for greatness, she would open her arms to embrace it.

A loud laugh accompanied splashing from the nearby bend in the stream. Carol turned her head.

She saw Derek coming up the valley carrying a fishing pole, his orphaned bear cub in tow. The little fellow loped happily alongside the ranger, whom he had accepted as his adopted mother. The bear cub raced forward a few paces, got distracted by the sound of the stream, then dived into the water in a vain attempt to catch a fish.

"Ha, ha," said Derek. "I can see I'm going to have a hard time catching anything with you along, Lonesome."

Hearing his name, Lonesome splashed happily out of the stream, coming to a halt by Derek just in time to shake himself vigorously, spraying a healthy amount of water onto the ranger. Derek bent down and threw his arms around the plump black cub, rolling around with him on the ground. The two continued to wrestle for several minutes, oblivious of Carol's presence behind the falls.

The wrestling match broke up when the little bear discovered some tasty berries growing among the bushes. Taking his chance while Lonesome was preoccupied, Derek picked up his fishing pole and moved to sit on a large rock on the bank.

Baiting the hook, he tossed the line into the water. In the span of a few moments, he landed his first fish.

As he leaned over to take the hook out of the trout's mouth, two furry brown paws draped over his shoulder while a long tongue licked his right ear. Derek laughed and tossed the fish back over his shoulder, onto the bank. His friend deserted him.

For most of the morning, she watched the pair. Finally, Lonesome was full and Derek was able to fill a stringer with fish to take back to the cooks. Carol looked forward to the addition of fish to their diet over the next few days.

After Derek left, she made her own way back to camp. As she approached her wagon, she heard a loud ruckus from the mess area. The sound of pots and pans clattering accompanied angry yells.

She rounded one of the wagons and saw Jock, her father's fattest cook, advancing toward a flour-covered bear with one of his butcher knives. As he was about to get in striking distance, Derek's boot caught him full in the midsection.

The fat man doubled over with a *whoosh*.

Turning toward Derek, the enraged cook bellowed, "Out of my way! I'm going to kill that animal!"

"You try it, and we're going to have to find ourselves another cook," Derek said, glaring back at him.

Carol stepped between the two men.

"Knock it off. Both of you! Derek, take Lonesome and put him where he can't cause any more trouble. As for you, Jock, I don't want to ever see you threaten that little bear again. He's just a baby."

"That baby did as much damage to my dinner as a herd of stamped-ing cattle!" Jock snapped.

Then, realizing to whom he was talking, Jock inhaled deeply. "I'm sorry, Lorness. It's just that the little monster had me so mad I couldn't see straight. I'll get over it."

She reached over and patted him on the back. She turned to see Derek leading the cub away by the scruff of his neck. The little fellow gazed up at him with such a forlorn look that she could not keep from smiling. Just then, Derek glanced back and, for the briefest moment, she thought she saw a hint of a smile play across his features. Then he turned and was gone.

The next several days passed too quickly for Carol. She had not real-ized how much she had needed to relax. The rest seemed to be improv-ing everyone's spirits. Broderick even rotated the rangers back in, a few at a time, for a break. She spent the time hiking, hunting, and practicing her spells. Hawthorne seemed duly impressed with her mastery of the fire elemental, although he warned her to maintain vigilance at all times when dealing with such a being.

She thought that this particular day was even lovelier than the ones preceding it, with a hint of change in the air. Tall thunderheads chased thin clouds across the sky, obscuring the higher peaks from view.

Rafel ordered everyone to prepare for a rainy night, and so most of the people scurried about, improving on the drainage ditches around their tents. Carol walked around her own tent only to conclude that she'd done a fine ditch-digging job the first time.

She walked over to the mess area as the first few drops of rain began to plop down here and there, sounding much louder than normal in the darkness. Jock looked up from where he knelt, trying to start a campfire.

"Ah, and a timely arrival it is," he said with a smile. "Perhaps Lorness Carol would not mind saving me the struggle of trying to strike a flame in this wind."

"Jock! I'm surprised at you. You've been spying on my practice sessions."

"And I am truly impressed."

Carol smiled. "With flattery like that, perhaps I can find it in my heart to lend a helping hand."

—⁊⁊⁊—

The underground audience chamber beneath Hannington Castle was ancient and vast. The room descended in rows of stone benches from all walls toward a large square area in the center. From that area, a twenty-foot black pyramid arose, hundreds of candles lining its tiers. A spiraling set of steps wound their way to a throne.

Carvings of elementals adorned the seat's back and sides, crowded with arms stretched outward in supplication, as if eager to do their master's bidding. The throne had been carved from the orange wood of a swamp willow, prized for its connections to the planes of air, earth, fire, and water.

Kragan sat atop this perch, gazing out over the small group below. Three were human. The others were vorgs, except for the massive grun Tarok, who stood ready to deliver the latest update on Kragan's army outside of Lagoth.

"Master, the army stands ready for your orders. All is in a state of readiness." Tarok's voice echoed through the room.

"How many?" Kragan asked.

"A hundred thousand strong await your orders to march from Lagoth."

"What a shame that King Gilbert ordered most of his troops west after High Lord Rafel's rebel band. He has just handed Tal over to me."

As if on cue, Commander Charna entered the room.

An angry glint shone in Tarok's red eyes as the muscular she-vorg shoved her way past him. Kragan motioned with his hand, signaling for the group to leave. Tarok departed last, closing the door, leaving Kragan alone with Charna.

Charna spread her arms wide as she approached the dais. "I never thought I'd be standing in the labyrinth beneath Hannington Castle, at least not before burning it down."

"You'd better watch yourself around Tarok, Charna," Kragan said. "One of these days I may just turn him loose on you."

"I'd have him screaming for mercy and release before he died. But enough small talk. I've scouted the western border of Tal, and there aren't enough soldiers there to even slow our army down.

"There was one odd caravan heading west toward the desert, quite large and heavily guarded. One of my subcommanders was fool enough to attack it and suffered defeat. He should have known better than to come back alive."

"Where is J'Laga?" Kragan asked. "I expected you to bring the wielder to see me when you came."

"Oh, he was with me all right. But I left his sorry carcass rotting in a cave several weeks' hard travel west of here."

"Wha-at?" Kragan slammed his fist down on the black marble. "How did it happen?"

"We ran into some bad luck named Blade. I really wanted to bring you his head, but that turned out to be . . . difficult."

"Deep spawn, I've waited far too long to step on that son-of-a-whore. But Blade is a nuisance, not a real threat."

"Tell that to J'Laga," Charna snarled. "He had a rather startled look on his face as Blade cut him down. That maniac attacked a whole group of us, killed some of my best fighters."

Kragan got up and climbed down from the pyramid to clap his hand on the she-vorg's shoulder. "It's been a long while since we hunted together. Would you care to accompany me this night?"

"I stand ready."

Kragan led the way up the pyramid to the back of the throne. He pressed one of the nude figures, and the throne slid forward to reveal a stone stairway, leading down. Charna followed him into the dark hole. The two moved easily through the darkness for a time, negotiating a maze of turns and twists, finally coming to a stop before a granite wall.

"Grab my hand," Kragan said.

Charna complied.

The two of them stepped through the wall, which had acquired the consistency of mist, and into the night beyond. They had emerged at the base of a cliff, far below the castle. The city of Hannington lay just to the north, but Kragan turned east, leading Charna through a wooded area and down into the farmland beyond. They stood together in the darkness watching the twinkling lights of several small farms.

"Take your pick," Kragan said.

"I like that one," Charna said, pointing to the leftmost homestead. "It has a cheery look."

The two of them moved rapidly down the hill, crossing a field of late-season wheat. As they got close to the farmhouse, a dog began to bark. Behind it, the door opened to reveal a strong young man in work clothes. Over the man's shoulder, Kragan could see a comely woman peering out.

"Don't worry, Anna," the man said. "It's just that fox again. I'll go check it out."

The man stepped outside, closing the door behind him. He signaled to the dog. "Go on, Lance. Go get that fox."

The dog came running toward the outhouse, behind which Kragan and Charna stood. As it caught sight of them, it snarled and leapt over the trough. Kragan's casting met the attack, snapping the canine's neck in midair, sending it to the turf with a dull thud.

"Lance. Lance. Where are you, boy?" The man continued to walk toward them.

As he came up alongside the outhouse, Charna stepped out. Upon seeing the vorg, the man blurred into motion. With surprising swiftness, he swung the small hand ax in his right hand. Charna caught his wrist in midair, twisting the farmer's arm violently and slamming him into the side of the outhouse. Charna's knife brought the man's howls of pain to an end.

As the woman opened the door, Kragan stepped inside. "Good evening, Anna."

Once more his mind reached out. Glowing orange bands crawled around the woman's body, binding her hands to her sides and lifting her off the ground. Charna entered the house as Anna came to rest about two feet above the floor on a far wall.

"What have we here?" Charna asked, gesturing toward the far corner.

Kragan's gaze followed the gesture. Seated on a narrow bed, her small hands still rubbing the sleep from her eyes, sat a little girl.

"Looks like we struck gold at the very first house."

Kragan walked up to where the terrified woman hung suspended in the air. As he leaned in, she spat directly in his face. He calmly reached up and wiped the spittle away. "I was planning on taking you first. But now you get to watch what we do to her."

The defiant woman began to speak, but a casual flick of Kragan's mind cut off the sound.

The wielder reached out to caress the girl's face. His mind cast outward for one of the greater fire elementals. Taking a deep breath, he gathered his will and spoke a single word.

"Jaa'dra!"

—⁂—

Standing beside the fat cook, Carol reached out with her mind for Jaa'dra, producing a flame that spread evenly under the pyramid of kindling, holding the fire long enough to allow the wood to catch. Suddenly Jaa'dra wrenched violently, almost breaking her concentration. Another jerk and her mind made contact with that of Blalock. Surprise rocked her as she felt Blalock's sudden burst of exultation, accompanied by a more powerful assault from Jaa'dra. Blalock had grabbed the fire elemental while she had control of it, and now the king's wielder was throwing his entire will into helping Jaa'dra overcome her.

Flames crawled outward to form a circle around Carol. As she fought to keep them back, long strokes of fire reached out to her body. Despite her best efforts, she realized that she could not withstand Jaa'dra's and Blalock's combined will. Suddenly a spear of flame leapt up to pierce her left shoulder, liquid heat etching an intricate brand into her flesh. Carol expunged the agony from her brain, pushing desperately against the fire, but with no effect. Her mind churned. Unless she did something very soon, she would die.

She centered, casting her mind out from her body in one sharp effort, feeling Jaa'dra's sudden delight. She had committed a wielder's cardinal sin. She had projected while spell-casting, her consciousness no longer anchored to her body, thereby ensuring elemental possession.

Her mind hurtled across the leagues of dark desert, drawn toward her target even as the elemental raced after her. Following Blalock's mind-link back to his body, she passed through the roof of a small farmhouse, her consciousness wrapping the wielder like his black cowl. And along with her consciousness came Jaa'dra.

Blalock staggered backward, one side of his head engulfed in a raging inferno. Recovering his concentration, the wielder forced the fire elemental away from his body, driving it back to the netherworld from which it had come. Blalock's knees gave way, and a massive she-vorg threw a blanket over him to snuff out the flames. As Carol's mind propelled itself back to her body, she caught sight of a woman running from the farmhouse, a young girl clutched tightly in her arms.

Carol stepped out of the circle of dying flames to see Hawthorne's fire-lit silhouette round the wagons at a dead run, his robes flapping out behind him.

Her legs buckled. As the world faded away around her, she reached out toward him, the smell of her own cooked flesh wafting into her nostrils as the ground rushed up to her face.

26

While he could remember many bad storms, Gilbert had never heard or felt fury equal to the one that had held Hannington Castle in its grip for the last two days. Wind did not whine through the cracks in doors and shutters. It howled, a wounded animal spewing out all its pain and anger at the world.

Although the quality of the workmanship in the castle was exquisite, the angry wind found its way through each chink in the mortar, every crack in the wood. It scurried along the hallways, picking up the dust from the floors in little eddying whorls, as if trying to grow baby storms into replicas of their mother outside.

If it had not been for the lightning that crawled across the sky, sending barrages of thunder to shake the mighty walls themselves, Gilbert would have thought the wind loud. Instead, he felt relief when he could hear the wind.

Gilbert paced across his chambers, barely seeing the form of the wielder who was the object of his ire. "Damn you, Gregor. Is this your idea of handling Blalock?"

Gilbert's scowl deepened. "What was it you said to me all those weeks ago? 'Do not worry, sire. I will do what I have been longing to do all these years. I will handle Blalock.' Wasn't that what you told me?"

Gregor failed to respond.

The king stopped his pacing to kick a chair across the room, almost striking Gregor, but it was not sufficient to break the infuriating old man's silence. To think he had allowed himself to believe that Gregor had succeeded in driving Blalock away. After all, the dark wielder had disappeared for several weeks with no word of his whereabouts.

But Blalock's return had been unpleasant enough to put an end to all the king's wishful thinking. The left side of the dark wielder's face had been nearly burned away, the flesh having melted and run, leaving bone and teeth exposed. Only a wielder of Gregor's power could have inflicted that kind of damage upon Blalock.

But despite his disfigurement, Blalock reasserted his authority with a vengeance. And now this.

"I want to know something. What news did the messenger bring Blalock that put him in such a fury that his storm of anger threatens to pull down our very walls? You can at least tell me that. No?"

Gilbert spat at the stone floor. "What good are you? What earthly good have you done for your king other than to make things worse than they were before you confronted Blalock?"

Gilbert came to a sudden stop in front of the ancient wielder, kneeling down and reaching out a hand to grab the man by his bearded chin, forcing his face toward the king's own. "Do you not understand that you are the only power that now stands between me and Blalock's madness?"

Despite the presence of his king's face only inches from his own, Gregor remained as the king's men had found him weeks past. His arms hugged his knees to his chest. His eyes, as white as hailstones, had rolled back into his head, as if they could no longer bear to look outward. The wielder's lips moved, but no sound issued forth. Gilbert leaned in close, his ear almost touching the old man's open lips.

In the king's bedroom, on a gold-inlaid nightstand, Gilbert had the large spiral shell of a creature that had once lived in a faraway sea. It gleamed with a mother-of-pearl sheen unlike any the king had seen before, a gift from one of the nobles who had sought to win his favor with such baubles. By holding it to his ear, just so, he could almost make out the sound of those faraway waters crashing against an unknown shore. So lonely. A haunting symphony.

Gilbert thought as he held his ear up against the open mouth of the wielder that he could just make out such a haunting symphony. But this was instead the echo of undying discord, the howl of a spirit whose torture knew no end.

27

Colder weather encroached as the caravan moved through the high pass, the snow-covered peaks blocking views to the north and south. Deer, antelope, and buffalo grazed in abundance.

Carol had been unable to cast even the simplest of spells since the incident in which she had received the fire brand. What had Hawthorne called it? The Mark of Jaa'dra. She pulled open the collar of her blouse so that she could look at it. Not a scar, but an incredibly detailed elemental self-portrait, almost lifelike. When she allowed herself to study it closely, flames seemingly leapt along the body of the fire elemental, its eyes following hers.

She had been incredibly lucky. Elementals only marked their slaves at the moment of possession. After that, the branded individual was forever lost, in thrall to the being that ruled her mind, a mind forever trapped on the plane of its master. She thought it an adequate description of the deep.

As far as Hawthorne knew, no one had ever been marked with such a brand and retained their own free will. For that reason, the wielder had been very harsh to the cook, the only other person to see the mark before Hawthorne had covered it and carried Carol off to his wagon. The spell the wielder cast wiped all memory of that day from Jock's mind.

"No one else can be allowed to learn of this," Hawthorne told her. "If they discover the mark, your own people will believe you are possessed by the elemental, and even I could not blame them. I believed it myself until I found no trace of its influence upon you. What you accomplished in that encounter is impossible."

She had promised Hawthorne that she would be careful not to allow anyone to see her bare left shoulder. Unfortunately, the mark wasn't her only symptom from the encounter with Blalock and Jaa'dra. She had developed a mental block that she could not overcome. Every time she tried to cast a spell, the pain she had felt as the flames knifed into her body came crashing back in, destroying her concentration. Hawthorne had tried to help her through the problem but had been frustrated in his attempts.

She glanced up at the wispy white clouds that glazed the sky high above, looking as if strong winds had ripped off small tufts and stretched them like taffy. The day had been mild with only a hint of a breeze, but now gusts whipped the grass and billowed out the canvas. Beneath her blouse, her shoulder throbbed. As she faced out into the chill wind, she had the strangest impression that it bore her malice.

—⁓—

The hexagonal room at the top of Hannington Castle's tallest tower had six windows through which the afternoon breeze swept in from the west, cooling the perpetual burning in what remained of the left side of Kragan's face and scalp. In the weeks that had passed since, he had discovered that the daughter of the Endarian Prophecy had been under his nose for more than twenty years.

He had actually seen her fifteen years ago when Rafel had brought his daughter and son to Hannington Castle for a gathering of noble families. But then she'd been only seven and bore little resemblance to the woman she had now become, the same one who haunted his dreams. Through pure dumb luck, he had encountered her when they had both reached out to control Jaa'dra. Kragan had stood on the very brink of killing the woman as Jaa'dra tattooed its flaming elemental mark on her left shoulder. But then she had broken the rules and projected her mind from her body while contesting with an elemental.

Somehow, she had propelled her mind to his body, and Jaa'dra had arrived almost simultaneously, melting away the skin from the left side of Kragan's face. He recalled the pain, and the memory stoked his hatred.

But before the inferno, before she had projected, Kragan had seen the distant mountains through her eyes. Although the intervening distance and the wards placed around Rafel's camp prevented him from determining her precise location, he had recognized those peaks. And during the long weeks of Kragan's recovery, he had calculated how long it would take Rafel's caravan to climb toward that mountain pass.

Rafel may have stopped along the way to rest and restock his supplies, but Kragan had no doubt that the lord and his followers were now well up into those heights, aiming to get through the high pass before winter set in.

As Kragan looked out to the west, he raised his arms out before him, half of his face twisting. He could not cast a major spell over such vast distances, but he could change the weather pressure here, shifting the flow of air from the frozen seas that lay far to the northwest. And as that wind rushed in across the Glacier Mountains, it would bring an abundance of moisture.

Yes. Winter in the high mountains was about to make an early appearance.

—⁓—

Rafel called an early halt and had the caravan circled in a gentle swale, but it offered little protection from the biting breeze that grew colder by the moment. The rangers returned with packhorses loaded with firewood scavenged from the ridge to their east. The cooks set about lighting fires within the circle. A boy ran up to tell Carol that her father had called a council meeting. The meeting began soon after she arrived at Rafel's wagon.

"Yes, sir, it looks like we're in for a real bad one," Derek said. "The signs are the worst I've ever seen. My best guess is that the snow will hit us by midnight. How long it'll last I don't know, but if the way the wild animals are acting is any indication, it's going to be with us for quite a spell. I'm sorry I couldn't have figured it sooner when we could have had a chance to find some shelter."

"You did the best you could do," Rafel said. "Gaar, get your men moving and group the animals in tight. I want every bit of shelter we can get put together before the brunt of the storm hits."

With those final instructions, everyone moved out to aid in getting the caravan prepared for the coming storm. As nightfall descended, Carol walked around the inner perimeter of the encampment. The wind howled through the caravan, ripping loose canvas that had already been fastened and breaking tie-downs. The workers no longer made significant progress, struggling to just stay even.

She shivered beneath her thick coat. Ice pellets stung her face and rattled against metal pans. She was now forced to lean into the wind to avoid being blown over. A sudden gust knocked Carol sideways just as a scream rose above the wind. She turned toward the sound to see a young boy pinned beneath an overturned wagon. The boy's mother stood beside him, yelling for help. Rushing to where he lay, she knelt beside the child.

Only the boy's head and chest stuck out from beneath the wheel, his breath coming in rattling gasps that left a bloody froth dribbling from the corner of his mouth. Several men grabbed the frame and lifted, setting it back up on its wheels. Before they could reach the boy to lift him, Carol restrained them. She couldn't tell the extent of his internal injuries, but she feared that they were so serious that moving the child might kill him.

"Go get the surgeon," Carol yelled. One of the men turned and ran off in the direction of the surgeon's tent. "And get me blankets. Quickly!"

She grabbed the covers as they were brought and carefully wrapped them around the small boy.

"It's okay," she said soothingly as a moan escaped from his lips. "We're here with you. You're going to be just fine."

The boy's eyes remained wide but relaxed just a little at the sound of her voice.

Another gust of wind rocked the wagon.

"Come on!" one of the men yelled. "Get the damned thing staked down."

Carol felt a large hand on her shoulder and turned to see Kelvin, the surgeon, motion for her to let him kneel in her place. Moving aside, she shifted up to stroke the boy's head.

"What's his name?" the surgeon asked as he removed the blankets and began to methodically examine the boy's injuries.

"Will," the weeping mother managed. "His name is Will."

Another gasp escaped the boy's lips, where fresh blood had begun to freeze at the corners of his mouth.

"Take it easy now, Will," Kelvin said. "Don't worry about a thing. I'll have you fixed up good as new before you know it."

Hawthorne arrived and provided a magical light for the surgeon to work by. After several minutes, Kelvin informed them that it was okay to move the boy, but that he would need to be placed carefully on a stretcher. This was quickly constructed by folding blankets over two long poles. Finally, the men moved the child onto the stretcher and carried him off to the field surgery wagon, accompanied by Kelvin and his mother.

Carol didn't have long to worry about the child. As she watched him being carried into one wagon, the top was blown off another. Men scrambled to hold down ropes while others worked with hammers and stakes. The ice pellets gave way to sheets of blowing snow so dense that Carol lost sight of the cook fires. Struggling against the wind, she made her way across the compound until she bumped up against the roped-off corral. She gasped. It was so cold that her lungs felt as if steel straps constricted her chest.

She worked her way counterclockwise around the caravan's innermost circle. The lurching of the wagons in the wind scared her, but not as much as the numbing cold. If it was this bad inside the inner circle, what must it be like on one of the outer vehicles?

Lifting the flap of Hawthorne's wagon, she ducked inside. The old wielder had arranged himself on a pallet and appeared to be deep in meditation. She was about to leave the wagon to avoid disturbing him when he spoke.

"Come in, Carol," Hawthorne said. "I have been preparing myself for the task that lies ahead."

"You look exhausted," she said. "You need rest."

"It'll have to wait for another day," Hawthorne said, shaking his head so that his long beard wagged. A fresh gust of wind shook the bed, sending snow swirling in through the flap. The candle wavered, but remained lit. "Do you hear what is going on out there?"

"Hear it? I was just out in it. I didn't think I was going to find my way to you."

"It's going to get worse," the wielder said. "Much worse. This storm is not natural. I feel Blalock's hand in this."

"What? That's not possible."

"I'm afraid it is. Listen to me. I want you to go to your father. Tell him to erect shelters inside the perimeter, where people can huddle together. In an hour, I am going to begin casting the spells that I hope will enable us to survive this storm.

"I am going to partially block the wind from entering the perimeter while I work to keep the fires going. During the remainder of the storm, no one can be allowed to disturb me unless I am taking a rest. I'm going to need every bit of concentration I can muster to maintain the spells."

"But you can't do it by yourself. Let me help you. Draw upon my strength as you did before."

"I've tried. I can't penetrate the blockage you have erected inside your mind. Right now, I need you to do as I ask. Go on."

Carol nodded and crawled back out into the storm. It was now so dark that she could only see the faint glow of the fires visible as halos through the swirling snow. Stumbling blindly forward, she reached her father's tent, finding him and Gaar inside.

She informed her father of Hawthorne's intentions. As soon as the words were out of her mouth, Rafel signaled to Gaar and the warrior plunged from the tent to disappear in the direction of the rangers and the makeshift corral. Carol started to follow him, but her father restrained her.

"Let Gaar do his job while I meet with my commanders. I need you to visit each family and spread the knowledge of what is about to happen. Nobody is to be allowed outside the perimeter unless I or Gaar order it."

Carol took a deep breath and once again stepped out into the storm. By the time she finished telling all the families what would be done, Gaar and the rangers had moved the remainder of the horses and other animals inside the circle of wagons and had roped off corrals away from the scores of cook fires.

The cooks were having a terrible time trying to keep the fires going, and she believed that they would have gone out had not Hawthorne's spells kicked in. Suddenly, the wind died down to a gentle breeze within the compound and the fires flared high, accompanied by a great cheer from the entire caravan. But the exuberance did not last long. Despite the easing of the wind, the cold was dreadful, and the snow continued to fall heavily. Half a foot of the powdery stuff already covered the ground, with occasional three-foot drifts.

Long after midnight, with feet that felt like blocks of ice, Carol stumbled back to her wagon. She found Jake and Lucy sound asleep, wrapped in a pile of blankets and coats in the bed. She pulled off her wet parka and boots, then crawled into the pile with them.

Despite the number of blankets and the body heat of the two others, the cold seeped in wherever her weight mashed the sleeping pallet flat against the wood floor. No amount of rearranging seemed to make the slightest improvement in this situation. She eventually managed to get some sleep by rolling over whenever the side that was down became too chilled.

When Carol awoke, she was unsure of the time. From the cracks between the canvas flaps she saw a dim, cold daylight. She poked her head farther out of the covers and then, like a frightened turtle, pulled it back in. If such a thing was possible, the morning was even colder than last night. Not hearing anyone calling for her to get up, Carol closed her eyes and dozed off once again. She did not awaken until Jake crawled out of the blanket mountain.

"G-g-g-good m-morning, Lorness," Jake said. "I thought I would get a cup of hot coffee. Can I bring back an extra for you?"

"I need to get up and out myself. The coffee would be cold before you could get it back here, anyway. Is it still snowing outside?"

Jake lifted the flap a little. "Just barely, but jeesh, it's waist-deep where it hasn't drifted. Outside the circle, I see some drifts even taller than the top of our wagons."

Carol shivered, then summoned her courage and struggled out from under the covers. "Aaah. This coat is frozen. I hope I can get close enough to the fire to thaw it out."

"Don't worry," said Jake. "I'll muscle open a path for you if I have to."

Her laugh produced little puffs of condensed breath that changed to tiny snow particles. Her laughter ceased when she learned the state of her boots. The wet leather was stiff as a board, causing great difficulty when she attempted to slide her feet into the boots. She cursed her thoughtlessness in not sleeping with her boots under the blankets to let them remain warm and dry from her body heat.

She lifted Hawthorne's canvas flap and peered inside. She gasped. Her mentor sat cross-legged on a small pallet in the center of the bed. His gray hair and beard were frosted white, and the skin of his face had gray patches where frostbite had begun to set in. Carol crawled inside the wagon, moving up beside the wielder, trying to avoid producing any additional distraction that might break his concentration. Beads of sweat stood out on Hawthorne's brow, and some of these had run down his face, forming little icicles in his eyebrows. His eyes stared off into the distance, focused on the unseen elemental with which he contended.

Assailed by panic, Carol sucked in a deep breath. How long had her old friend been like this? The thought that the wielder would have his concentration so occupied that he would be unable to keep himself warm had never crossed her mind. She cursed herself as she set to work, gently wrapping blankets around him.

As she worked, the desire to attempt to fight through her mental blocks to magically warm Hawthorne grew unbearable. She seated herself and began the centering meditation. Her mind focused on her body, relaxing its parts one by one before turning inward. Suddenly fire exploded in her left shoulder, searing her brain with agony.

She clenched her teeth to prevent the scream that built inside her from bursting through. Then the agony was gone. Tears welled in Carol's eyes as she stared down at her left shoulder. The fire and pain were only a memory.

Returning to Hawthorne's side, she stared into his haggard face. She wept silently in worry and frustration, then wiped away her tears and crawled back out of the wagon. Past the guard and toward the cook fires, Carol pushed her way through the deep snow. She signaled to the two cooks who were busy preparing hot soup.

"Gerald, Sam. I want you to get several large kettles and fill them with hot stones. These are to be brought to Hawthorne as soon as they're ready. Set them inside his wagon as quietly as you can. I want them replaced hourly. Pass the word to the other cooks. Do you understand?"

The two cooks nodded their heads, but she made them repeat the instructions she had given them. She also made sure that they understood that she wanted the other cooks to repeat the instructions aloud when they changed shifts. Then she made her way to her father's command tent, disappointed to find it empty. She stopped and looked around.

The snow had begun falling more heavily again, but the breeze inside the circle had died out. Her attention turned to a large group of soldiers standing in formation over by the horse corral. As she approached the group, Carol saw that both her father and Gaar were present. Gaar stood in front of the assembled officers, giving orders in a loud voice.

"And I want every bit of snow inside the perimeter shoveled into big piles," Gaar thundered. "I expect to be able to walk back and forth between wagons and the cook fires without so much as having to shuffle through an inch of the damned stuff. I refuse to have the women and children feel that they cannot make it to the fires, is that clear?"

"Yes, sir!" The reply thundered through the camp.

The old warrior pivoted. Carol made her way to where they stood, her father turning toward her as she spoke.

"I don't know how much longer Hawthorne is going to be able to maintain our protection from the storm. His physical condition is deteriorating, but I'm afraid that if I try to feed him some soup or even water, I'll break his concentration. So I've got the cooks putting heat pots near him on a schedule. It's not much, but it's the best I can manage."

Rafel pounded his fist into his open palm. "How could it come to this? Because I could not imagine Hawthorne overcome by a storm, I paid no attention to his needs. If he succumbs, I fear that the rest of us may follow him into the deep."

"I do not mind dying in battle," said Gaar, "but I don't like the idea of freezing into an icicle."

Unable to express her own feelings of guilt, Carol made her way back across the perimeter, passing a large number of soldiers working with shovels to clear paths through the snow. She turned onto one of the paths and followed it as close to Hawthorne's wagon as she could before having to trudge back out into the deep snow again. Carol crawled silently between the flaps, pleased to find the interior warmer and Hawthorne looking less strained. He no longer had the frost in his beard and eyebrows, although there were still gray patches of skin on his face. She settled down on the mat beside him to wait and watch.

The night passed uneventfully. The heat kettles cut some of the chill, but the temperature was not what Carol would call comfortable. She looked down at her mentor without trying to stop the tears that trickled down her cheeks. For one who had been so full of herself only weeks before, to be struck so low felt both just and terrible. And now, all she could do was sit here and cry.

Hawthorne looked frail, presenting a cloudiness in his eyes that she had never before seen. She longed to take his hands between her own and warm them, but she didn't. Instead, she sat close, watching, worrying, and hoping that the terrible storm would soon end.

But the storm raged on, and as the hours passed, the old wielder weakened. She continued to sit with him between excursions outside to ensure that the families were doing the work that would keep them from freezing.

Toward the end of the week, sickness began to spread through the camp. The sound of incessant coughing came from at least a quarter of the hundreds of wagons that formed the caravan. The surgeon informed Rafel that most of these were only bad colds, but he expressed concern that, if the cold spell lasted much longer, pneumonia could set in.

On the fourth day of the storm, Hawthorne's protective shield began to falter. The first evidence was a gust of wind that howled through camp, driving a horizontal sheet of snow before it. Carol had just come out of her father's tent when the wind hit her, almost knocking her down with its unexpected fury.

Alarmed at this breach of the wielder's defenses, she ran toward Hawthorne's wagon, slipping and plunging into a bank. She scrambled back to her feet, gasping as a wad of snow slid down her neck.

When her racing footsteps brought her to him, she found the wielder slumped over on his side, his breath coming in ragged gasps. A sudden severe fit of coughing doubled him over. At the same time, the wind whipped the canvas flap, lashing Carol across the face with the tie-down rope.

When she put a hand to her cheek, it came away bloody, but she ignored the wound. Climbing inside, she wrapped her arms around Hawthorne's shoulders, laid his head on a pillow, and covered him with blankets. The wind howled, making the guard outside struggle to tie the flap back into place.

Carol was terrified. In desperation, she grabbed the wielder's flint and tinderbox, and struck a flame to light his thick, white candle. Then she set it to Hawthorne's side.

His eyes stared ahead in an unseeing stupor, his pupils mere pinpricks in the gathering darkness. His hands felt like ice between hers, and no amount of rubbing seemed to help. The old man's chest heaved, and his eyelids fluttered.

"Carol?" Hawthorne rasped.

"I'm here," she said, trying to keep her voice steady.

"Listen to me. I've done my best. Hopefully it will be enough to get our people through this storm. But from this point forward, the caravan is in your hands."

"What are you talking about?"

"I know that Rafel is as good a leader of men as there has ever been. But there are forces taking shape in this world against which he would be powerless. To battle those, he must rely on you."

"Don't be silly," she said. "You'll be around to take care of such matters as always."

A smile flitted across the old man's lips.

"Look at me with your eyes and not your heart. I'm afraid that you are now this caravan's only wielder. Buried within you is a talent the like of which I had never imagined. You just have to find it again. I have faith in you."

The eyes of the old wielder suddenly widened in fright, focused on something behind her. His look spun her around, certain that something evil had just snuck through the canvas. But all that confronted her was her own shadow dancing on the inside of the canvas. She turned back to Hawthorne to see him raise his right hand, palm outward, as if trying to fend off an attacker. When his hand dropped into his lap, Hawthorne shuddered. Then, with one last rattling breath, the wielder lay still.

Outside, the wind howled as Carol hugged the old man to her breast, cradling his head in her arms as she cried.

She had possessed the ability to save Hawthorne but had failed in her attempts to use her powers. Because she had been unable to conquer her fears, she had allowed Blalock to kill her mentor.

The wind howled through the canvas, but as she slowly rocked Hawthorne's body back and forth, Carol barely felt the cold.

28

Endar Pass—Northern Glacier Mountains
YOR 413, Mid-Autumn

As autumn advanced on the high plains northwest of the Mogev Desert, thunderheads filled the afternoon sky. They swept by with a drenching downpour, swirling winds, and cascades of lightning and thunder, leaving a chill that raised the gooseflesh on Arn's arms.

"That's it!" Kim's exclamation brought the other three riders to a halt. "Endar Pass!"

Arn stared hard in the direction Kim pointed. At first, he could see only the rolling plains disappearing in the blue haze to the north. Then he became aware of a subtle difference in the distant sky. He began to see how the plains became rougher country that gave way to twin peaks that towered over the silhouette of mountains.

"I never thought that I'd be so glad to see mountains," said John.

"To us, it is nothing less than sacred ground. You will have the privilege of being the first humans since the Vorg War to be allowed to set foot inside the valley." With a toss of her head, Kim urged her horse to a trot.

Despite the increased pace at which they traveled, the mountains remained an elusive goal. The plains gave way to foothills and steep valleys that blocked the travelers' view of the high country. Periodically, the riders would crest a rise to see the mountains change from pale blue to purple, and finally to dark green. The scrub gave way to juniper and then pine, which scented the cool, thinning air.

Ty trotted up beside Arn. "Have you noticed that we're being watched?"

"We have been since we entered the foothills," Arn said. "It's odd that I haven't seen who's watching us. That's never happened to me before."

"Don't worry," said Kim. "It is my brother and some of the Endarian scouts. They have been observing us to see if I am in any danger. If they had decided that I was, you would have all been dead by now."

"Maybe. Maybe not," said Ty, resting a hand on the carved handle of his ax.

"Word will have reached my mother of our presence," said Kim, ignoring Ty's remark. "She will send a party to greet us. You will have to excuse them if they are a bit gruff. It is rare that we welcome humans into our lands."

"It will be a real pleasure to be able to meet others of a race that could produce one such as you," said John, who over the months of travel had never stopped complimenting the Endarian princess.

By afternoon the mountainous terrain had become more rugged. Kim led them along a rocky but well-traveled trail. It wound along through the mountains, rising steadily and, at times, steeply up the mountainside. Arn began to feel closed in by the forest. The dense woods suddenly opened into a clearing, through which a rushing stream cut a path. Kim held up her hand to signal that this was the place she had selected to camp for the night.

As they dismounted, a group of Endarians rounded a bend in the canyon and strode rapidly toward them. They were tall, slender, and dark-skinned, with ebony hair that hung almost to their waists. They moved with a fluid grace that Arn remembered from his previous encounters with their kin. All of the Endarians were clad in garments of a light color that seemed to shimmer and change as they moved.

Kim ran to the nearest of the Endarians, threw her arms around his neck, and kissed him fondly on the cheek. Arn noted that she was the only brown-haired Endarian in the bunch. That, combined with the lighter shade of brown of her skin and eyes, highlighted her heritage.

She released her grip on the Endarian and began a conversation, the nature of which Arn could not quite make out. After several minutes, she stopped talking and led the Endarians to her companions, holding tightly to the leader's hand as she came.

Arn glanced at John, noting the pained expression etched into his face despite an obvious effort to hide it.

"Galad," said Kim, "I would like you to meet my good friends and saviors, John, Ty, and Arn. My friends, this is my brother, Galad."

Arn heard a barely audible sigh of relief from John. "We're so glad to meet you," he said, stepping forward and extending his hand.

The tall Endarian stood still for several moments, examining his sister's traveling companion with eyes almost as dark as John's.

John lowered his hand.

When Galad spoke, his voice carried none of the warmth he had just shown his sister.

"Our mother, Queen Elan, sends her greetings and offers her most profound thanks for the rescue of her daughter. For tonight, you will camp here under the protection of my scouts."

Galad gestured toward another grim-faced Endarian. "Tomorrow, Jalal will escort you into Endar Pass. But my mother would have me bring Kim to her side tonight. Until tomorrow."

Galad inclined his head slightly, then turned. He and Kim ran back the way he had come. The grace with which they moved reminded Arn of deer running along a mountainside. In seconds, they rounded the bend in the trail and were gone, leaving the three humans staring after them in amazement. Arn realized that they weren't actually running faster than speedy humans or vorgs, but far more effortlessly. Now that he thought about it, Arn realized he had not, until now, seen Kim run.

The Endarians who remained behind began preparations to camp for the night. They lit a fire, although Arn could not quite make out how they completed the task. Flames seemed to leap from rocks without any sign of fuel. The Endarians spread food and drink before them and then departed, leaving the small company to themselves.

"Why don't they eat with us?" Ty asked.

"Odd reception, all the way around," said Arn.

"Kim didn't even say good-bye," said John.

Arn heard the worry in his voice.

After finishing their meal of dried fruit and a surprisingly good flatbread, the three men settled down to sleep. Arn woke before sunrise to find that breakfast had already been laid out for them. He awakened the others, and the company ate as heartily as the night before.

Arn finished his portion just as a group of Endarians walked from the woods with Jalal in the lead.

"Come with us," he said.

The trio packed their things, mounted their horses, and followed Jalal around the bend in the canyon as the rest of the Endarian warriors fell in behind them. The trail climbed rapidly, exiting the forest to carve its way along the face of rocky cliffs. As they climbed, Arn could see that they were moving up toward a pass between the twin peaks that appeared to have once formed a single mountain. The peaks looked as if they had been split asunder by a giant sword slicing through naked stone. Only a lonely, gnarled pine had managed to maintain its purchase on the bare rock.

The trail curled around the side of the cliff, barely wide enough for two horses to walk abreast. Arn glanced over the edge to his right and was rewarded by the sight of a winding stream in the canyon far below.

He could not be certain how far down the drop went because of the mist that shrouded the canyon bottom.

The group continued along the rock wall for several hours, climbing steadily. As they rounded a final bend, a sheer cliff closed off the canyon. The river leapt over the edge of the precipice to fall several thousand feet to the floor of the canyon below, creating the veil of mist. The trail disappeared behind this plume of water.

Arn leaned forward in his saddle. He could not make out where the trail emerged on the other side of the falls. The sight pulled forth an eerie feeling that he failed to shake, as if he were approaching the edge of the world. The feeling grew stronger as he got closer to the falls. The Endarians led the way forward, pausing as they entered the mist so that Arn and his companions had to pull their mounts to a stop lest they run them over. As he caught a querying look and a "What is this?" glare from Ty, their guides disappeared into the thick fog. So Arn urged Ax forward.

Suddenly, he was aware of something pressing against his entire body, almost as if the mist did not want to allow him entry. Ax continued forward, but for a moment the horse seemed to have slowed considerably. But then the feeling passed, and rider and mount were moving naturally again.

The mist swirled so thickly in the air that Arn could no longer see the trail beneath him. Only the steady *clip-clop* of Ax's hooves on stone assured him that they remained in contact with the earth.

The journey through the mist lasted much longer than Arn had anticipated. He began to wonder whether the passage of time was real or a distortion caused by the feelings that engulfed him.

As the riders emerged from the mist, a valley descended before them, dropping between forested ridges until it came to the edge of an azure lake. Mountains surrounded the lake on all sides, sending tree-covered fingers of land out into the water. Sandy beaches also stretched along the shore. Flowered meadows spread out between ancient groves of pine. High up on the slopes above, groves of white aspen replaced pine. These, in turn, gave way to snow-covered peaks.

Yielding to a sudden impulse, Arn glanced back, catching his breath as he did so. The terrain rose toward more snowcapped peaks, but there was no sign of the mist from which he and his group had just emerged.

The country grew ever lovelier as they approached the lake. The color of the pines was unlike any that Arn had seen before. The trees had a strange mixture of blue and green needles, along with a hint of yellow near the heath. Wildflowers bloomed wherever the sun's rays could force their way through the trees to the ground, an odd occurrence for that time of year.

As the riders descended the ridge, the valley curved north and widened to reveal a stunning close-up view of the lake. Endarian forms dotted the southern lakeshore. He was surprised to see some of them standing several hundred feet out in the lake with water rising only to their knees. Several boats glided across the surface farther out, their gossamer sails billowing in the gentle breeze. And then Arn noticed the ivory fortress that rose up in the lake's center.

The structure was a thing of wonder, with gleaming white walls that rose hundreds of feet into the sky and brilliantly-colored pennants that flapped from the tops of four towers.

A single bridge, also of the same white stone, crossed a wide expanse of water, connecting the south shore to the Endarian castle and the city that spread out to the north. Endarian warriors lined this span, standing erect along both sides of the bridge. Others moved along the tops of the outer castle walls, staring down at the approaching formation from their elevated vantage point. Arn could just make out other figures watching from windows in the high inner towers.

Arn's study of the fortress was interrupted by the sight of a large group of Endarians emerging from the trees near the lake and making their way toward the riders at a rapid jog, several hundred strong. They poured from the forested ridges on both sides, many with long swords slung across their backs, while others carried bows and quivers full of arrows. The Endarians guiding the group of riders signaled for them to stop and wait where they were. Then the guards moved forward to meet the advancing warriors.

"I don't like the look of that," Ty said. As he fingered the handle of his ax, his palomino stallion snorted and pawed the ground.

"Sit tight," Arn said.

"If they'd wanted to kill us, they could have done it long ago," John said.

"Unless they wanted to keep the meat fresh for tonight's barbecue," Ty said.

"Endarians don't eat humans," John said.

"Did you ever think that Kim might have left something out?"

"Kim has been a loyal companion, and you denigrate her at the first chance, you dog. I ought to—"

"Perhaps you two should tone down the hostilities," Arn said.

The Endarians closed in around them. A particularly statuesque fellow in gray signaled for the riders to follow him. The Endarians turned toward the lake, falling into a great column a dozen warriors wide, with the three human riders at its center.

The formation with which the riders moved came to a halt and parted to allow the gray-clad warrior to lead the human riders between his compatriots. Up ahead, the fortress rose. Traces of mist hovered just above the azure surface of the surrounding lake. A flock of geese ascended from the western shore, settling into a familiar V formation as they winged their way to the south.

The bridge crossed the water in a gentle arch. But when the horses stepped out on it, no sound rang forth when hooves struck stone. Arn cocked his head to listen. The other sounds in the world around him continued. He could hear the faint honking of the geese and the louder sounds of horses breathing and leather creaking. Only the *clip-clop* of hooves striking stone was missing.

Arn studied the castle walls as they drew ever closer. They looked strangely smooth, and he found it difficult to see the corners. Arn redirected his attention to the bridge, which was constructed of the same material.

Up close, this effect was even more pronounced. Only where the stone was silhouetted against the water below was there a clear delineation of edge. In fact, studying the material made him slightly dizzy.

The gateway into the fortress yawned before them at a distance of about a hundred paces. There was no drawbridge, nor was there any sign of a portcullis that could be lowered across the thirty-foot-wide opening. He could clearly see through the tunnel into a grassy courtyard on the far side where a small group of Endarians waited.

The riders' Endarian guide paused for several seconds as he entered the passage. When Arn moved up beside the guide, he again felt a sudden pressure much like what he had felt in the tunnel behind the waterfall. The feeling passed, and he and the others continued down the tunnel. The odd sensation repeated itself as they stepped out into the inner courtyard.

Arn blinked and squinted as his eyes readjusted to the bright sunshine, which seemed much lighter than when he had entered the tunnel a few moments before. In fact, the sun seemed slightly higher in the sky than it had been just a moment ago. He looked around. The thick outer walls of the fortress arced away behind him, gradually curving inward.

The party of Endarians that they had seen through the gate stood about fifty paces in front of them. Kim stood between her brother and a stunning woman, clad in shimmering blue. Several other Endarians stood just behind these three. A broad smile lit Kimber's features, and she raised her arm and waved, a motion that John mirrored. Just then three young Endarians trotted forward.

"We will take your horses, gentlemen," said one of the serious youths.

The three companions dismounted, lifted their packs off their mounts, and turned the horses over to the Endarians. Much to Arn's surprise, Ty's stallion snorted with pleasure as one of the Endarians ran a hand over its muzzle. The big horse turned and followed the boy toward a distant stable, accompanied by the other Endarians and horses.

Arn slung his pack over his left shoulder and walked toward the waiting group, with John and Ty beside him. Kim ran forward and threw her arms around John's neck in a hug that he heartily returned. She released her embrace of John to quickly hug Arn and Ty as well.

"My friends," Kim said, "I would like to introduce you to my mother, Queen Elan."

The queen in the blue gown stood almost as tall as Ty. She stepped forward and Arn bowed to kiss her extended hand.

"We are deeply honored, Majesty."

The queen inclined her head.

John followed Arn's example, but as he stepped backward from the kiss, he stumbled and would have fallen had Arn not reached out to support him. His face reddened, but a kindly smile from the queen seemed to reassure him.

Arn held his breath as the queen turned to Ty, wondering whether the unpredictable wild man would do something that would embarrass them all. But Ty responded with all the grace of a nobleman, copying Arn's motions as if he had been born to them.

"I would like to welcome you all to Endar and to express my personal gratitude for saving my daughter's life and for safely returning her to me," Elan said. "It has been ages since a human last set foot inside this castle.

"You must all be tired from your long journey, so Galad will usher you to your room and allow you to clean up and rest before dinner. Tonight, we shall hold a grand banquet in your honor. I will leave the difficult discussions until tomorrow."

The queen then turned and walked across the park toward one of the many gardens, accompanied by all her party save Galad. As the group strolled off, Kim turned and waved once more. Then she disappeared behind a hedge.

The three men followed Kim's brother as he led them off toward the palace. While flowers had been the central theme of the park, water became the dominant feature as they approached the palace facade. Waterfalls, lily ponds, fountains, and geysers produced a lilting melody that Arn found hypnotic.

This gave way to steps a hundred feet wide, leading up a terraced embankment and to the wide palace doors. The walls of the palace were of the same white stone, although the doors and other fixtures were of wood, intricately carved and inlaid with scenes of animals, trees, and mountains. These carvings had been painted so that the scenes appeared to be lifelike, such that Arn felt as if he were looking at an actual landscape. He almost expected to see the animals raise their heads at the approach of strangers, but they did not. The feeling passed as the doors swung open.

Arn, Ty, and John followed Galad into a ballroom larger than any Arn had seen in Hannington Castle, the walls of which were decorated with delicate tapestries. The far wall of the ballroom was glass and looked out over an inner garden completely enclosed by the palace. At the center of the ballroom, a white set of stone steps spiraled upward.

Fascinated as he was, Arn did not have much time to study the room, for Galad led them rapidly up the stairway. The odd coloring of the stone made it so difficult to see the edges of the steps that Arn had to concentrate in order to avoid stumbling and plunging down to the ballroom floor. John and Ty seemed to be exerting similar levels of concentration in their ascent as Galad moved up the stairs with Endarian grace and the ease of long familiarity.

They reached the top and followed Galad down twisting corridors lighted by a soft glow given off by the stone walls, floor, and ceiling. The hallways they traversed, wide enough for three to walk abreast, offered no decorations other than the intricately carved wooden doors that the men passed on either side.

After several minutes of negotiating narrow corridors and stairs, Galad led them through a door and into a large room with a fireplace and hearth in the center of the far wall. Comfortable rugs covered the floor and a massive window opened onto a balcony on the left side of the space. Three pallets with heavy quilts lay spread out before the fireplace.

"Kimber said that you three would prefer to stay together," Galad said. "If that is not the case, we can set up different rooms for you."

"This will be fine," Arn said.

"Bath facilities are through that door," Galad continued, pointing to a door on the right-most wall. "We have also provided clean garments in the closet. I will give you some time to freshen up and relax from your journey. Then, just before sunset, you will be escorted to the Feast of Welcoming. Until then . . ."

Galad turned and strode out of the room.

"Well, what do you make of that?" Ty said as he walked to the doorway and glanced down the hall. "Kim's brother sure is a cold bird. I get the distinct feeling that he isn't too happy about us being here."

"He was happy to see Kim," said John, "but as far as he's concerned, we should have turned back after we dropped her off."

"And did you hear Queen Elan's comment about difficult discussions ahead?" said Ty.

Arn paced slowly across the room with his hands behind his back. He paused to stare out the window. "I'm not sure what kind of reception I was expecting, but this is not it. Something is wrong here."

"I say we leave before we get our throats cut," said Ty.

"I'm staying," said John. "Kim isn't about to let anyone harm us, and I can't believe that Queen Elan would, either. Did you see the look on her face when she thanked us for saving Kim's life? That was true gratitude."

"Yes, and something else that I couldn't quite put my finger on," said Arn. "Regardless, leaving now is out of the question. Some kind of Endarian magic was operating in that fog, so we probably couldn't find our way out if we tried. Let's sit tight and play the part of welcomed guests."

—⁓—

The three men slept the afternoon away on the comfortable pallets. When Arn opened his eyes, he saw the orange ball of the sun hanging just above the mountains. He yawned and stretched.

A knock on the door brought him to his feet.

"Come in," he said.

Kim's lithe form stepped into the room. She was clad in a green gown that glittered with a translucent sheen. She had laced delicate white flowers into hair that cascaded down her back.

"Hello there, sleepy ones," she said.

At the sound of her voice, John scrambled to his feet.

A groan came from the spot where Ty lay atop his pallet. "Go away and come back tomorrow."

John's foot struck him in the ribs.

"I have come to inform you that the feast will begin in one hour," Kim said. "Though all of you may not like the idea, please wear the fresh clothes that hang in the closet."

She shot a glance toward Ty. "I am sure that they will fit, but I warn you not to be startled. Endarian garb has rather unusual properties. I will be back to escort you after you have had a chance to get ready."

She turned and walked out the door, closing it behind her.

"Damn it. I didn't even get a chance to say hello," said John.

"We should prepare for dinner," said Arn.

The three men stripped out of their clothes and took the new pants and shirts from the hooks where they hung. Ty's startled exclamation pulled Arn's eyes to him.

"What in the deep?"

The green trousers that Ty had pulled on were now scarlet, with just a hint of black threading its way through them. As he slipped into the shirt it also changed color, the thin veins of black becoming more predominant in its cloth. When John put on his clothes, the scene repeated itself, except that John's attire acquired a deep blue.

Arn stared down at the green outfit that he had draped across his left arm. He slipped it on. The color shifted and faded, leaving the cloth as black as Slaken's blade, although he thought he saw a transitory shimmer of red shifting across its surface.

"Wow." A low whistle escaped from John's lips. "It looks like these clothes are designed to tell them something about us."

Arn strapped his knives to his body.

The three men finished dressing and settled down to wait for Kim's return. They were soon rewarded with the sound of a tap on the door. John opened it.

"You three look lovely," she said as she stepped back to observe her traveling companions. Her gaze lingered slightly longer on Arn than on the others, but she made no comment.

"Shall we go?" she asked. Arn gestured forward, and Kim guided them through the winding passages and back down the spiral staircase. She led them across the large ballroom and back out through the front doors. The early evening air was brisk, and Arn was surprised to find that the light Endarian clothes kept him warm.

Perhaps a hundred Endarians stood in the grassy park, clustered in small parties. Kim guided them toward the largest of these groups.

As they got closer, Arn could see Elan talking intently with an ancient-looking fellow clad in pale green. His hair had gray streaks, and his frame was bent. The old Endarian was so thin that Arn thought that a strong wind might blow him away.

As Kim led them along the edge of the garden closest to that group, Elan turned toward them.

"Ah, it is good to see you clean and rested," the queen said. "Quite an improvement."

"I must compliment your tailors," said Arn. "These clothes are by far the most comfortable I have worn. I hardly know what to think of the color, though. I hope you do not think that my heart is as black as this cloth."

"Black does not necessarily indicate evil to us," said Elan, "but let us not discuss such weighty matters at the moment. We are here to celebrate, to make merry."

With that, she turned and raised her hands. A hush fell across the park. The queen signaled to Kim, who guided her friends to a place beside Elan. The small groups of Endarians moved to form a circle on the grass so that the queen and her party sat nearest to the palace. With twilight taking hold, Arn was barely able to see those gathered on the far side of the park.

Queen Elan reached out, palms up, and other Endarians ventured forth to set trays of food illuminated by fist-size, lighted globes before the seated assemblage.

The evening passed quickly. Arn felt tempted to overindulge on the delicious venison, bread, and wine, but he resisted. A glance to his side informed him that Ty and John were unconcerned with such worries. Between courses, singers performed, and though he did not understand the language, the music pulled forth visions of times long gone, when Endarians roamed these lands in far greater numbers. The poignant sense of loss affected Arn most deeply.

He had just pushed away his plate and leaned back when he felt a hand on his shoulder. Looking around, he was surprised to see Elan.

"Come. Walk with me," she said.

"Certainly, Majesty."

Rising to his feet, he strolled beside the queen through one of her many gardens before entering a wooded portion of the park. A number of Endarians darted between the trees parallel to their course. They were so quick and blended so well with the grove that Arn almost failed to detect them.

The queen halted and turned toward him. "It is time that you learn the reason that your reception was somewhat less than a warm one," she said.

Arn waited, saying nothing.

The queen began to slowly pace as she spoke, her hands intertwined in her garment. "We Endarians are an ancient race. Up until four hundred years ago, we numbered in the millions and spread throughout the forests of the north. At that time, there arose an evil beyond telling, an ancient wielder known as Kragan, whom we believed long dead.

"Kragan sought to spread his power through the destruction of the Endarians. The war that followed decimated my people and shattered the great kingdoms of men. In the end, Kragan, along with his city-state of Lagoth, was destroyed in a conflagration of spells that created the Mogev Desert.

"The surviving Endarians, who numbered but a fraction of their former strength, returned here to our seat of power to recover. For some time, we were able to do just that, to console ourselves over our terrible losses with the knowledge that we had destroyed the threat Kragan posed.

"But a little over thirty years ago, a great horde of vorgs swept out of the northeastern planes to ravage the land. King Rodan of Tal sent a young warlord named Jared Rafel as an emissary, offering an ancient

Endarian document as tribute as he sought to forge an alliance between our peoples against the vorg.

"I would have refused him audience had not a member of the Endarian High Council been with the scouting party that first encountered Rafel. That councilor recognized the importance of the ancient scroll and brought Lord Rafel before me and the council. After much consultation, we determined that an alliance with the humans would be mutually beneficial."

"And the scroll?" Arn asked.

"We turned it over to our wisest archivists. Ever since that time, they have studied it in an attempt to understand and verify the prophecy it contained. The prophecy was written in an ancient variant of the Endarian dialect. Its phrasing caused considerable disagreement in its interpretation. But one thing is very clear: the prophecy has correctly predicted every major historical conflict, including both the Kragan War and the Vorg War.

"There is also general agreement in the high council that Kragan will rise again, that his fate is somehow linked to Rafel's human daughter. That is part of the reason that I sent a party of Endarian warriors, led by my own daughter, to find Rafel and summon him here."

Queen Elan paused, her dark eyes sparkling in the moonlight, their intensity foreboding.

"Blade, I know who you are and what you do. I know that Rafel saved you from the gallows when you were but a child. I know the dark legend that you have become. You are no doubt aware by now that your knife does not shield you from Endarian magic."

"I am."

"Then you should know that we believe that the ancient scroll foretells that you will play a key role in determining whether the prophesied ray of hope lives or dies. Whether or not you will end up saving or destroying her is open to debate."

"How so?"

"Consider this," Elan said. "An Endarian princess is sent to summon Rafel to Endar. The princess is captured by the vorg, but before she can be seriously harmed, an infamous assassin rescues her and, along with his two barbarian companions, returns her safely to her mother, the queen of the Endarians. An intriguing coincidence, would you not agree?"

Now the chill Arn had felt was replaced by a growing tension in his muscles.

"I understand what you're implying," he said.

"There is a faction among my advisors who believe that this is all too convenient. They say that Blade has used far more intricate schemes to reach his other targets. They tell me that I cannot afford to take chances with one such as you."

"If I were them," Arn said, "I would be telling you exactly the same thing. Knowing my reputation, you're foolish to risk my presence here."

"Maybe I am not taking as big a chance as you think."

"If you mean the bowmen positioned in the trees, they could not keep me from killing you if that was my intent."

The queen's laughter caressed his ears, a mix of condescension and trust.

"Oh, Arn. Over the years, I have learned to trust my judgment of others, and while it might be possible that someone like you could fool me, I rather doubt it. No. I think that I will allow you to play out your part in this, trusting that your role shall be for the good."

Arn felt his body grow less rigid. "That's . . . good to hear."

"Besides," said Elan, "I will have the entire season to observe you before you and your friends depart. The winter storms will soon close the mountains beyond Endar Pass. To leave here before spring would mean certain death."

The news that he was trapped here for the next few months left Arn momentarily speechless.

Seeing his consternation, the queen placed a hand on his arm. "Let us rejoin the others. During your time here you will learn more of the prophecy of which I have spoken, and you will have the chance to make up your own mind as to its meaning." She stopped and pointedly gazed at the assassin again. "I suggest that you take full advantage of this opportunity."

Then Queen Elan turned and led Arn back to the feast. Throughout their walk, he sensed her Endarian bowmen gliding silently through the moon's shadows.

29

Hannington Castle
YOR 413, Mid-Autumn

The cowled figure shambled along, painfully working his way down the hallway that led to the secret entrance into the chambers hidden beneath Hannington Castle. Kragan stepped through the stone wall, emerging inside the bedchamber. A half sneer warped the face hidden beneath the cowl.

Moving to the statue, he placed a hand on the branded shoulder of the marble woman. He mumbled as he moved, drawing a variety of lesser elementals to place magical markings on the floor surrounding, working up the concentration necessary for what he was about to attempt.

He stared at the marble figure, the image of the prophesied she-wielder who had haunted his dreams all these centuries. And no matter how many images of her he created, he'd never found her. Until now.

Kragan trembled. She was strong, much stronger than he would have imagined she could be at this stage of her training. Pain shot through his head as he remembered the firestorm that she had rained down. He spat, hitting the white marble idol. The decision he'd made was one he'd been forced into. For the power he would need to defeat her, he would have to take the ultimate risk. If he survived, Rafel's daughter would pay for what she'd done.

Kragan moved to the front of the white figure. He mumbled an incantation, and the marble changed to flesh and blood, no longer a stone figure. It was a living woman, the image of the prophesied one.

His mind reached out into the elemental mists, going deeper. He found himself in a chamber that glowed with a dull-red heat, a glow that cast slinking shadows within corners and niches. The only thing Kragan could see clearly was the outline of a reclining form stretched upon a couch before the fire blazing in the hearth. He braced himself.

The figure rose from the couch to tower over him, grabbed him by the throat, and slammed him into the wall. Kragan gasped as the air rushed from his lungs. He forced himself to look at the primordial, Kaleal. What the wielder beheld—a massive, bronze-skinned being with slitted, golden eyes exuding sensuality and power—took away what little breath remained in his chest.

A low rumble that sounded something like a laugh worked its way out of the primordial's throat.

"Kragan. You have survived quite long for a human, but your arrogance is about to hasten your demise. Yet I can see that you have already taken a beating. Is it vengeance that made you so desperate to confront me? Has the desire for revenge clouded your awareness of my power?"

Kragan struggled to speak, but only a squeak made it out of his mouth. Summoning all his will to protect his throat from the primordial's squeezing fingers, he fought to avoid losing consciousness.

"Kaleal! If you kill me now, you will lose the one thing that I can give you that you can otherwise never have."

As Kaleal tightened his grip again, overpowering Kragan's will, the wielder felt the blackness close in around him, distorting his vision to a tunnel that narrowed as he watched. Then the primordial relaxed his grip. Kragan felt his face smack the stone floor. A fit of coughing racked his body. When he looked up again, Kaleal stood over him, waiting.

"Frail one, what is this great thing that you desire to give me that I am incapable of taking? There is nothing in your world that I want."

A wave of exhilaration shot through Kragan. He had the primordial's interest. "Isn't there? I'm relieved to hear that you are not upset that the one of prophecy walks the earth unmolested by you. Are you biding your time before you attempt to crush her?"

Kaleal's slitted pupils widened, his lips curling back to reveal fangs. "Do not dare to play games, wielder. Get to the point now, before I decide my curiosity is not worth this trouble."

"Very well. I am talking about the prophecy of the Endarian, Landrel."

The primordial slammed his fist into a wall. Stone fragments flew across the room.

"And it was Landrel who bound you here without access to the world of men and Endarians, all those thousands of years ago, was it not?"

A pause. "Yes."

"I believe that part of the prophecy dealt with you while part of it dealt with me, and yet another dealt with the witch. You cannot escape from this trap unless you are willingly called forth by someone with sufficient skill. Unless I am mistaken, you have already had the unfortunate opportunity to test yourself against the will of the witch, as have I. Yes, I see it in your face. Now to my offer. I will release you from this trap and give her to you."

"You fool. As soon as you arrived I was free. If I choose to possess your form, I will once again walk freely through your world."

"Yes, and you will be free to face her once again, most likely with more discouraging results."

The primordial paused for several moments, studying Kragan as if he were prey.

"What I offer you," Kragan said, "is a partnership in which we share this body and use our joint wills to subdue her."

"And what do I gain from this arrangement, little wielder?"

"You get your freedom to roam my world, toying with it as you please, except in matters pertaining to my interests, and you get the prophesied witch to possess and do with as you will."

Kaleal stroked the golden fur on his head, his eyes never leaving Kragan. His decision was unexpectedly swift. "The bargain is made." A cruel smile settled on the primordial's lips. "But you expect me to enter a body like that? I think not."

The mists dissolved, and Kragan found himself back in his bed-chamber, standing across from a ghostly projection of Kaleal.

"Prepare to receive me," said Kaleal.

A fog descended on Kragan, swathing him in a boiling mist that entered his body through nose and mouth. His chest heaved outward, and his lungs seemed to burst.

Then the mist was gone, replaced by a red film that covered his eyes, a film formed by bursting vessels of blood. Kragan's body convulsed on the floor. He thrashed about, crashing into the wall and then the statue standing in the center of the room. He squirmed into a ball and hammered his head against the floor in a vain search for oblivion. He cried and begged for death.

Ever so slowly his body changed, gaining in height and breadth. Tendons and tissue rippled into place, stretching his skin until it burst, only to reknit itself, then burst again. Gradually the cycle slowed, the skin thickening, taking on a bronze hue that eliminated all traces of the scars that had covered much of Kragan's body.

As the pain began to recede, Kragan lay still on the cold stone, not caring that he was covered in vomit and excrement. At last he struggled to his feet. Suddenly he stopped, staring into the large mirror that hung on the far wall. It was as if he had never really looked at Kaleal before. The naked body that stared back at him from the glass stood tall, a lustrous feline form of strength and speed. He flexed his toes and fingers, noting that as he did, curved claws extended, retracting again as he relaxed. But his head pleased him the most, his scars having vanished. As he stood there staring at the image, a deep murmur arose from within.

Kragan felt the primordial within him, speaking, plotting, manipulating. A broad smile settled across the wielder's new features. The balance of power in this world had just taken a turn.

30

On the first day of winter, Carol looked over the encampment at the valley the rangers had discovered, a thousand feet below the pass where Hawthorne had died, watching the people go about the daily duties that their lord had imposed upon them. Through a regimen of hard work, Rafel kept the survivors busy and alive. They had lost two hundred and seven people, thirty-two of them small children, as they fought their way through the deep snow to reach this sheltered place where they could survive the winter.

She bowed her head at the thought. They certainly hadn't endured autumn well.

Broderick's rangers performed daily miracles, returning from their hunts with venison to keep the people fed. The remainder of Rafel's legion of two thousand soldiers cut and hauled trees to build shelters and stoke the fires that kept the survivors warm and cooked their food.

Every day Carol struggled to break through her mental blockage so that she could come to her people's aid, and every day she cursed herself for her failure to do so. As the new year approached, storms came and went, but these were of the ordinary kind. And down here, away from the pass they had left behind, the snow that accumulated melted off between occurrences. The camp was muddy, damp, and miserable, but less so with each passing day as every able-bodied person worked to improve the structures and walkways that had begun to take on the appearance of a crude town. The people had even given the locale an unofficial name, although it was not one of which High Lord Rafel approved. Mud Flats.

As Carol ended her rounds, checking on the health and needs of every civilian within the caravan, she prepared to make another try at spell-casting. She took the most direct route back to her tent that was possible while remaining on the network of log walkways. She raised the flap and ducked inside, pausing to light a candle before letting the flap fall closed behind her. Like the other tents and shelters within the compound, the floor was covered in a thick layer of pine fronds, but she had augmented this with the rug she had taken from Hawthorne's wagon. In the center of this she set the candleholder, seated herself cross-legged on the rug, and allowed her eyes to adjust to the dim light.

Having thought long and hard about the mental problem preventing her from accessing her magic, she had recently reached a conclusion. Her issue was basic. Carol found herself unable to achieve the level of meditation necessary to control even a minor elemental.

But that knowledge had given her hope. After all, meditation had always been one of her greatest strengths. She could remember the process. Overcoming this disability only required discipline, practice, and persistence. And perhaps a fortified mental sanctuary to where her mind could retreat.

Carol inhaled deeply. She steadied her pulse and began the meditation. She was floating, pulled from her body by the wind. She willed herself upward, through the clouds. Something sped up after her, something that she could not allow to catch her. Her will pulled her onward, faster and faster, higher and higher, until she arrived at a temple atop a snow-covered mountain. She rushed inside, slamming the heavy doors behind her. As she closed the huge bolt that barred the entryway, something slammed into it from outside. Carol staggered backward. The door had to hold, at least long enough for her to do what she needed to do.

The battering on the doors intensified, but Carol ignored it, turning her attention back to what she had come here to accomplish. Her mind was clear and sharp, a feeling she had not experienced since the mark of fire. She could do this.

Reaching out toward the elemental plane of air, she could sense its occupants and focused her attention on the weakest of these. But as she prepared to touch the mind of Wreckath, a massive blow split the doors of the mind sanctuary she had constructed.

She reached out for the air elemental. It appeared, but at such a great distance that she could not make contact. With all her will she thrust her mind outward. Another terrible blow struck the door, shattering part of one panel. In desperation, she pulled Wreckath to her. Almost there, she had just touched it when pain exploded in her left shoulder, pulling a ragged gasp from her lips.

Carol was back in her tent, her heart hammering the walls of her chest as if she had just sprinted across the valley. After several moments, she rose to her feet.

She had failed today, but she had gotten much closer to success, and that renewed her hope. Tomorrow she would try again. And she would not quit trying until she demolished the obstruction in her mind to be the wielder Hawthorne had believed she could become. She owed this to him and to her people. And she owed this to herself.

In the meantime, she hoped that High Priest Jason's prayers for an early spring would be answered.

31

Endar Pass—Northern Glacier Mountains
YOR 413, Late Winter

Arn stood among the trees, not far from the shoreline, taking in the incredible view of the white fortress city in the lake and the arching bridge that connected it to the southern shoreline. With spring and the start of the new year still two weeks away, a warming trend had begun, sending the snow retreating up the nearest hillsides. Soon, the snowbound mountain passes would reopen, and the time of departure from Endar Pass would be at hand.

Kim, John, Ty, and Arn would resume the quest to find Rafel and his human daughter, with Queen Elan's blessing. Although Kim's brother, Galad, and his scouts would accompany them down the western side of the Glacier Mountains and into the Endless Valley, they would not journey with this little band. After extensive argument on the topic, Arn had convinced the queen and her top advisors that the key to success was to avoid attracting the kind of attention a large armed force of Endarian soldiers would attract. And that this group of four had successfully completed a long journey through dangerous country only served to make his point.

Seating himself beneath a tall spruce, Arn leaned back against the thick trunk. The thought of Rafel pulled Carol into his mind. He wondered how she would react when she saw him again. The prospect of such a reunion both frightened and thrilled him, emotions that somehow felt new. Prophecy or not, Arn would have sought Carol out after the discovery of Lagoth. And now, after Endar, no earthly or elemental force would stop him from protecting his love from the wielder who hunted her.

ACKNOWLEDGMENTS

I want to express my deepest thanks to my lovely wife, Carol, without whose support and loving encouragement this project would never have happened.

I also want to thank Alan and John Ty Werner for the many long evenings spent in my company, brainstorming the history of this world, its many characters, and the story yet to be told.

Many thanks to my wonderful editor, Clarence Haynes, for once again helping me refine my story.

ABOUT THE AUTHOR

 Richard Phillips was born in Roswell, New Mexico, in 1956. He graduated from the United States Military Academy at West Point in 1979 and qualified as an Army Ranger, going on to serve as an officer in the US Army. He earned a master's degree in physics from the Naval Postgraduate School in 1989, completing his thesis work at Los Alamos National Laboratory. After working as a research associate at Lawrence Livermore National Laboratory, he returned to the army to complete his tour of duty. Today he lives with his wife, Carol, in Phoenix, where he writes science fiction thrillers—including The Rho Agenda series (*The Second Ship*, *Immune*, and *Wormhole*), The Rho Agenda Inception series (*Once Dead*, *Dead Wrong*, and *Dead Shift*), and The Rho Agenda Assimilation series (*The Kasari Nexus*, *The Altreian Enigma*, and *The Meridian Ascent*)—and the epic Endarian Prophecy fantasy novels.